Praise for *The Exact Opposite of Okay*

'Funny, unapologetic, and shameless in the best possible way, this is a YA heroine (and a book) that you've never seen before' Louise O'Neill, award-winning author of *Asking for It*

'Sharp, funny and important' *Buzzfeed*

'Acerbic, honest and very funny, it's an unapologetic look at slut shaming' *Bookseller*

'This is an unapologetic and hilarious teenage feminist . . . Her relationships with both her friends and lovers are expertly drawn, with a particularly sharp take on "the Friend Zone", and the call-to-arms ending is well-earned. I utterly adored this book.' *Irish Times*

'Excellent feminist novel which explores clichéd attitudes to sexuality . . . a much needed young adult novel' *Irish Examiner*

'This book will make you laugh out loud, nod in agreement, cringe with recognition, and stand up and cheer. I adored it' Katherine Webber, author of *Wing Jones*

'Brilliant. Hilarious. Important. Pick this up and spend the rest of your life wanting to be best friends with Izzy O'Neill' Samantha Shannon, author of *The Bone Season*

'I loved it. Hilarious and feminist (and full of foofers)' Keris Stainton, author of *If You Could See Me Now*

'I LOVED this book! A really smart, relevant and switched-on exploration of teen sexuality, gender and slut-shaming' Katherine Woodfine, bestselling author of *The Sinclair's Mysteries*

ALSO BY LAURA STEVEN

The Exact Opposite of Okay

A GIRL CALLED SHAMELESS

LAURA STEVEN

ELECTRIC
MONKEY

First published in Great Britain in 2019
by Electric Monkey, an imprint of Egmont UK Limited
The Yellow Building, 1 Nicholas Road, London W11 4AN

Text copyright © 2019 Laura Steven

ISBN 978 1 4052 8862 0

A CIP catalogue record for this title is available from the British Library

68225/001

Typeset by Avon DataSet Ltd, Bidford on Avon, Warwickshire
Printed and bound in Great Britain by CPI Group

Egmor   y.
We air   s.

To Nic – the most fun-loving, straight-talking, bird-squawking, queen-saving, bigot-slaying, take-no-shit witch-hunter I know

Hello. Again.

Hello again, my dear pals. Turns out that several of you are actually quite interested in the utter debauchery and chaos that is my life, including but not limited to: international sex scandals, kissing beautiful brown boys, and overzealous eyebrow tweezing. This interest comes as quite a surprise, on account of Ajita telling me roughly fourteen times per day how dull I am, and yet here I am, gallivanting bravely onward, hoping that I haven't somehow run out of jokes in the two months since my last blog post.

On account of the fact I have the memory span of a pair of oven mitts, and I'm willing to bet a bunch of you guys are in the same forgetful boat, I thought [read: my editor thought] it would be a cool idea to do a recap of what happened last time we hung out.

If I was in any way a skilled author, I would attempt to weave all this seamlessly into the first quarter of the book, but since I'm essentially just copy and pasting my old blog posts into a Word document and adding valuable retrospective insights in square brackets, the weaving seemed like a lot of hard work. So, as ever, I'm taking the easy option, but this also makes it the easy option for you, dear reader, and consequently we now all have more time for the important things in life, like laughing and nachos. Cool? Cool.

1. Things started out pretty normal. By pretty normal I mean I was an impoverished orphan living with my eccentric grandmother Betty and our wiener dog named Dumbledore. You know, the way all classic fairy tales start out.

2. And then the Big Bad Wolf ate Betty and stole her identity. Wait, no, that's not right. Gimme a sec.

3. Ah yes. My charming little friendship tripod, comprising of me and my best friends Ajita and Danny, was thrown into a tailspin when Danny decided that after eighteen years of watching me poop on FaceTime he was in love with me. A sentiment I did not reciprocate – I was about as attracted to Danny as I am to coffee tables, which is precisely not at all. However, this did not stop him from attempting to buy my affections with all manner of gifts, including but not limited to fancy chocolate, Coldplay tickets, and the classic "please-fall-in-love-with-me-and-suck-my-penis-at-your-earliest-convenience" flowers.

4. Around the same time this unrequited love business was going down, I slept with Zachary Vaughan, a Republican senator's son, on a garden bench at a party. Oh, also I slept with another dude that night, Carson Manning. He and I are now in a relationship, but that is by the by.

5. Anyway, senator's son. A few days later, I sent him a nude picture, because I wanted to, which should not be too difficult for you to grasp. Then, along with a candid in-situ photo taken mid-hump on the garden bench, someone leaked said nudey pic online, creating a charming website called Izzy O'Neill: World Class Whore. This is a completely a-okay thing to do, since there are no laws against revenge porn in my state. [Revenge porn: the practice of distributing intimate or explicit photos or video of someone without their consent. Just as an FYI.]

6. Said senator's son received little to no backlash for said nude picture, because that is the way of high school and also of the world. He also performed a catastrophic cafeteria speech declaring his innocence, which ended up being filmed [because high school] and sent to local media outlets. And since his dad is, you know, his dad, a Republican senator and all-round dick, the footage immediately went viral quicker than, I don't know, the bubonic plague.

7. The website creator turned out to be Danny. I mean, looking at it all laid out like this, it was pretty obvious all along. But, as you may remember, I am not the sharpest erection in the shed/brothel. Conveniently, it took me roughly the length of one book to figure out my jilted best friend was behind the vicious website.

8. Some other stuff that happened: I accidentally outed my other best friend Ajita and nearly destroyed our relationship forever. But miraculously she forgave me, and together with our new friend Meg we launched a platform called Bitches Bite Back aimed toward calling out all the misogyny and nonsense we face on a daily basis.

9. I signed with a hotshot screenwriting agent in LA after being kicked out of a comedy-writing competition because of the nude pic's media coverage. Huzzah!

10. And I finally learned to open up about my feelings and stop using humor as a defense mechanism. As you can tell by this super-serious and not at all sarcastic introduction, it's going great.

So settle in, folks, for we're about to embark on another awkward (and oftentimes calamitous*) adventure together. And

* Betty bought me a thesaurus for Christmas. Didn't have the heart to tell her you can use one online for free. Lest she think her thoughtful gift was purchased in vain, I'm going to

who knows? Maybe I'll actually get round to telling you the story about the old folks' home break-in this time.

---

be using some more intelligent words from now on. You lucky devils. Or should I say "fortuitous Mephistopheles"?

Monday 2 January

The thing about sex scandals is that you never quite get used to your grandmother having seen you naked.

I mean, obviously she's seen me naked before. She used to bathe me and clothe me and rub baby oil on my butt. But that was a whole year ago! [I did tell you my jokes may have gone downhill.]

You know what I mean, though. Once adolescence strikes, your parents/legal guardians are highly unlikely to see you au naturel, especially if your nipples are of the pierced variety. Unless of course you have a nude picture leaked to the nation, à la Izzy O'Neill, in which case your bare tits and foofer are sort of on display to millions of people, forever and ever until death do us part.

It's been a month or two since the media got over the whole fandango, and Betty has never ceased to be a supportive angel, but every single morning, without fail, I sit down to breakfast and immediately picture her picturing me. You know. *Me*. As in, a euphemism for my genitalia.

Which is ludicrous, because if I were Betty I would have immediately poured hydrochloric acid into my eyes had I seen my teenage granddaughter naked. Or as a less extreme solution, just tried to scrub the image from my memory as best I could. [And I'm in luck, because Betty's memory is not all that great these days. I still remind her of the time she left her keys in the toaster and nearly murdered us all.]

The usual smell of waffle batter – just about to burn around the edges – and the sound of an upbeat pop song fill the kitchen. Betty and I perform our usual routine: she cooks, I make coffee. She sings along to the radio incorrectly. Dumbledore the dachshund loiters without shame. I can almost hear him praying Betty drops some sausage on the ground, but for once he's outta luck.

It's see-your-breath cold in here, because we can only afford to have the heating on for a couple hours a day, and it doesn't make sense to waste our allowance in the morning when Betty's about to head to work and I'm returning to school for the first day back after the holidays. So we're both wearing two bathrobes each, to keep frostbite at bay, and Dumbledore is wearing the delightful wizard's robes Betty knitted him for Christmas. I don't think he fully appreciates the effort she went through to fashion a Gryffindor badge out of yarn scraps, which is rude, but he is a dog so I suppose we shall let him off the hook on this occasion.

"Looking forward to getting back to school, kid?" Betty asks completely earnestly and without a trace of sarcasm. Does she truly have no idea how traumatic the school system has become? No, because she's a hundred years old and thinks an Instagram is a unit of measurement used by supermodels when purchasing cocaine.

"I guess," I say, because I do not have the time nor the energy to explain, yet again, why education is a cruel and unusual punishment for being born. "Although I've loved having so much free time to work on my script."

And it's true. Having three weeks off school to polish my screenplay to within an inch of its life – with the help of my new agent [!!] no less – has been the stuff of dreams. I almost can't believe that I actually have to go back to Edgewood and complete my senior year. For a hot minute it actually started to feel like I was a real screenwriter, and polishing scripts was my new normal.

One day, O'Neill. One day.

"You know, you're going to have to let me read it at some point," Betty says, scraping cheap sausages around a frying pan. They splutter aggressively, protesting their own low pork content. "You go on and on and on about your script and your agent and how you're essentially Quentin Tarantino but with better boobs, and yet will you let your dear old grandma read the damn thing? Will you heck."

[Guys, there is no way I'm letting her read it. My screenplay

8

– a comedic, gender-swapped *Pretty Woman* with a myriad of distasteful sex jokes – is a whole other level of inappropriate. And no matter how filthy the old bird is, and no matter how much she would find the whole thing hysterical I do have some boundaries. I know. It was a shock to me too.]

A billow of steam erupts from the waffle iron. The kettle whistles just as I'm done scooping instant coffee and sugar into big purple mugs. I pour, Betty scrapes. We're a noisy but well-oiled machine. A little *too* well-oiled in Betty's case. While a good layer of insulation is generally a good thing for an older lady, sky-high cholesterol not so much. So she's supposed to be cleaning up her diet, but the token punnet of grapes we bought to appease her fascist of a doctor is molding happily on the windowsill.

Nonetheless, I don't want her to die or anything, so I spoon a tiny bit less sugar into her mug than usual. New year, new Betty, and all that crap. I top it up with enough creamer that she hopefully won't notice.

But the old bat takes one swig and spits it dramatically all over Dumbledore. His Gryffindor robes are splattered with subpar coffee. He blinks in confusion, then raises a tiny little leg like he's high-fiving the air.

Betty turns to me, aghast. "What is this crap? I raised you better than this."

Honestly, there must be three fewer granules of sugar than

9

normal. It's like a poor-man's *Princess and the Pea* reboot.

"Calm down, Hans Christian Andersen," I retort. "I'll get you more sugar."

She just stares blankly at me. "Hans Christian who?"

See? Education is a total and utter waste of everyone's time.

2.55 p.m.

The singular upside of the whole sex scandal fandango is the absurd surge in subscribers to Bitches Bite Back – specifically our weird, poorly directed sketch comedy. We're a few hundred YouTube fans shy of breaking 10,000, which is all kinds of bonkers.

Today's sketch, penned by yours truly, is about an army of sex dolls who become self-aware and seek revenge on their creepy owner, who not only uses them for some Messed Up sexual shit, but also likes to pretend they are his maids, and beats them when they do not adequately complete household chores. Many of his lines are direct quotes from famous politicians, actors and sportspeople who've been accused of abuse. He is an amalgam of all the horrible men in the world, and deliberately nameless and faceless in a way that implies he could be anyone. [Social commentary with dirty jokes = my MO.]

Weirdly, no dudes were up for the challenge of playing said Creepy Owner, so I have carefully constructed an understudy out of two trash cans and a trenchcoat.

This time, I've written a speaking part in the sketch for our new $^{13}/_{10}$ excellent human pal Meg, who has never acted before but has always shown a massive interest in our YouTube channel. She was actually a fangirl before we became friends, which is all kinds of sweet. Even though she was unsure about participating to begin with, I candidly filmed her chatting to Ajita, and she ended up loving the way she looked on camera – and didn't hate the sound of her own voice as much as she expected to. So she agreed to be our newest actress, and proceeded to text me five times a day over the holidays asking *exactly* how a sex doll would pronounce the word "vagina".

We've also managed to recruit most of the girls from theater to play crazed sex dolls, and freshman Fern Fournier – a ridiculously cool French-Japanese girl with awesome stage makeup skills – has agreed to give everyone a Crazed Sex Doll makeover. I did try going to the Mac counter in town and asking if they'd be up for the challenge, but apparently Crazed Sex Doll, while a name of one of their overpriced lipsticks*, is not a makeover style they're familiar with.

So now there are twelve of us on the makeshift set in Ajita's basement, thanks to the general awesomeness of Ajita's parents, who not only had a ramp installed so Meg had a hassle-free way of visiting, but who also provided coffee in an industrial-sized vat suitable to power a dozen hellbent sex dolls.

---

* Not really. It's that artistic license thing.

Fern has set up a mini makeup station beside the pool table, and is currently working her magic on Meg – who also loves makeup, and is chattering excitedly about contour palettes. The rest of the girls are changing into matching costumes we cobbled together from the drama department at school.

The only downside of no longer being friends with Danny is the fact he was the sole provider of fancy filming equipment. Ajita managed to find some basic tripods and collapsible reflectors online, but we're sorely missing the expensive camera and array of microphones. So we're just having to make do with Ajita's parents' DSLR.

Ajita and I are in the process of moving the sofa to make room for an army of sex dolls to assemble. [Another one of my strange sentences that doesn't give off a great impression if you take it out of context.] From the corner of the room Meg's girly giggle cuts through the sound of eight sex dolls running lines. Ajita shoots a weird look over to where Meg and Fern are fawning over a new shade of lipstick, then fluffs a cushion slightly aggressively.

"You okay?" I ask as quietly as I can – which is easier said than done when you have the voice of a malfunctioning foghorn.

Jaw gritted, she rearranges a fallen cushion, not meeting my eye. I'm pretty sure if you listen closely enough, you'll hear the sound of Ajita grinding her teeth down into bleeding stumps. [That was an unnecessarily brutal mental image.] "Yeah.

It's just . . . I don't know, dude. You could've asked me before you wrote Meg such a big part. It's meant to be our joint sketch show, you know?"

This is not what I was expecting. Like, at all. And to be honest, it kind of rubs me the wrong way. Why would I need to ask her permission to have Meg in a sketch with us? I've always written all the material for our skits. Writing isn't her thing, and she's never shown an interest in it before.

This level of pettiness is pretty out of character for her, and I'm on the brink of calling her out when something stops me. Something oddly guilt-shaped. Because after everything that Ajita forgave last semester – after I accidentally outed her to the entire world and she welcomed me back into her life with open arms – I have no right to feel mad at her over a tiny niggle like this. So instead of prodding her for an explanation, I say, "Okay. Sorry. Next time, I'll ask you first."

At this point Meg comes over to where we're sitting, pops the brakes on her wheelchair, and asks, "Do I look okay?"

Ajita paints a falsely bright smile on her face, worlds away from the agitated expression of three seconds ago. "Do sex dolls have regional accents?" She says it with the exact inflection of "Is the Pope a Catholic?" as though phrasing a rhetorical question, except in this instance, there is no clear answer.

13

6.04 p.m.

Just as we're packing up after a successful afternoon of shooting, Meg wheels over to me, tinfoil choker round her neck and giant grin spreading from ear to ear. I look up from the lens I'm trying to force into the wrong case and return the smile. This was her acting debut and judging by the look on her face she's hooked.

"Izzy!" she exclaims, breathless with excitement. "This was so, so fun. Thank you so much for letting me be in a sketch!" Her makeup still looks flawless; pillar-box red is so her color.

"Dude, you're *so* welcome," I say. "You were awesome. Like, was this really the first time you've ever acted? Or are you actually in a world-famous improv troupe and just wanted to hustle us?" I mean it too. Meg's got a natural knack for nuance and didn't overact at any point, which a lot of beginners do. I'm totally writing her a bigger part in the next sketch. With Ajita's blessing of course.

Speaking of the devil, Ajita re-enters the room from the top of the stairs, clutching half a dozen cans of soda awkwardly to her chest. She tiptoes down the stairs one at a time, like she's sneaking downstairs for a midnight snack and trying not to wake her parents, and looks more terrified of dropping the soda cans than if they were live grenades. Reaching the middle of the room five decades later, she lays most of them down on the sofa like newborn infants, then tosses one to me. I catch it and hand it to Meg, then catch the subsequent can she hurls my way. We both crack them open simultaneously with an aggressive puh-tsshhhhh, i.e. the most satisfying sound in the world. [With the possible exception of bubble wrap and/or sexual moans. Not that the two are in any way related. Or, you know, they might be. I don't know your fetishes.]

Ajita taps the lid of her own can with purple-painted nails. "What're you guys talking about? My impeccable camera skills? Which, BTW, are literally of an Emmy standard at this point."

"Something like that," I say.

"Are we really just going to skip over Ajita saying BTW out loud?" Meg snorts, shooting Ajita a playful look. "We all know how inaccurate her spoken text slang can be."

I freeze for a second. Will this rub Ajita the wrong way? I mean, she didn't even seem to want Meg here in the first place. But I need not have worried.

"Whatever," Ajita says, swigging her grape soda. "I still maintain that LMAO should be pronounced *luh-mao*, like a dish at a Chinese restaurant. Yes, good evening, waiter, I'll have the pork *luh-mao* with a side of egg-fried rice, please. That kind of thing."

Meg giggles so hard her shoulders start to shake, and Ajita looks extremely pleased with herself, licking grape soda off her lips with her freakishly long tongue, which has the potential to look seductive and yet actually just looks like a slippery pink snake is climbing out of her mouth and ravishing her face.

Tuesday 3 January

8.25 a.m.

Waiting for Ajita at our usual halfway-to-school meeting point is borderline life-threatening, on account of the fact it's colder than the dark side of the moon. I don't even know if the dark side of the moon is particularly cold, but I've always got standoffish vibes from the moon in general, so let's just assume its temperature is appropriately frosty.

When she eventually arrives, Ajita is all wrapped up in that Rory-Gilmore-meets-Paddington-Bear duffel coat of hers. Without even saying hello, she greets me with an eloquent, "What the fuck is even the point of it being this fucking cold if it's not going to fucking snow?"

"Who knows?" I reply. "I have a feeling the moon is to blame."

She thrusts a paper cup of coffee into my mittened hand. I smile gratefully and take a sip of scalding peppermint mocha. Because really, is it even winter if you don't add obnoxious flavorings to your favorite caffeiney beverage?

She readjusts her wooly hat and takes a swig from her own

cup as we start dragging our heels in the direction of Edgewood. "Dude, if I haven't said it before, your beef with the moon is not normal."

"Yes, Ajita, you have said it before. And I feel like, as a vegetarian, you shouldn't take beef's name in vain. By the way, did you know the plural of beef is 'beeves'? I learned that in the thesaurus Betty got me."

At this point Ajita's phone buzzes, and she smiles as she reads a text. And if I didn't know any better, I could swear she's tilting the screen away from me so I can't see who she's texting. I pray to the peanut butter cup gods that it's not Carlie, the wannabe Victoria's Secret model she crushed on last semester. For one thing, the girl voluntarily ate salads of her own free will, which is how I immediately knew she was an ax murderer in disguise. For another, she bitched about Ajita behind her back, and I ended up pouring cold tomato soup over her perfectly groomed head in the middle of the cafeteria. So there's that.

Ajita and I chatter our usual nonsense for a quarter of a mile or so, but I can tell she's feeling a little weird too. So I decide to vocalize my own apprehensions. [How thesaurusy is that sentence?]

"Hey. It's kinda weird how we graduate from high school this year, right?" I say nonchalantly, staring at my feet. My thrift-store Doc Martens — dark red with black laces — are hella scuffed round the edges.

"Right," she agrees. "And that this is the last time we'll ever meet up after winter break to remark on the passage of time."

School is weird. For so many years it feels infinite, like you'll never be anything other than a high-schooler. It's so intrinsic to your identity, and while you can imagine what you might do beyond it, it mostly feels like it'll never happen. And then senior year hits, and suddenly everything you do is the last. The last first day back after summer. The last New Year's Eve as a schoolkid. And, someday pretty soon, the last peppermint mocha on the walk to Edgewood. It's exhilarating, but also terrifying. Because school is all we've ever known.

I decide Ajita will not appreciate my lyrical ruminations on the circle of life, so instead I just say, "So. What bitchy things are we going to do today?"

Since we started the Bitches Bite Back website a couple months ago, word has slowly started to spread about what we're doing. Which is shouting, mainly. Shouting about all the things that make us angry, and inspiring other teenage girls to do the same. A whole bunch of shouting. As well as a roster of feminist sketches, we now have a handful of weekly contributors, who write articles and personal essays on an all manner of feminist topics, and our daily hits are now in the high hundreds rather than the low, well, zeroes. We're actually heading to Martha's Diner tonight to have an informal meeting about the tech side of things, which Meg is way savvier about than Ajita and me, who mainly project-manage the shouting. [Is that an official job title? Project Manager (Shouting Division)? It should be.]

10.26 a.m.

There's one reason I *am* happy to be back in school: Carson Manning.

Even though we've been texting and video-calling a ton, we haven't seen each other in person at all over the holidays. He's been working like a madman, doing extra shifts at the pizza place to help his mom cover Christmas expenses. His mom's douchebag of a partner left them in the lurch a few months back, and since Carson is the oldest the onus has fallen on him to pick up the slack and bring in some extra income.

From what I can gather his mom would love to go to work and provide for the kids, but since there are so many of them, the cost of childcare would far outweigh whatever she earned salary-wise. A common catch-22.

So yeah, Carson has been working double shifts most days, and spending whatever limited free time he has with his family, enjoying the holidays as best he can. Which I totally get. But selfishly I'm still super excited to see him this morning.

We haven't even exchanged gifts yet. We set a ten-dollar limit on account of our severe brokeness, but I think I knocked it out of the park nonetheless.

I mean, I think I did. No matter how well you think you've

nailed someone's gift, the moments before you actually hand it over are hardcore nerve-wracking. And you suddenly think, oh my God, I took it too far, they're going to think I'm a crazy stalker, this is too much, it's *too* thoughtful, please can a giant seagull just swoop overhead, nosedive onto my face, and carry me away in its beak. Or something.

Since we don't have first or second period together, we've arranged to meet by my locker for a smooch and a gift-giving ceremony. And I'm kind of . . . nervous? Well, it's more like anticipation. Either way, the butterflies are real. Except butterflies makes it sound cute, whereas in reality it feels like my insides are being squashed through a colander and made into pasta sauce. Anyone for some *fettucine al intestino*?

The hallways are even more hubbuby than normal, with tons of other reunions and gossip sessions taking place. I wave goodbye to Ajita, take a drink at the water fountain, rub a stubborn smear of dirt off my Doc Martens, and try to steady myself for seeing Carson again. Honestly, why am I so nervous? He's my boyfriend. He's into me. That won't have changed in the last three weeks. Will it?

Jeez. I was never this insecure pre-scandal.

I'm rummaging around in my locker, looking for a peanut butter cup I know I left here before the holidays, when two arms snake round my waist from behind. "Hey, you."

And just like that the butterflies melt away, joining my

intestines in pasta sauce heaven. [Another strange sentence. I'm not even sure context helps us here.]

I twist round in his arms, and our faces end up startlingly close together. Not that I'm complaining. Because his face is my second favorite face. [Ajita would literally flay me alive if I in any way suggested hers did not occupy the number-one spot.]

He kisses me softly on the lips, smiling as he does, so it's really more of a bumping together of grinning mouths. A tooth clash, if you will. He smells of acrylic paint and fresh air, like he always does, and his head isn't as freshly shaven as usual, so there's a short layer of black fuzz everywhere. I'm very into it.

"Hey," I murmur in what I hope is a seductive voice, but in reality I probably just sound baked. "Long time no see."

"It's been what, a decade?" he asks, and he's grinning so wide, and it makes me really happy that the sight of my face and the sound of my weird stoner voice is enough to make him do that.

"At least two, I'd say." I take a deep breath and then add, "So I got you something!"

Except he says the exact same thing at the exact same time, like they do in movies, and it's all so cringeworthy but I just do. Not. Care. Because all those cheesy romance tropes I used to take the piss out of? Turns out they're pretty great.

"You first," Carson says, ever the gentleman. [Or probably just because he wanted to receive his gift first, to judge

22

whether or not the one he got me was better. I see your game, Carson Manning.]

"Okay, hang on a sec." I reluctantly wriggle free of his half-hug and rummage around in my locker. My hands hit pay dirt. "Found it!" Triumphantly I emerge with the rogue peanut butter cup I'd been hunting down before he arrived.

He gasps extravagantly and claps his hands to his cheeks. "Your last peanut butter cup? I know you're into me and all, man, but . . . you really like me *that* much?"

I scoff. "Absolutely not." I quickly unwrap the cup in under 0.2 seconds, seasoned professional that I am, and shove the entire thing in my mouth before he can protest.

Then, mouth full of claggy peanut butter, I bring out the *actual* gift, and the butterflies return with a vengeance. The gift is wrapped in tinfoil, because a) do you even know how expensive wrapping paper is? and b) tinfoil saves you money on Sellotape, and c) your gift looks like a spaceship. So it's a win all round.

He snorts, actually snorts with laughter, and pulls his gift out of his backpack. And wouldn't you know, it's also wrapped in tinfoil. Romance, Gen Z style. We're broke, woke, and unusually innovative when it comes to gift-wrapping solutions.

Plus our presents are also almost exactly the same size and shape. Like. What.

As he unravels the tinfoil on his present my chest pounds. It's the moment of truth. Is he going to think I'm the ultimate weirdo? Or is he going to be charmed by my lunacy?

The tinfoil drops to the floor, and he squints as he tries to read the handwritten Post-it note I've stuck on the front of his gift in explanation. To be fair, since I type basically everything, my handwriting is more akin to ancient hieroglyphics than the Latin alphabet, so it does take him some time to decipher.

What I've attempted to write: "To share with Colbie and Cyra".

Colbie and Cyra are his youngest brother and sister – they're five and three respectively.

Carefully he peels the Post-it note off the cover of the hand-made picture book I've made him, and the moment he reads the words on the front cover, he collapses into a fit of laughter.

Where do you hide a poo in a zoo?
by Izzy O'Neill and Carson Manning

"Man, that's hilarious," he cackles, shaking his head in astonishment.

I had the idea last time I visited Carson's house before the holidays. Even though there are ten kids living there, and it must be crazy difficult to keep them all fed and watered and clothed, Carson's mom Annaliese has curated the most awesome collection of kids' books.

Arranged by age group on the bookshelves in the living room, she's picked up funny picture books for her youngest, magic realism and middle-grade fantasy for the primary-school kids, a ton of sci-fi for the older teens. She's even got well-worn book box sets of both *Lord of the Rings* and *Harry Potter*.

And honestly, it made me so emotional to see it. Because I never had that. Betty did an incredible job raising me, don't get me wrong. I'll never stop being grateful to her for all the sacrifices she made just to make sure I had a good life. But a mini library in my house? I can't even imagine how cool that would have been.

When I spoke to Annaliese about it, her face lit up. She told me about how a lot of the books were hers from when she was a kid – all the Enid Blyton originals, all the Roald Dahl classics, the full *Chronicles of Narnia* – and how, over the years, she's always tried to pick up one book a month from a thrift store. No matter how broke she was, she could always find a quarter somewhere to bring home a new book, even if it meant she went without dinner that night.

Isn't that the most amazing thing you've ever heard in your life?

So while I was agonizing over what I could possibly get Carson for under ten dollars [and also the fact that I didn't even have ten dollars], I thought . . . why not write a kids' book for him to share with his siblings?

I bought a landscape A4 notebook with a hard cover and blank pages, did some word art on the cover – as best I could with my non-artistic abilities – and then wrote all the text throughout the notebook. Due to my abysmal handwriting, it took me *days* to write it all out in neat block capitals with a black sharpie, but, honestly, it looks pretty cool.

Each page is told from the perspective of a different zoo animal who's done a poo and wants to hide it inside their cage. So it's kind of educational, because kids learn what every different zoo animal's poo looks like [because this is the kind of important wisdom the education system neglects to impart], and also interactive, because the kid gets to help the animal find the best place to hide its poo according to its surroundings.

[I know. My brain is weird.]

"I thought you could do the artwork for it," I say, gesturing to the blank spaces beneath the text I've written. "Since I have the sketching ability of a drunk toddler. I mean, I could probably stretch to painting the assorted poo variations, but when it comes to the actual animals and their environments I might be a little challenged."

Again he shakes his head, and he actually looks a little emotional. He wraps me up in one of his trademark bear hugs, and squeezes me real tight, and all the painstaking hours of dreaming up different voices [and poos] for fictional animals are suddenly worth it.

"I love it," he whispers in my ear, and for a second my heart flips, because I think he said something else, but then he adds, "And my mom'll love it too." Pulling away slightly, he kisses me tenderly on the cheek and says, "You're the best. How am I supposed to match that?"

He takes a deep breath almost exactly like the one I took before presenting him with the book, and hands over his own tinfoil-wrapped efforts. A wave of excitement hits, but also confusion. This gift isn't just similar in size and shape to mine — it's identical.

Frowning in confusion, I peel away the foil to reveal the back of the exact same notebook I bought Carson, except this one is portrait instead of landscape. I flip it over to see the front, and gasp.

Carson has painted over the original plain cover with his own artwork, and OH. MY. GOD.

It's like a collage, except every single component has been hand-painted by him. There's the Hollywood hills in the background, an old school movie theater, palm trees, a bucket of popcorn, a ticket stub with the title of my movie on it, a film reel, a director's chair . . . and me.

I'm right in the center of the painting, clutching a script to my chest. I have huge movie star sunglasses on, but my hair is still the same unruly blonde mess it is right now. The stompy dark red Doc Martens are on my feet, but I'm wearing a sundress in the LA heat. In the drawing I'm smiling from ear to ear, like I am right now, and he's even matched my slightly wonky front teeth to perfection. But I don't look as terrifying as I often think

I do; I look beautiful. The wild hair and crooked teeth just make me look even more so.

"I don't know what to say," I murmur, completely blown away by the effort he's gone to.

"Do you like it?" he asks, looking shy for probably the first time in his life. "It's for all your screenwriting notes. For when you inevitably fly to LA to meet a ton of hotshot Hollywood producers about your script." A funny kind of smile. "Hopefully it'll make it harder for you to forget me, right?"

"Like I could ever forget you!" I say, with enough force that he knows I mean it despite the jesting tone. I look back down at the notebook, at the broad, colorful brushstrokes and vivid detail. "I *love* it, Carson. Really."

And then a nice little silence ensues in which we just . . . look at each other and smile. Then he leans in for a real kiss, and the clamor of the hallway dims. I'm painfully aware of the fact I smell like hours-old coffee, but he either doesn't notice or doesn't care. His lips are soft and minty, and his warm body presses against mine, and oh. *Oh*. I desperately want to not be in a public place right now.

Yeah. Being back in school definitely has its perks.

2.36 p.m.

I forgot about the whole inconvenient learning thing you have do. There I am, quite happily daydreaming in math class about what it's going to be like when I win my Oscar for Best Original Screenplay, when I am rudely interrupted.

"Miss O'Neill, are you listening to me?" Mr Wong seems to be saying from very far away, except he's not far away, he's right in front of me, wiggling his wooden ruler two feet in front of my face. [Fortunately, in this instance, wooden ruler is not a euphemism.]

It transpires that I am not, in fact, listening to him. And yet somehow I get the impression that's not the answer he's looking for. So I lie. "Yessir, absolutely I am."

"Right. So you *do* know how to calculate the circumference of a trapezoid?"

I mean, really. If they're going to pretend we'll need all of this shit in the real world, they could at least try and make it believable.

6.01 p.m.

We're sitting in Martha's Diner, which still has all its holiday decor up, but please don't go picturing a charming Santa's grotto. Giant frosted wreaths hang in the windows, which are all steamed up with sweat and condensation, and an obnoxious tinsel tree stands in the center of the room. Almost every available surface has been assaulted with a spray can of fake snow in a dogged attempt at festive cheer, yet it just makes it look like the ceiling fans have dandruff.

Martha's is famously shameless in how long it drags out the holidays. I'm pretty sure it'll all still be here come summer solstice. The staff are still wearing Rudolph ears too. Well, all except Betty, who put hers in the waffle iron in protest, burned them to a fuzzy felt crisp, then played the Forgetful Old Person card. God love her.

Anyway, the diner is still a good place to host a highly feminist business meeting. [Milkshakes and matriarchy, the classic combination.] You just have to look past the slightly unprofessional three-foot-high elf in the doorway, who greets diner patrons with an aggressive and insistent "Happy Holidays!" Only I think its batteries are running low because it sounds more like "herpy her-ler-derrs". It's literally a real-life meme at this point. Ajita put him in the meeting minutes under Any Other Business last time, just for the laughs.

I dunk my forefinger into the whipped cream on top of my strawberry shortcake shake, ignoring the relentless drone of "Jingle Bell Rock" playing from the speakers behind our booth. Since she's the designated minute-taker for this meeting, Meg pulls a pretty floral notebook out of her satchel, which she has completely covered in New Orleans Saints patches. Seriously, the girl is NFL obsessed. She's promised to teach Ajita and I the rules of football sometime, and while Sportsball™ is not generally my cup of tea, I'm happy to invest in it a little if Meg wants to be able to share her passion with us. We got her hooked on *SNL*, so I guess it's only fair.

I watch as she notes down who's present for the meeting: Izzy O'Neill, Ajita Dutta, Meg Martin, Derp Elf. Meg's handwriting is all swirly and loopy and makes everything look awesome, except it takes her a million years to do. I want to crack a calligraphy joke at her, but I just don't know if we're at the ruthless piss-taking stage of our friendship yet. Even though it's my way of showing affection, I don't want her to think I hate her or anything. Cos I don't. She raises the cool level of our group by a factor of seven, with her sportsball knowledge and all.

"Okay, without further ado, let us begin!" I announce. "Meg, what's our first order of business?"

She clears her throat theatrically. "At the end of the last meeting we decided the first topic on our agenda this week would be —"

There's an ungodly clatter from the kitchen, as though Thor has dropped his hammer from a great height, and the swinging double doors burst open. The hostess who's been serving us all night storms out, tossing her apron over her shoulder dramatically. I mean, aprons don't weigh very much, and it just kind of wafts to the ground like a poorly made paper airplane, so it's a bit anticlimactic. But still, I appreciate her penchant for histrionics.

The chef comes yelling after her. "And if you don't like it, don't come back!"

"Wasn't planning on it," the hostess hisses, practically in

Parseltongue, before slamming out the main entrance and huffing down the street. The derp elf bids her farewell completely unironically.

With the exception of our friend Derp there's utter silence across the entire diner. Like, total quiet. You could hear a centipede fart. [Do centipedes fart? I doth not know.]

The chef, a beady-eyed Bostonian fellow with an igloo of a gut, addresses the rest of us with a healthy dose of both derision and desperation. "Any of you on the market for a part-time hostess gig?"

Silence creeps over the diners like a snowy blanket as the idea forms in my head. With a part-time job Betty and I could finally stop teetering on the knife edge of bankruptcy. We could eat actual literal fresh vegetables, and meat that isn't part sawdust. I could even start a savings account. Imagine!

And so I rise to my feet. "I volunteer as tribute," I say, voice clear and confident.

"Er, what?" Chef Man huffs haughtily, folding his arms across his snowdrift of a chest. He looks disgruntled. [Can you be gruntled? Because that's a highly entertaining word.] "Look, do you want a job or not?"

"Affirmative, sir. Absolutely I do. Very much."

"Good. You start Friday."

"Roger that, sir," I reply, unsure why I'm behaving like an army cadet all of a sudden. Thankfully I resist the urge to salute and/or begin leopard crawling toward the kitchen.

With that he barges back into the kitchen, so forcefully the swinging doors are almost wrenched from their hinges. I sink back down into the chair, blinking with disbelief.

"Dude. That was awesome," Ajita says, patting me awkwardly on the shoulder. Physical affection is roughly as appealing to her as squatting on a cactus, so I appreciate the gesture.

There's a faint buzzing in my ears. I assume this is what adrenaline feels like, but as a person who has never participated in sports I cannot be sure. "What in the actual name of fuckery?" I ask, stunned.

"Eloquent as ever," Ajita congratulates me.

"Seriously. I've tried to get a job since the day I turned fourteen. How was that so easy?"

"I'm trying very hard not to make a joke about your mom being easy," Ajita replies.

"Considering that my mother has been dead for over a decade, I appreciate your self-restraint."

Honestly, I cannot believe this. I have a job. I mean, there's every chance I could royally screw up training. This is me we're talking about. If I lay eyes on a tub of Greek yoghurt, for example, I may just start rocking in a corner due to post-traumatic stress. [This is an in-joke from Book One. If you recall, I accidentally touched my foofer after chopping chilies and had to seek relief in a pot of . . . Well, you get the idea.]

But if I manage not to ruin this gig like I do all other facets of my existence, I might actually have money for the first time in my life. I may actually be able to pay for my own milkshakes, for once. Like, I'm not going to go crazy and stop leeching off Ajita's Netflix account or anything, but still. Think of the possibilities. A new toothbrush! Bras with underwires! Limitless potential!

"So, where were we?" I ask, not wanting to derail the Bitches Bite Back meeting by turning my entire life round. "Something about website wizardry and . . . corum fodes? Or forum codes, even." I'm so excited the words are falling out of my mouth like potatoes.

However, at some point between me turning my life round and my potatoey sentence Meg has blanched pure white. Ajita, who's sitting on the same side of the booth, peers over her shoulder at the laptop screen, immediately beginning to chew the inside of her lip.

"Oh fuck," she murmurs, horror written all over her beautiful face. "Um, Iz . . ."

Immediately I'm terrified it's something to do with my scandal. The website has resurfaced, or the nudes have been picked up by another gossip site, or Senator Vaughan is back on his soapbox about family values. Familiar dread blooms in my gut, cramping painfully.

"What is it?" I ask, too scared to even crack a joke about the fact Meg is so tense she looks like she's trying to pass a kidney stone.

"Another girl's nude leaked," Ajita mumbles. "It's bad. Oh shit, no, not just a nude. A sex tape. Oh . . . oh fuck."

Meg goes to turn the laptop to show me, but I gesture frantically, shaking my hands no. "Please. Don't. I can't look. I don't want to."

"I get it," Meg replies softly.

"Who is it?" I ask.

"Another senior. Hazel Parker. You know her?"

I shake my head, but then realize her name is familiar. "She's a cheerleader, right?"

"Judging by the pompoms, I would assume so," Meg says gravely.

Acid churns in my stomach. "Is it on a blog? Or YouTube?" I remember the World Class Whore website Danny made to publicly shame me, and it's still so fresh I can feel the sharp pangs of horror all over again.

Ajita shakes her head. "A group chat. They added everyone from school." Sure enough, one glance at my phone shows a bunch of new notifications from a group chat entitled "Hazel 'Pompom' Parker." After the original video, which I blur my eyes in order not to look at, there are a few dozen comments – mainly from guys, because guys – about the nude. Critiques of her body, her technique, and, inevitably, the eggplant emoji followed by the water squirt emoji. Her friends from the cheer squad have posted angry messages demanding that the chat is deleted or they'll go to the police, but that just makes me feel even more sick. There's nothing the police can do when revenge porn is legal.

Oh God. Hazel made some shitty comments online when my garden-bench picture was leaked. Something about how shameless I am, about how dirty my behavior was. And now the same thing is happening to her.

A dark, spiteful part of me feels an iota of satisfaction at the way the world has dealt her revenge, but the bigger, overwhelming part just feels terrible for her. No matter how shitty a person she is, she doesn't deserve this. Nobody does. Sympathy crests in my chest.

What's Hazel doing now? Has she seen it yet? Or is she enjoying her last moments of blissful ignorance before her world is turned upside down?

I remember the way I felt when the nudes first dropped. Disbelief, along with roiling nausea and a desperate desire to wake up and find this is all just a bad dream. And the paranoia, sharp and immediate. The feeling that every single person I made eye contact with had now seen me naked, from the principal of Edgewood to the homeless man who sleeps rough on our housing estate. My skin crawls at the memory, as vivid as the day it happened.

No. I wouldn't wish this on anyone.

"Are you okay?" Ajita asks. Her teeth work away at her inner lip. Meg's eyes are wide and sympathetic. Their pity makes me feel two inches tall.

"Yeah, fine," I lie. Then, despite my best efforts to bury it deep down in my chest, emotion explodes through me in savage waves, so intense it leaves me gasping for breath.

Anger. White hot, furious. Pure, unfiltered rage, so potent and visceral it makes me feel more wild animal than teenage girl.

Nothing is ever going to change. No matter how well our sex-doll sketches go down, no matter how many chords we strike with the BBB fanbase, this shit will continue to happen to girl after girl after girl.

I grip the table, knuckles whitening like the flames inside me. I want to smash something, want to feel something shatter in my fist. I eye the glass pepper shaker longingly.

"This is going to keep happening as long as it's legal," I spit out. "Teenage girls are going to keep having their lives ruined, and if they're over eighteen, the douchebags who leak their nudes are totally off the hook. It makes me sick that you can ruin someone's life and face no consequences."

"Maybe if we keep going with Bitches Bite Back, we'll make guys see that –"

"No, we won't," I burst out, interrupting an alarmed Meg. I pound my fist on the Formica table, cutlery rattling in its jar. "We won't make guys see anything. We don't have the scope."

Ajita and Meg exchange a worried glance. I don't think either

37

of them have ever seen me like this. Honestly, before the scandal, I wasn't an angry person. Self-absorbed and immature, maybe, but I've never felt this way before. So easily irritated, so quick to erupt. It's like my blood has been replaced by molten lava, scorching me from the inside out.

The noise in the diner is dimmed by my rage. My heartbeat pounds in my ears as I try to sharpen the anger into a point, try to focus my blistering energy into action.

How can Bitches Bite Back stop this? Writing blog posts and launching forums isn't enough. We need to take real action. But how? We're just teenagers. We have no power.

But that isn't true. I think of the marches organized by victims of school shootings, kids like me who wanted to channel their pain and grief into change. Could we organize a protest maybe? Our town is small, but if enough women and non-awful guys got behind it . . .

No. It's not enough. Those victims had a clear goal: stricter gun control. Our message would just be: hey, maybe stop being such unbelievable cretins toward young women?

So . . . we should do the same. We should demand comprehensive revenge porn legislation. It's the only thing that would provide an adequate deterrent for guys seeking to destroy a woman's reputation. These laws already exist to varying degrees in other states, but the South in general is yet to follow suit. And with far-right senators like Ted Vaughan in office, change is unlikely to happen anytime soon.

Yet a plan is formulating in my mind. I'm aware I've been sat in silence for several minutes, and things round the table have gotten a little awkward, so I lay my palms flat on the sugar-dusted table, fingers splayed, and say, "I have an idea."

"Always dangerous," Ajita says. "Go on."

"I think we need to arrange a meeting with Ted Vaughan."

Meg blinks twice in quick succession, pushing her glasses up her nose. "The senator?"

"The father of the dude you banged on a garden bench?" Ajita adds.

I nod once, solemn as a nun. "The one and only."

Nothing is ever going to change. Not unless we force it to.

Wednesday 4 January

7.45 a.m.

Despite last night's wild sequence of events – namely landing a job and experiencing severe second-hand pain on Hazel's behalf – I leave the diner and walk home in good snuff. [For the uninitiated, this is entertaining old slang for "in a good mood". I am not sure if you can culturally appropriate Middle Ages England, but if you can, please send the Tudors my apologies.]

We spend the rest of the BBB meeting drafting an email to Ted Vaughan's office, requesting a meeting to discuss the state's condemnable lack of revenge porn legislation. We even use words like "legislation", to give off the illusion of savvy. The BBB email account pings immediately with an auto response: someone will get back to us in three–five business days. The impatient imp who nests inside my skull wants to march down to the office right now and demand they see us this very instant, but I beat down the *imp*ulse [geddit?] for once. We all know I'm not fantastic at will power, or generally behaving like an adult in any way, shape or form.

So we must consider this show of spectacular restraint a win.

Having a plan makes me feel fierce and determined, rather than angry and helpless. I cling to it like a life raft.

Hazel's sex tape is the talk of the town. The guy who leaked it – a former jock nicknamed Bakehead on account of his well-documented pot habit – is apparently her ex-boyfriend. He cheated on her, she wouldn't take him back, so he sent their sex tape to everyone he knew. She filmed it in trust, and that trust was shattered.

Lots of girls have left the group chat in a show of solidarity, but plenty haven't. The follow-up messages are now into the hundreds. The majority are lewd, crude and skin-crawlingly vulgar, although there are a handful of brave souls who've chimed in and called out the guy who started the group chat, labeling him a pitiful bully and a pathetic, immature dick. But those are few and far between. It's mainly water-squirt emojis.

Carson, God bless his soul, commented saying, "Hey, man, this is uncool. Delete it, right now." It remains undeleted, but I appreciate his sticking up for Hazel nonetheless – because as soon as he does a few of his teammates follow his lead. It's nice seeing guys actually call each other on their bullshit, and even nicer when it's your boyfriend leading the rally cry.

Even Danny – who has abstained from the general internet since I found out he leaked my nude pictures to the entire world – has heard the news, on account of the fact it's a small-ass town, and you can't even take a dump without your neighbor speculating over its consistency.

Despite the fact we haven't spoken in months, he messages me the following:

Hey. Heard about Hazel. Hope you're both okay.

I sigh and shove my cell phone back in my pocket, breathing in the crisp winter air and vague scent of log fires. I don't think there is a Pulitzer Prize for uninspiring text messages, but if there were, I think this dry-as-toast attempt would definitely make the shortlist.

In fact, all this text does is stoke my fiery rage. No, neither of us are okay, and it's all your fucking fault. How dare you massage your own conscience like this.

To be honest, I don't even care about Danny. I know who the good people in my life are, and he is not one of them. His support, or lack thereof, means nothing to me anymore. [Hold that thought, past me.]

Even though we have a plan of action and having an outlet for my anger is already alleviating its intensity, I'm still dreading school today. I can't watch Hazel suffer like I did. I can't go through the stares and the whispers and the laughs all over again. My emotional armor isn't robust enough – there are chinks and holes from the open fire it endured for months on end.

But I'm an O'Neill. We get by. We always have, and always will. So instead of letting fear and anger paralyze me, I'm going to go into the kitchen, make coffee for Betty and me, and tell her the news about my new part-time job. I'm briefly concerned the excitement will cause her to shit herself right there in the kitchen, so I take a mop just in case. The last thing we need is Dumbledore using a poop as a chew toy. Again.

RIP, couch. May angels lead you in.

3.17 p.m.

School is nowhere near as bad as it has the potential to be, which is probably the first time those words have ever left my mouth/ fingers.

Hazel stays home. I don't blame her. Rumors are flying around about the awful shit that's happened to her since the tape was sent around. She was instantly fired from her weekend job at Hollister, and her ultra-religious parents have grounded her so severely that she's not even allowed to be on the cheerleading squad anymore. She's an honors student, by all accounts, with lofty career ambitions. Does she feel like her future has been snatched away from her, like I did? Like I still do, in my darkest moments?

At least Hazel's friends seem to be rallying around her. The squad are on a letter-writing campaign – to Hazel's parents, begging them to let her back on the team, and to Hollister HQ, demanding she get her job back. Carson's teammate's mom knows a guy who's high up at Abercrombie & Fitch, and offers to reach out to him explaining the situation. Baxter and a couple other guys on the soccer team corner Bakehead and threaten to kick his teeth in if he doesn't delete the group chat. He obliges, thank God, but the damage is largely done. The tape is burned into everyone's minds forever – and saved to camera rolls all over town. It's only a matter of time before someone shares it wider.

As a general rule people suck. Hazel's locker has been adorned with pompoms, flimsy underwear and a strip of condoms. Ajita, Meg and I help her friends hastily tear all of this down and stuff it in an overflowing garbage can, to the soundtrack of many loud "booooooo"s from the assortment of teenage dirtbags around us. The entire time we're working, chills run up and down my arms, pooling in the palms of my hands. Watching this unfold all over again is like a waking nightmare I can never outrun.

At lunch I take myself away to the restroom and huddle in the cubicle, typing out an email to Hazel using her school address. I remember the way the scandal made me feel so alone, as though nobody else on the planet, much less in this tiny town, could understand the pain of what I was going through. If I can save Hazel from that intensely lonely sensation, it'll be worth it.

Hey Hazel,
I just wanted to say that I'm so sorry you're going through this. I know it feels like your entire world is crashing down, like you might die from the shame of it, but I promise it gets better. It really does. People have very low

attention spans and will honestly forget about it way quicker than you think. Even if you wind up on BuzzFeed, like yours truly.

If you do ever want to talk to someone who genuinely gets what you're going through, I'm always here. It's not that I think I'm the authority on the situation – of course I'm not. I can only speak from my own experiences, and I know everyone is so different. But yeah, I understand what this very specific pain feels like, so if there's anything I can do just let me know.

Izzy

Look! Not one single trace of sarcasm in the entire two paragraphs! Better text Ajita a dirty joke, stat.

Hey. Why does Santa Claus have such a big sack?

Her reply buzzes almost immediately.

I don't know. I don't celebrate Christmas, you culturally insensitive asshole. Xo

Me: **Okay, well, the answer was because he only comes once a year, but you've kind of ruined the moment.**

6.45 p.m.

Betty's working late tonight, and Ajita is going to some kind of tragic athletics meet with her hideously talented brother Prajesh, so I decide to spend the evening working on my screenplay. My agent just sent me notes on the revisions I did over the holidays, and I'm excited to roll up my writerly sleeves and get stuck in.

However, just as I've boiled the kettle for a literal gallon of cocoa, there's a knock at the door. Carson.

"Hey," he says, smiling, cute as a button in his pizza place uniform. He's still wearing the pepperoni-themed baseball cap, even though he hates it. He knows it makes me smile, so he wears it whenever he can. I will never get tired of his sausage. [Yes, this entire paragraph was leading up to that innuendo. Why am I like this?]

"Just finished work?" I ask, leaning in for a smooch. He smells of oregano.

"Nah, I just wear this for kicks," he mumbles, lips pressed against mine.

Dumbledore dashes restlessly round our ankles. He's hyper with pent-up energy, since I haven't had a chance to take him out properly over the last few days. Reluctantly I pull away from Carson. "Hey, I need to walk the pooch. Wanna come? It's fine if not. If you've gotta get home or whatever."

He bends down to play-wrestle with Dumbledore, who pants excitedly. "Nah. I'll come with." The dog immediately rolls onto his back in mock defeat, and wriggles in delight as Carson rubs his chubby little belly.

"Awesome," I say. "I'll just grab his wizard's robes."

To his credit Carson is completely unfazed by this. He's

immune to my family's weirdness, which I sort of kind of love about him. [Don't tell him I used the L-word in a sentence describing him, because I work very hard on my reputation as an aloof sloth-type figure, and don't want it to be ruined now.]

While we walk to the nearby park, I fill Carson in on both the BBB and the job developments. "Anyway, the combination of the two almost rendered my darling grandmother incontinent. Thankfully she managed to control the situation, which is good, because the last thing we need is a medical emergency."

"How would that be a medical emergency?" he asks. "Do I even want to know?"

"I meant for Dumbledore," I explain, shoving my hands deep into my pockets, still clutching Dumbledore's leash. I watch him waddle ahead of us, little buttocks bouncing up and down, determined to show off in front of Carson. "Speaking of medical emergencies, have I told you about the time I had a tumor in fifth grade?"

His eyebrows shoot up into his beanie. "You had a tumor? How could I not know that?"

I maintain a serious expression. "I mean, it turned out to be a gummy bear lodged behind my uvula. But it *could* have been a tumor. At least it gave the ER folks a good laugh."

Carson snorts extravagantly. "You got taken to the emergency room for a malswallowed gummy bear?"

"Firstly, 'malswallowed' is not a word, although it should be, so thank you for the entertaining new vocabulary. Secondly, in my defense, it was a fizzy gummy bear. That shit stings. Anyway, the school nurse was convinced I was dying. I wrote my will while waiting for the CAT scan."

Carson's dimples make an appearance as he grins. "Oh yeah? And what was on this will?"

"I requested a Viking burial, and left my worldly possessions to a rhino sanctuary I saw on a documentary that day. I'm not sure why I thought a herd of orphaned rhinoceri would have use for my Justin Bieber CDs, but there you go."

By the time we arrive the park is almost deserted. It's around midway between my housing community and Carson's place, and it's like something out of a post-apocalyptic movie. The swingsets and slides are rusty and worn, and there's a rocket-shaped jungle gym graffitied with ugly slurs. The sandboxes are equal part tiny rocks and cigarette butts. There's a swimming bath that hasn't been used in years, so has been transformed into a charming skate park/drug den hybrid. And yet at this time of year, with the moon shining on the sparkling layer of frost coating the park, it's weirdly beautiful. And, you know, harrowing.

The whole place is empty, because it's way too cold for even the most hardcore teenage delinquents. We leave Dumbledore to roam around and do his business. He promptly takes a piss against a Confederate statue. Good dog.

Carson and I pull up a pew on a memorial bench, dedicated

to the only properly famous guy from our neighborhood — a celebrated anti-apartheid protester who died in a South African prison. [I've always found it ridiculous how the powers that be decided he was only worthy of a bench, not the entire park. I'd give him the entire state, if it were my call to make, which is probably why it is not my call to make.]

"Anyway, at least now we'll be able to afford pet insurance, with this new job of mine," I announce merrily. "Dumbledore can eat all the delicious turds he likes. And, hey, maybe I can afford a new toothbrush! Mine has had alopecia for several years now."

"Shit, things have been so bad you can't afford a toothbrush?"

I shrug. "I'm used to it. Many apologies that you must kiss this improperly washed mouth of mine."

Dumbledore ambles back over to us, dropping a carefully selected rock at Carson's feet and looking up expectantly. He's a rescue dog — obviously, because how the Dickens could Betty and I afford a pedigree dachshund — and he's always had a rock fetish. He often carries them home with him in his cheek pouches, like a hamster, and nestles them into his dog bed with him. Bless.

Carson picks up the rock and throws it in the direction of the permanently lopsided seesaw. Dumbledore chases it as fast as his tiny legs can carry him, which is not fast in the slightest. Since it's pitch dark, finding the same rock again should keep him entertained for a while.

"Man, I had no idea things were ever that desperate." Quietly he adds, "I wish I could help out more. I'm sorry."

"Don't ever apologize for that," I say, louder than I mean to. He looks taken aback by my belligerence. [Belligerence! Check out that thesaurus usage!] "I just mean you have your own shit to worry about," I add hastily, softer now. "You shouldn't have to take care of me too."

"But I want to. You're cold?" he asks, watching my leg bounce up and down in a bid to warm up. He takes off his oversized sweater and hands it to me, flashing a strip of toned brown belly skin as he does, and I feel a familiar jolt of longing.

Although maybe I just have a thing for benches at this point.

9.14 p.m.

With Betty not around to crow about water bills I take a longer, hotter shower than usual, before spending the night the way I planned to: editing my screenplay. I mean, right after I finish writing this blog post. And checking social media. And making hot cocoa. The scandal changed many things about me, but not my talent for procrastination.

Finally, after completing the most pointless and unnecessary of tasks, I curl up in my tiny single bed and get to work, throwing my hair up into a messy bun. Instagram girls somehow make messy buns look like the sexiest thing on this earth but I assure you mine just makes me look like I'm wearing a swimming cap, which is not my dream aesthetic. [No offense if you're reading this, Michael Phelps. Which I don't know why you would be, but still.]

Friday 6 January

9.51 a.m.

Since I stayed up half the night manically whizzing through script edits – writing in a new character and removing another entirely – I'm glad our first class of the day is drama. It's the only thing I'm remotely good at academically, and we never have homework because Mrs Crannon is one of those blessed "learn-by-doing" advocates. So I can coast by pretty easily on zero winks of sleep.

We're studying the script of *Guys and Dolls* in prep for our midterm exams. Unfortunately studying theater is not just about goofing off on stage and attempting Jazz-era Brooklyn accents. We actually have to write essays on things like narrative arc, which if you ask me is incredibly unreasonable, although as an aspiring a screenwriter it's probably a useful exercise. So we're sitting in a circle in Mrs Crannon's classroom and doing a read-through from the playbook before we start analyzing and breaking everything down.

I've been cast as Miss Adelaide, one of the two female leads, while Ajita is a Nepali Sarah Brown, because Mrs Crannon is not one of those absurd people who use "historical accuracy" to justify their racism. She's also cast a Chinese-American girl called Sharon in the famously white male role of Lieutenant Brannigan. This decision angered Danny greatly, as he's been relegated to an ensemble part. He's still stewing about it now. In fact, if he stews for much longer, he's in real danger of becoming a casserole.

Mrs Crannon has dashed backstage to grab a stack of fur coats to help us get into character, and also because the radiators are broken so the classroom temperature is currently subzero. When she left she told us to start the read-through without her, but of course, as a roomful of lazy/horny teenagers, this is not the course of action we ultimately take, instead opting to chat among ourselves on topics of our choice. For instance, I'm chatting to Ajita about the possibility of lip-syncing my singing parts, because although Miss Adelaide is an alto role, I still cannot hit the high notes without sounding like a meerkat with a softball bat shoved up its ass. Right when I'm doing my very best meerkat-with-a-softball-bat-shoved-up-its-ass impression, much to Ajita's delight and merriment, Danny chooses this precise moment to come over to us.

Ajita's euphoric expression takes on a vaguely murderous vibe as she watches him approach, but still the useless shrew does not think to warn me about the incoming douchebag. So I'm still howling "aaaaayyeeeeeee-yeeeeee-yaaaaaaaaahhhhh" when he taps me on the shoulder.

"Hey, Iz," he says as woodenly as, I don't know, a didgeridoo.

My skin bristles at the use of my old nickname. Shouldn't he have lost nickname privileges when he systematically ruined my life?

"Daniel," I say coolly to illustrate the point in my patented passive aggressive manner.

He's wearing that ancient Pokémon T-shirt I got once him. It's been washed so many times that the Pikachu's face is vaguely haunting. "You didn't reply to my text."

"Didn't I?" I reply, milder than a chicken korma, even though the mere sight of him is enough to send me into a rage-induced coma. [Does that rhyme? Should I abandon screenwriting to pen profound and poignant poetry? Rupi Kaur makes it look very easy.]

"Uh, no." Danny scratches a tiny scab on his upper arm, and the top layer comes away. He winces as poppy-red blood blooms in its place. GOOD. BLEED, DOUCHEBAG. [I did warn you about the rage.] "Anyway, just wanted to say that I'm here. You know. If you need anything. Which you probably don't. But, uh, yeah."

"She's fine," Ajita butts in. "Carson and I have her back. Anything else?"

At the mention of Carson's name Danny's benign demeanor is shattered. He stands up straighter and injects some venom into his voice. "Right. Fine. Sorry for wasting your time then." And he flounces away again. I'm trying to think of something funny to say about flouncing, but I'm tired as hell. Maybe one day I'll stop hating Danny as much as I do right now, but that moment seems very far in the future indeed.

"You know, sometimes I think I might miss the guy," I mutter to Ajita, who's staring viciously at Danny's back as he walks away. "But then I remember his personality and think better of it."

12.59 p.m.

Holy guacamole and for the love of nachos! We're grabbing lunch in the cafeteria when all three of our phones ping with an extremely exciting email notification at the same time. I immediately drop mine into the bowl of soup in front of me.

We got a meeting with Ted Vaughan's office! A political staffer is going to sit down with us next week to discuss our concerns. Gahhhhh! We genuinely did not think this would happen. I'm literally already nervous.

Part of me is glad we're not meeting with Vaughan himself. After everything he's done since the photo emerged of me banging his son on a garden bench – all the high-and-mighty speeches about family values and degenerate youths – I don't think I'd be able to resist launching across his desk and tearing out his esophagus with my bare teeth.

Anyway, I'm distracted from the nerves somewhat by the rescue mission we must now perform to recover my phone from its oniony fate. Ajita fishes it out the bowl with her bare hands and I rinse it off in my cup of water, which is admittedly not the wisest move but you remember the thing about me not being the sharpest erection in the shed/brothel?

Thankfully Meg produces a bag of dried rice from her purse, and we shove my phone into it for the foreseeable future. When I enquire as to why on earth Meg was carrying said bag of rice around with her to begin with she merely replies: "I've been friends with you for, what, three months now? And this is the fourth time you've dropped your phone in soup."

She has a point.

2.04 p.m.
Phone now successfully resuscitated, we're leaving geography class when Carson crops up behind me and squeezes my shoulders. I jump a little, like I've received a mild electric shock, but soon relax when I see it's him. [For some reason I'm more easily startled since the sex scandal. I have no idea why, but it's like I'm constantly just a tiny bit on edge.]

He's wearing his hyperactive puppy expression in full force, and opens our conversation with, "So is it just me, or is Mr

Richardson even more Peru-obsessed than usual?" [Context: our geography teacher once trekked Machu Picchu, and not a single class goes by without some kind of reference to his journey of a lifetime. Like, if anyone can find a way to relate glacier formations to the Temple of the Sun, it's him.]

"Do you think we should tell him it's highly offensive for a white man to dress as an Incan emperor?" I ask. Not that he's done this yet, so attached is he to his staple uniform of plaid shirts and beige chinos, but give it time.

Carson laughs his smooth, easy laugh. "You all set for diner training tonight?"

"Think so," I say, just as a bubble of nerves pops in my belly. "Just picked up some plain black pants at a thrift store, and they'll provide me with a couple shirts. So I think I have everything I need uniform-wise."

We stroll toward Carson's locker, where he's picking up books for math. "You'll be great."

I slip my hand into his and give it a grateful squeeze. "Thanks. Although as a bona fide slacker in all things, I'm marginally concerned at having to perform actual manual labor. Do my limbs even work that way?"

He laughs and drops my hand so he can enter his locker combo. "You're no slacker, O'Neill. Just selective in what you spend your energy on. However, they do know you gotta be fed every half-hour else you turn into Medusa incarnate, right?"

I shove him playfully, and he shoves me back, and then I'm squealing as he grips me in a bear hug and pretends to eat my shoulder, and oh God we're one of those obnoxious couples everyone hates but I just don't care because it's so fucking nice.

In all seriousness I'm actually excited to start work at the diner. Betty and I are no strangers to being poor. We're not. Things that other people take for granted – things they consider necessities, like batteries for the TV remote – are luxuries to us. And to be fair I've never known any different, so it doesn't bother me that much. We get by.

For me and Betty what it comes down to is this: we've always managed to stay afloat, and that's all that matters really. But now, with me working too, maybe life will be better than just staying afloat. Maybe we'll be able to go out to the movies, or get takeout from the fancy Chinese restaurant uptown. The thought makes me fizz with excitement. It really does.

I mean, I'd even resigned myself to being poor forever. Poverty is a cycle, by design. Let's take shoes, for example. Reasonably wealthy people can afford to buy a decent pair of shoes made from leather or, I don't know, dragonhide, which will last them a few years. But the lower working class cannot. We buy cheap, terrible shoes made from awful materials and stitched together by exploited southeast Asian kids. And they fall apart within months, and we have to buy more cheap terrible shoes because we need shoes, damn it, and we end up spending way more than the wealthy middle-class people ever did. All because we couldn't afford the initial upfront cost of a $100 pair of shoes. So we stay poor, because we're forever using our only slivers of disposable income plugging the shoe-shaped holes in our lives. It's impossible to ever save money, to ever work yourself out of the poverty pit. Because shoes.

Anyway, "shoes" is starting to not sound like a word, so I'm going to move on. TL;DR, bring on my first ever shift.

3.42 p.m.

The perks of spending half my life at the diner and being bought overpriced milkshakes by Ajita is that training is actually pretty straightforward. I already know the menu inside out, and also the price list, because that's what happens when you have no mullah. You look at the price before the actual item.

Anyway, it transpires that the only thing I really need training on is the till system, but as a digital native who's grown up with intuitive technology skills, it's a breeze. So after three and a half hours of training, now I'm sitting in the back wolfing down some chili cheese fries. Betty never mentioned the free food! This changes everything. In fact, I might never leave the diner. I was here all the time anyway – at least now I'm getting paid for the privilege.

Once I get off break, I'm going to be shadowing another hostess just to get a feel for how she manages her section of tables, and I've also been charged with taking down the Christmas decorations when it gets quieter later. Part of me will be sad to see the derp elf go. He really does bring a certain level of festivity/insanity to proceedings.

Do we think anyone will notice if I leave him front of house to play hostess while I hide in a corner and work on my screenplay? If you strain extra hard, it does almost sound like he's saying, "May I take your order?" instead of "herpy herr-lerr-durrrssss".

Although if you don't strain quite hard enough, it more resembles "herpes her like dicks", so that's perhaps a bit of a gamble. Back to the drawing board we go.

7.24 p.m.

So I'm crouched behind the tinsel tree, trying to find the best way to dismantle its clunky base, when Ajita and Meg arrive in the diner, greeted by the increasingly dogged drone of the derp elf.

The petulant third-grader inside of me is all, "RUDE! How dare they hang out without ME? I hope they both break out in hives!" And the even more petulant second-grader inside of me is all, "How dare Ajita give me shit for inviting Meg to act in our show, then betray me like this?"

In any case, even though they must've come in here to pay me a visit, they don't see me wedged under the tree with my ass crack on display to every Google Earth drone in the state. Nor do they appear to be looking for me particularly hard. Instead they just park up in a booth nearby and chatter away about what burgers they're going to order.

"I feel like you can't go wrong with a chicken mayo," Meg says. "I mean, usually I would posit that any and all lettuce has been summoned to this earth by Lucifer himself. But you can't beat a bit of crunchy iceberg in a southern fried chicken burger."

"Fair point," Ajita agrees. "On behalf of vegetarians everywhere, I accept your stance that lettuce is the devil's work. In fact, I believe every vegetable on this earth, up to but not including the humble potato, is just plain arrogant. Like, they know they're nutritious. They know they're better than you."

I feel a sharp pang of . . . something. Maybe FOMO [Fear Of Missing Out, if we have any grandmas in the house], but I don't know, it's a little more than that. Why is this bothering me so much?

8.52 p.m.
Lol, never mind. Period just started. As you were.

9.04 p.m.
After I clear up the tinsel debris and whizz through the rest of the decoration removal, and obviously stop and say hey to Ajita and Meg for as long as possible without being hung, drawn and quartered by my manager, I head back to the kitchen with several

buckets of potatoes to peel and leave in water for tomorrow, which is a great relief. I'm irritable and exhausted and my feet hurt from pounding hard tiles, so to be in a quiet corner of the kitchen alone is a blessing from above. Literally if you asked me whether I would rather have sex or peel vegetables right now, I would be elbow deep in potato skins before you'd even finished your sentence. [Does "elbow deep in potato skins" sound vaguely rude to you? Or am I just delirious at this point?]

Seriously, though, I have all new respect for Betty after just one shift. If my eighteen-year-old body is struggling by the end of a ten-hour shift, how must hers feel?

This is all just reinforcing the fact that I can't possibly go to college come fall. I need to stay in this sleepy little town and work in the diner every day, so that Betty can finally retire in peace. I can write screenplays on my days off, or on my dinner breaks, or in the small hours of the morning while the rest of the town sleeps. Like some sentimental hipster type.

Oooooh, I might go full Romantic poet à la Samuel Coleridge. I mean, I'm not sure he moonlighted as a pancake chef, but he had the right idea. Do we know anyone who can hook a girl up with some opium?

10.59 p.m.
Sweet angel Carson Manning meets me after my shift to walk me home. He even brings me a leftover pizza from his own shift.

A customer unfathomably ordered Hawaiian pizza, on account of the hallucinogens they were clearly under the influence of, then came to their senses and amended their order to the hugely preferable pepperoni pizza. But not before the chef had already put the first pizza in the oven. So now I have the original Hawaiian pizza in my possession, and I'm too hungry to shun the presence of pineapple on the world's greatest food. [Well, world's greatest food apart from nachos. Omg, are nacho pizzas a thing? If not, can we make them a thing? Who do I have to call to make this happen?]

"So how'd it go?" he asks as we walk side by side back to my apartment. He's still in his pizza-themed polo shirt, though he's thrown on a hoodie and a beanie hat to keep his noggin warm.

It's still super cold out, but not too cold for me to practically inhale the first few slices of pizza. Carson holds the box open for me like it's a silver platter while I cram fistfuls into my mouth.

"It was all right, I guess," I say through a mouth of pineapple atrocity. "Angela seemed largely unimpressed by my character as a whole, but I think as long as I steer clear and mind my business, it'll be fine. Plus, free food, so. Not too many complaints. Which is strange, because you know how much I enjoy the act of complaining." I lick my fingers wolfishly.

As we keep walking through the frosty night silence blooms between us. And, as usual, my default reaction is to fill it with a joke or a story – anything to avoid awkwardness.

"So Ajita and Meg came by tonight," I start, crunching through a pizza crust with more vigor than is strictly necessary. "Ajita had some interesting sentiments regarding the inherent arrogance of vegetables, though she made some allowances for potatoes. Your thoughts?"

As he always does, he considers this statement with utmost sincerity. "I concur, man, I concur. Like, have you even seen a parsnip? Ain't no more high-and-mighty vegetable than a parsnip."

I fumble in the box for another slice of pizza, and am mildly astonished that I'm down to the last piece already. My eating talents never fail to amaze me. "But you will concede that potatoes are, by and large, the humble champions of the vegetable arena? You know, in modesty terms."

"I don't see that they have a choice, my dude," Carson says, shaking his head in mock sadness. "After all, intense modifications gotta be made to the humble potato in order to make it worth eating. Roasting, mashing, frying. A sorry state of affairs, man, and certainly nothing to brag about."

My bad mood is evaporating with every step. I think part of me has always worried that I'd never find a guy whose sense of humor was as compatible with mine as Ajita's. Like, what if you only get one soulmate, and my best friend is mine?

And yet every single second I spend with Carson reminds me that I've somehow hit the jackpot, and my boyfriend makes me laugh just as much as my favorite pal does. [Please hide the flaying equipment from Ajita. She is not above torturing me for the above statement.]

11.34 p.m.

Betty is asleep when I eventually get home, snoring like a manatee with a head cold. Although Carson offers to stay and hang out for a while, I can tell he's just as wiped as I am, and looks pretty relieved when I give him a get-out-of-jail-free card. So we bid each other farewell at the gates, knowing we won't get to smooch again until school on Monday.

This weekend marks a full two days of back-to-back shifts for both of us, and I'm already ready to drop at the mere thought. And also still feeling a little homicidal from earlier. Currently fantasizing about impaling Angela on a broomstick. [As Ajita suggests, my murder fantasies have definite Count Dracula vibes these days. Vlad the Impaler: the role model you never knew you needed.]

Still, I'm so nearly finished with the final screenplay edits, and I want to get the polished version to my agent before she inevitably realizes I am a fraud and drops me, so I decide to spend the next few hours putting in some more work.

My eyes sting with tiredness as I fire up my laptop. I consider making hot cocoa, but everything aches and the thought of doing anything physical, anything at all, is enough to make me give up and resign myself to a cocoa-free writing session.

Dumbledore curls up in my lap, sensing my exhausted, periody, done-with-the-world mood, and gently licks my knee as a means of easing the fury. This probably sounds gross, but in all honesty I will take any comfort I can get right now, even if it means having my stubbly legs moistened by a tiny canine tongue. I try not to think about the fact he's probably just having a good suck because my skin tastes of diner grease and sweat. Yum.

At first, doing a round of dialogue polishing is like trying to get a post-rigor-mortis corpse to perform a limbo. [Good grief, my imagery is dark in this post. Send in the nuns, for I require a cleansing.] Usually I read dialogue aloud to myself to get a feel for what sounds natural and what sounds clunky and jarring, but since I don't want to wake Betty, I have to settle for a low mumble, which does absolutely nothing to illuminate the subpar sentences. Le sigh.

After twenty minutes of quasi-productivity, I rub my sleep-deprived eyes and blink at the screen through the bursts of kaleidoscopic light caused by pressing my fingers into my eyelids with too much vigor. [Anyone else used to think they were the only ones who could do this? Or did I just suffer from snowflake syndrome as a child?]

My phone vibrates under the pillow, and I pull it out. A reply from Hazel Parker. The lump of defective muscle in my chest — commonly referred to as a heart in normal homo sapiens — twinges as I read.

Hey. Thanks so much for reaching out. It means a lot. Kinda feels like my life is over now, you know? I wanted to be a doctor. No med school will take me seriously after this. My parents won't even look at me. I can't stop crying. Can we meet? My friends have been awesome, but they don't really get it :(

I do a funny little whimpering noise, and in the ultimate show of disrespect Dumbledore glares irritatedly up at me, furious that I dare interrupt his knee-sucking bliss, then leaps off the bed and makes a point of humping my stuffed teddy collection, looking me straight in the eye the whole way through. [Honestly, that dog has such an attitude problem at the moment. Total angsty *Order of the Phoenix* vibes.]

Swallowing the stubborn ice cube bobbing in my throat, I fire off a reply to Hazel, saying I'm more than happy to meet up outside of school and talk her through everything. Then I bury my face in my pillow and resist the urge to scream, digging my fingernails into my palm until hot crescents are burned into my skin.

The rage ebbing and flowing through me for the last few days won't leave. I'm angry, angry for Hazel, angry at Danny, and angry at myself for not being to stop this happening again. And, to top it all off, my sausage dog is penetrating the ear of my favorite teddy bear.

After I regain a normal breathing rhythm, I turn my

attention back to the screenplay, but the fury is like a dam for my creative energy. I can't think past the scalding adrenaline, the uncomfortable edge it gives my heartbeat. The screen blurs. My pulse thuds. There's an acrid, bitter taste in my mouth. Even as the least active person in the northern hemisphere, I have the sudden urge to throw something, to smash a plate, to punch a wall. Anything to let out some of this jagged energy.

Sunday 8 January

10.46 a.m.

After a long-ass Saturday spent working in the diner – thankfully without any major run-ins with Angela, the woman single-handedly keeping the town's tanning salon afloat – I spend the rest of my Saturday night finishing up the remainder of my screenplay edits and sending them back to my agent.

I will literally never get tired of saying "my agent". In fact, I may just start directing any and all enquiries I do not want to address myself to my agent instead. Izzy, would you please clean the burger-sauce spillage on Table Twelve? See my agent. Izzy, what's the square root of an octagon? See my agent. Izzy, woof-woof-woof? See my agent. [That last one is Dumbledore asking me to take him out for a walk, in case you are not fluent in dachshund.]

This morning I treated myself to a lie-in until roughly nine thirty, at which point my darling grandmother decides to blare her 90s rap classics CD at full volume. I shit you not, the woman still has a CD player. I think Thomas Jefferson was the leader of the free world when she first brought it home. In fact, allow me to recount a charming conversation that took place roughly two weeks after she purchased it from a pawn shop for $1.50.

Me: *Did you like the Ice Cube album I got you?*

Betty: *Mmmm, yes, very good.*

Me: *You didn't listen, did you?*

Betty: *Well, I didn't like to say anything, but . . .*

Me: *???*

Betty: *It didn't fit.*

Me: *What didn't fit?*

Betty: *The CD you got me. It didn't fit in the CD player.*

Me: *What are you talking about? All CDs are the same size??*

Betty: *Not the one you got me. It's fat and has square edges.*

Me: *. . .*

Turns out the crazy old bat hadn't even taken it out of its case. She thought the case *was* the CD. I despair.

Anyway, the long sleep must've paid dividends in terms of melting away my anger, because I'm actually feeling refreshed and full to the brim of ludicrous jokes this morning. The last week has sapped my comedic energy somewhat, like a laughter leech. But now I'm back to best and ready to perform patronizing wildebeest impressions at the drop of a hat. [If you've never seen my patronizing wildebeest impressions I feel bad for you, son. I got ninety-nine problems but a gnu ain't one? No, I don't know what I'm talking about either.]

1.24 p.m.

Carson and I take Dumbledore for another walk in the park, except now that there are more than a few inches of snow on the ground, Dumbledore cannot actually touch the ground through said snow. He just kind of sinks into the powder with a disgruntled yelp. So really, a more accurate sentence would be "Carson and I take Dumbledore for a carry in the park." I tuck him under my arm, dressed in his wizard's robes, and he admires the view from a great height.

We reach the park and I wipe the snow from a bench, taking a seat with Dumbledore in my lap. He lies on his back and demands, with his eyes, that I tickle his tummy at my earliest convenience.

Carson begins immediately making a snow statue, compacting snowballs together to make . . . something. Really, it just looks like a pile of snow in a weird shape. Not that I don't have full trust in his artistic abilities or anything.

"So how're things going at home?" I ask Carson, Dumbledore squirming in creepy ecstasy.

"Not bad, not bad. Oh man, did I tell you Colbie's super into basketball now?" He pounds snow into another tight ball and places it carefully. "Always stealing my jersey. Caught him checking himself out in the mirror while wearin' it, even though it was down to his ankles. Five years old, man, and already thinks he's the next LeBron."

"That's adorable. Has he ever, you know, played basketball?"

"Details." Carson smirks, green hoodie making his eyes look even darker, and I honestly want to smooch his face off. "I'm savin' up for one of those mini hoops for his bedroom wall. With the inflatable balls and whatnot. He'll lose his shit when he sees it. Man, I can't wait."

"You're so cute with your siblings," I say, breath steaming up the air.

"It's weird, y'know? We don't have the same dad or anything, but we're still so tight."

"You ever talk to your dad?" I watch Dumbledore's eyelids droop. "You don't mention him much."

His body stiffens slightly, but he bends down to disguise it. Picks up more snow, this time a smaller handful. Rolls it into a longer shape. "Nah, never. Ain't seen him since I was in diapers. Doubt I'm missin' much, from what my mom says."

The slightly ethereal snowscape makes me want to talk. Like, properly talk.

"Still," I murmur, "I know what it's like to have that weird hole in your life." The words feel horribly stark and honest against the quiet snow. But they feel right. Cathartic, somehow. I've always wanted to talk to Carson about this – this huge thing we share. I feel like it'll bring us even closer together, having that connection. Truth be told, he's the only person I've ever wanted to talk about it with. Ajita and Meg are amazing, but they can't ever truly understand what it is to lose a parent.

But Carson just shrugs. "Yeah, I guess."

He's obviously not in the mood for Properly Talking, which I get. I've spent 99.9 percent of my life in the exact same frame of mind. And yet disappointment surges in my chest. I guess that's something nobody tells you when they urge you to open up to the people around you. Sometimes the people around you just won't be in the right place to listen.

So I keep my sentimental thoughts about parents and absence to myself, tucked away somewhere below my ribs.

"Whaddaya think?" Carson asks.

He steps back to reveal his finished sculpture, and I frown trying to make out what it is. Definitely an animal, of some sort, but it's misshapen and lumpy.

"It's an alpaca, dude!" he says, looking offended.

"Sorry. I just find its facial expression a little . . . a-*llama*-ing."

"Oh my God."

9.18 p.m.

For some reason my evening shift absolutely drags, despite the fact Betty is also working, which is all kinds of weird. We're making a point of being overly formal with each other so our serpentine manager cannot accuse us of being unprofessional. I bow every time I see her, and she calls me Madam Hostess O'Neill, Probably One-Millionth of Her Name. I fail to see how we could possibly be any more professional than this.

But still. It. Is. Dragging. I think when you work the long ten-hour shifts they go quicker, because you're not constantly looking at the clock. You just accept that you're there for an eternity. But when it's shorter the temptation to clock-watch is so much stronger, because you're, like, surely I'm nearly done now? [This is obviously in my expert opinion, having worked a grand total of three shifts in my entire life.]

Also, while I'm peeling yet more potatoes, I cannot stop thinking about Hazel Parker. How is she feeling right now? Is she poring over the lewd comments, examining every inch of her naked body and sexual technique through the lens of public perception? Is she shutting herself away from the judgment of her parents, closing down when her friends try to talk to her about it? Has she stopped applying to colleges? Does she feel like I did – powerless and lost, like her whole future has been burned to the ground? I know how impossible it is to see past something like that. How nothing else seems to matter but the fact the world has seen you naked.

This meeting with Vaughan's office cannot come soon enough.

Anyway, it's still snowing outside, and Betty is doing a

hilarious Canadian accent for little to no reason, and it's only forty-two minutes until I can go home and have my knees cleansed by my pubescent dachshund. So all is not lost.

Monday 9 January

8.00 a.m.

Ajita, Meg and I convene in the school library to a) finally upload our sex-doll sketch and b) strategize for our impending political meeting with Ted Vaughan's office. [Oh my God, if the Izzy of three months ago could read this sentence, she would pass out from awe and disbelief, and Dumbledore would chew her face off as an afternoon snack. RIP, needlessly massive nose.]

There are a handful of our Hermione-esque classmates in here already cramming for midterm exams, and a singular grouchy librarian clutching her flask of coffee. Snow falls gently past the window, and there are around fifteen space heaters pumping out warm, stale air. We huddle in a quiet corner, cradling a giant box of Honey Nut Cheerios and taking it in turns to shove fistfuls into our mouths.

"I feel like Vaughan's the kind of guy who would respond better to facts and figures than to emotional anecdotes," I say, partially because it's true, and partially because I would rather stick rusty screwdrivers in my eyes than share my emotional anecdotes with the slimiest senator in Slimeland.

Meg jots this down in her notepad. Honestly, the girl takes notes almost 24/7. No wonder her GPA is roughly triple mine. "That's true. He's pretty unemotional as a human."

"So what kind of stats do we want to present?" Ajita asks. "Like, how many young women are affected every year? How much the trend has risen since the dawn of smartphones?"

"Yeah, those are good. But won't he still think, so what?" Meg counters. "Facts and figures are effective, but we need to show why those facts and figures matter. We need to give a reason for his stone heart to care. Otherwise we might as well be delivering stats on the color preferences of humpback dolphins."

"Aren't dolphins colorblind?" Ajita asks.

Meg snorts. "I don't think –"

"What about suicide rates?" I mumble, rolling a Cheerio between my thumb and forefinger. "How many victims kill themselves as a result of revenge porn."

I can feel them both staring at me, and I know I let more than a crack of genuine hurt into those words. Can they tell I'm thinking of my lowest point a few months back, when everyone had abandoned me, and I couldn't see a future beyond the scandal?

"That would work," Ajita says softly. For a second it looks like she might squeeze my hand, but since she finds physical affection as appealing as rabies, she settles for sticking a Cheerio up each of my cavernous nostrils.

10.15 a.m.

I have no idea whether I'm just projecting my own insecurities onto him, which I admittedly have the tendency to do, but I feel like Carson is mad at me.

Consider the following exchange:

*Me: Heyyyyyy! *throws arms round Carson by the water fountain**
Carson: No, Iz.
Me: What? Why?
Carson: Because I'm mad at you, that's why.

On reflection, maybe it ain't just projection. [I could *so* be a rapper. Or at least a rapper's lyricist, if that's a thing, because there's nothing cringier than a white girl rapping. As a white girl who frequently raps, I know this for a fact.]

Anyway, he issues that final sentence without a trace of aggression, so it's hard to know just how badly I've messed up. In fact, he's so calm he might as well be delivering a weather report.

So I say, "Okay, why?" which I feel is fair given the complete lack of context he has provided me with. And yet he looks at me like I have all of a sudden grown tree trunks as arms.

"You really have no idea, do you?" He stares at me as I run my fingertips up and down my arms in a panic, making sure they haven't developed a bark-like texture during the course of this conversation. I seem to be in the clear, thank God. [No offense to tree-men, or anything. I'm just not super into photosynthesis.]

"I must confess, I do not," I say, shifting uncomfortably. He's looking at me like I'm the world's biggest jerk. Which I might be. But I just don't know exactly why this time. [You might have noticed this, but I am not all that self-aware.]

He scratches the back of his neck with a paint-stained palm and turns away. "Forget it."

"No!" I say a little too loud, reaching out to touch his arm. The warmth of his skin radiates through his gray sweater. "I mean, if I've upset you, I want to know about it. So I can be better in future." When he still says nothing I whisper, "Please?"

I don't mean to use a soft voice to soften his mood – it's just the way the plea came out – but it has that effect all the same. "Fine. Let's talk at lunch, though, 'kay? I'm late for class. Meet you in the woods at twelve thirty."

Ah, the woods. The backdrop of all traumatic exchanges in the life of Izzy O'Neill. I would not be surprised if I ultimately die among those trees, such is the impressive track record of tragedy in that one foresty patch. In fact, I should preempt the universe's intentions for my demise and burn myself at the stake to get it over with. Joan of Arc made it seem enjoyable, in a martyr-y kind of way.

Riddle me this: How doth one buildeth thine own stake?

12.57 p.m.

The woods are like a snowy winter wonderland, which I suppose would make the pyre situation all the more dramatic, but before I can even assess the logistics of the plan Carson turns up. He's not wearing a jacket, and even he, the warmest-blooded of all warm-blooded humans, seems to be shivering a little.

"What's up?" he asks, with none of his usual affection. I must really have messed up. It's alarming how easy it is to inadvertently make someone hate you. [A lesson I really should've learned by now.]

"Not much." Snow crunching under my Docs, I close some of the distance between us. He stays stock-still as I walk up to him, eyes staring just over my shoulder. "Carson?"

It's eerily quiet in the woods, the falling snowflakes muffling every sound except Carson's mumbled, "Yeah?"

"Talk to me. What's going on?"

"That video you guys just posted on YouTube." He grits his teeth, biting back some of the annoyance he's clearly feeling. "The sketch. Did you write it?"

"The crazed sex-doll one?" I ask, surprised by the direction of the conversation. "Yeah. Why? You didn't like it?"

He laughs, but not like he thinks I'm funny. More in disbelief. "D'you really think all guys are that creepy and awful?" His condensing breath hangs on the air in feathery wisps.

"No," I say, staring at my hands. My fingertips are so purple

80

from the cold that they look bruised. "Of course I don't think *all* guys are creepy and awful. But, like I said the other night, I believe there are enough bad guys out there that women have a right to fear them, you know?"

Carson says nothing, just sniffs sharply against the cold.

"You're really mad at me about it?"

He shrugs.

"But why?" I ask as calmly as I can. Right on the tip of my tongue there's a rant about why the #NotAllMen argument is a steaming heap of elephant crap, but I want to hear him out on this first. He's a smart dude, and I value his opinions. "Talk me through it. Talk me through your anger. Because I don't get it."

At this he scoffs, kicking a hardened snowball with the rubber toe of his sneaker. Not in an aggressive way, just absentmindedly. But he still won't look me in the eye.

A fresh flurry of snowflakes dislodges from a nearby tree. "Of course you don't get it." His voice is as cold as the air between us.

A cramp of discomfort seizes my stomach. "Don't get what?" I nudge, after he doesn't elaborate.

A moment's pause. He weighs his words carefully, rolling them around in his mouth before they go any further. Then: "When you're a black guy everyone assumes you're violent and dangerous, or some shit, and it's like . . . you always gotta be proving them otherwise. Always gotta be calm even when you're mad."

I nod slightly while I let myself digest this, allow his words to sink in, but he mistakes my silence for something else.

"Sorry," he mutters. "I get that's not what you wanna hear. Forget I said anything."

"No! I'm glad you did. I'm just processing. Listening. Please, keep talking." I reach out for his hands, but he pulls away again. From the strained expression on his face I can tell this conversation has gone too deep, too fast.

I give him more space to talk, but eventually he just says, "You know what? Never mind. Let's get lunch."

It's tempting to push it further, tempting to push past the endless half-conversations I seem to have with him, but as we walk back to the cafeteria I decide to leave the ball in his court. If the Ajita stuff has taught me anything over the last few months, it's that not everyone is an open book. Hell, I'm the worst offender when it comes to laughing over my issues, never allowing a jokey discussion to get too serious in case it forces me to reveal vulnerability. So I get it. I do.

The more I think about it, though, the more I realize that Carson never properly talks about what's going on with him. Not really. He just shrugs, says, "Yeah, sucks," and then we move on. And yet there must be so much pressure bubbling below the surface that never sees the light of day.

We're yet to have our first major argument as a couple,

and I can't help but wonder how the hell we'll ever talk it over when we do. They say opposites attract, but Carson and me? We're cut from the same cloth. And that's either going to make or break us.

Tuesday 10 January

11.16 a.m.

I spend all of yesterday and most of this morning flapping about the thing with Carson. Was I an insensitive jerk filming that video? Is he super mad at me and trying to downplay his anger, like he says he does so often? I care so much that it makes me feel a little pathetic – a simpering high-school girl obsessed with whether or not her boyfriend is mad at her. But it's hard not to worry when he buries everything below the surface. I can never tell exactly how much damage has been done. [What an unbelievable hypocrite I am. Did past me really not see that this is EXACTLY HOW PEOPLE FEEL WHEN TALKING TO ME??]

As I stop by my locker after final bell I'm barely paying attention to what's going on around me, just staring at my phone and praying it'll ping with a message from Carson, while simultaneously rifling through my locker for a tampon. Then a nearby conversation makes my ears prick up.

". . . has a banging rack."

"Oh yeah. If I was gonna go to prison for nailing a teacher, it would be her."

An eruption of laddish whoops. "All. Day. Loooooooong."

"Wonder what it'd take to get her to pull a Parker? I can just see her with a pair of pompoms . . ."

Rolling my eyes, I turn to face the culprits. Unsurprisingly it's a group of freshmen jocks. It's always at this point in the year that freshmen start to get a bit cocky. I prefer them meek and intimidated like they are in September, starting a new school at the bottom of the pecking order.

"Or an O'Neill. I'm allllll about that garden bench fetish . . ."

I'm about to storm over and give them a world-class smackdown when none other than Zachary Vaughan – he of the garden-bench shenanigans – pipes up.

He's strolling alongside them, basketball spinning on his finger, when he hears them shit-talking and stops in his track. "Apologize," he says, cool and firm. He gestures to me. "Apologize right now."

Yes, you read that correctly. Zachary Vaughan. Son of a senator, receiver of my nudes, maker of ill-judged cafeteria speeches. Please place your tongue back in your gaping mouth.

"Fuck that," one of them says, laughing, albeit uncomfortably. The others jeer and squirm in equal measure, some staring at the ground, some making smirking eye contact with each other.

The original offender starts to walk away, but Zachary steps right in his path. "I was on the garden bench too. Don't see you giving me shit about it. So apologize, or I'll go tell coach you're out here harassing girls to make yourself look like a big shot."

What even? I'm impressed – and amazed – by Zachary's tone. It's forceful without being aggressive. I'm also impressed and amazed by the very act of him defending me, since we haven't spoken in months, and I do have a habit of telling him to have sexual intercourse with a cactus, but we'll get to that in a sec. [Not the cactus intercourse. The impressed amazement.]

The jerkwad who mentioned my name turns to me. "Sorry." His jerkwad friends make snorting noises, and he flushes bright red.

"There's a good boy," Zachary says. "Now scram." They scram.

Zachary starts spinning the basketball again, strolling in the direction he was originally walking.

"Hey," I manage to choke out before he passes me. "Thanks for that."

He stops and turns. Half smiles. "No problem. Sorry I didn't do it sooner."

I shrug. "It's okay." I turn to shove a textbook into my locker, and when I close it he's on the other side.

"I was a jerk when it happened. Blaming you and all."

"Don't worry about it," I say, surprising myself with how genuinely I mean it despite my general revulsion toward the Vaughan name and everything it stands for. I guess his minor douchebagdom pales in comparison to Danny's epic betrayal. "Besides, it's not like you got off easy."

He nods, looking thoughtful. Spins the ball on his finger once more. "Yeah. So how've you been? Since everything went crazy, and all. I hear Castillo gave you The Talk. The Lord our savior, Jesus hates blowjobs, all that."

I snort. "She did. You got it too?"

"Yup." He shifts his backpack on his shoulder, white polo shirt crumpling as he does so. I'm not sure why he looks like he's participating in a surreptitious drug transaction every time we exchange words, but he's on-brand as ever. "It was super fun. A wild ride from start to finish."

A glimpse of the sarcastic, funny Zachary I met on that garden bench shines through, and I can't help but picture him as his self-assigned patronus: a duck-billed platypus. [You know. A duck-billed platypus attempting to purchase crack cocaine.]

"Gotta say, I'm surprised Castillo bothered talking to you," I mutter. "Everyone else seemed to be obsessed with dishing out all the blame on me."

"Yeah." He stares awkwardly at the ground. "Again, I'm sorry it blew up like that. Really. It's not fair how they treated you."

This stuns me somewhat. "I . . . Thanks, Zachary. For you know. Not being too Vaughanish, for once."

He gives me a pained smile. "Yeah, well. Like I say, I know I acted like a jerk before. But I don't want you to think

I'm anything like my dad. Because I'm not, okay?"

The mention of his dad surprises me – does he know about the meeting? – but I just nod. "Okay."

He studies me carefully from beneath his stupidly long eyelashes. "I hope this Hazel thing isn't bringing it all back for you?"

I avert my gaze as I lie. "Nah. I'm cool. Thanks, though."

2.43 p.m.

Speaking of unexpected solidarity, a couple Hazel's cheerleading friends approach me after math class. They're wearing matching black sweaters with initials of their first names – F and Z – sewn on in pink felt. Petition to change their title to twee-leaders, all those in favor say aye? [Aye.]

"Hey, Izzy, right?" Z says, smiling warmly. She clutches her textbooks to her chest. "We're Hazel's friends. Zara, Faye." The other girl, a beautiful blonde with a long pierced nose waves awkwardly.

"Hey! How's she doing?" I ask, stuffing my pencil case into my overfull satchel and struggling to zip it up. The bag of rice I've now started carrying around with me rustles conspicuously, and I hastily shove it deeper so the twee-leaders won't witness my lunacy first-hand. There are a number of soup casualties already in the rice ward, including my phone charger and Meg's iPod.

"That's kinda what we wanted to talk to you about," Zara

says, tucking a thick black braid behind her ear. "She's not great. And we kinda just wanted to know . . . since you've been through it and all, we wanted to ask you if there's anything we could be doing to support her?"

Faye nods. "It sucks to see her this hurt. We'll do anything it takes to make her feel better." Her voice is sweet and fluffy, like cotton candy. It takes an inordinate amount of willpower not to eat her voice box.

TBH I'm finding it quite strange to be painted as the expert on surviving slut-shaming when I barely got through my own leaked nude alive. I thought if I was ever going to become a world expert on something, it would be innuendos, or the ideal ratio of cheese to salsa on nachos. But no, I'm a specialist on how to deal with your boobs and vajayjay suddenly being in the public domain. [Many times since the scandal I've considered a giant statue of the eggplant emoji instead of a tombstone.]

"Honestly," I say, finally winning the zipper battle, "it sounds super basic, but the best thing you can do is just to let her know over and over again that you'll be there for her. At my darkest moments it felt like everyone had turned on me. That was partially my own fault, but still. Never let her get to that point, okay? Oh, and keep calling out all the douchebags who mock her for it. Don't just stay quiet and hope it calms down without your input. We need as many people as possible to fight back against this shit."

Zara and Faye nod, staring at me with something resembling respect. It's a weird feeling, but one I could definitely get used to.

7.28 p.m.

Ajita's parents are out of town at some conference for hotshot surgeon geniuses, and Prajesh is at track practice, because even though it's -70,000 degrees outside he took a blood oath to his sadist of a coach and must dedicate his entire existence to running a four-minute mile. Or something equally pointless. [This makes it sound like I don't care about sports. It's not that. It's just that I don't care about sports.]

Because of this rare empty house situ, rather than being relegated to the basement like we are every other night in life, Meg and I are chilling in Ajita's fancy kitchen. Ajita has put on some background music, and there's a bowl of Satan's grapes, a.k.a. olives, on the giant marble island. In our entire millennium as best friends she has never done either of things when it's just me and her hanging out. All right, so that's partially because I refer to olives in such derogatory terms, but still. The background music thing. WTF. It's some depressing acoustic shit I've never heard before in my life, and even though I mime having an emotional breakdown every time a new song comes on, Ajita still does not get the hint. Honestly. You would think she'd be more in sync with my needs by now.

Anyway, she's not paying attention to my dramatic Marcel Marceau episode because she's too busy fuming about some of the dickhead comments we got on the sex-doll video.

". . . and then the bastard said you couldn't pay him enough money in the world to have sex with any of us, which, like, *good*, because we're high-school kids, but also, rude??" She's stuffing olives into her face without pausing for breath, licking the garlicky lemon juice off her fingers with her freakish St Bernard tongue. "Worst part is, that comment got over three hundred likes. Ugh."

"Mmmm," Meg murmurs in semi-agreement. Except she's not paying attention to Ajita not paying attention to me, because she's too busy smiling at something on her phone. It's like not-paying-attention *Inception*. [There I go again with my stellar rap lyrics. Someone get me a record deal, stat.]

Ajita trails off as she notices Meg not paying attention, which if you ask me is quite offensive, because there I am paying perfect attention to her.

"Hey, Fern just sent me this hilarious meme," Meg giggles, oblivious to the mind-bending clusterfuck of irritation surrounding her. "Wanna see?"

Judging by the look on Ajita's face, she would like to drive over to Fern's house and tattoo aforementioned meme to her face using a scalpel and a ballpoint pen, but instead she plasters the world's fakest smile on her face and says, "Sure!"

What the hell? Her tone and demeanor are uber tense. If I didn't know any better, I'd say . . . she has a crush on Meg? It would kind of explain her weirdness about me inviting Meg onto the sketch show. Kind of. In any case I hope she doesn't like Meg that way, because it seems like Fern has Meg wrapped round her little pinkie.

Anyway, the meme is a $^4/_{10}$ at a push. It's a dog playing *Guitar Hero*, which would be hilarious as a standalone image, but the meme-maker has taken it a step too far and added the words "Me trying to tackle Mondays", which is *so* five years ago. Meme evolution has left Fern behind clearly.

"Hey, shall we go over the plan for the revenge porn meeting one last time?" I interrupt. Our meeting with Vaughan's office is tomorrow, and I'm determined to put this abundance of rage to good use. "I know it's off-brand for me to have any kind of interest in planning as a concept, but I've had a sudden and severe personality transplant. Ajita, can your parents arrange a lobotomy?"

Wednesday 11 January

3.23 p.m.

Having sought prior permission to leave school early – God bless Mrs Crannon and her lax attitude to attendance taking – we catch a shuttle bus into the city for our meeting with Vaughan's office. As a public transport snob this displeases me greatly. [Apparently being a public transport snob is a thoroughly unreasonable and indefensible position for an individual living below the poverty line, but I still maintain that old bus smell is a violation of the Human Rights Act. Just because I'm poor doesn't mean I have to enjoy the scent of piss-marinated Cheeto dust.]

For once we have all dressed semi-smartly for the occasion. There are no Chucks in sight. Our English teacher nearly passed out when we walked into class this morning. Considering the fact I wore my pajama shirt to school yesterday, this reaction is entirely justified.

Today I've borrowed a floral blouse and tailored blazer from Meg, while Ajita looks every inch the *Vogue* cover girl in a fitted plum-colored dress and a beige trench coat. Meg is wearing the same pillar-box red lipstick she wore in the sex-doll sketch.

For one horrifying moment, we don't think Meg is going to be able to join us, since the bus that eventually rocks up doesn't have a ramp. When we ask the driver for one, he just mutters, "Sorry, broken. Budget cuts." So instead of waiting for the next bus, which would make us late for the meeting, Ajita and I lift Meg up the stairs ourselves. It takes a grand total of twenty seconds, but by the time we're done I am drenched in sweat, like I have just climbed Kilimanjaro. Ajita swears delightfully at the driver, blotting her own brow on a moldy seat.

We spend the bus journey looking over our notes and practicing the small speech we've prepared, which we based on some online resources about how to put effective pressure on your reps. I think we've done a stellar job, outlining our concerns in a concise way, providing statistics about how common the phenomenon is (and what impact it has on victims), and drawing on examples as to how other states have pushed forward with legislation. It's up to Vaughan's office to put together official proposals and whatnot; our main priority is making sure our voices are heard.

Once we've run over everything a couple times, Ajita turns to me, face painfully earnest, as though she's about to request a portion of my liver, and says, "Can you maybe not do that thing you do?"

"What thing?" I ask innocently in full Virgin Mary mode.

"The joke thing. You know, the thing with the jokes."

"I don't know what you're talking about," I gasp, faux-astounded. "I'm as serious as a coat hanger in the rectum."

Ajita nods gravely. "Thank you for illustrating my point so efficiently."

7.16 p.m.

So we arrive fifteen minutes early and are shown into a fancy waiting area. There are orchids dotting the tables, copies of the *FT* and the *Economist* stacked in piles, and there's a water fountain bubbling insistently in the corner. The air smells clean and filtered. After the nasal trauma of the bus journey it's a pleasant vacation for my nostrils.

All three of us fall silent, even though we're the only ones in the waiting area. Maybe it's the crisp professional environment, or maybe Ajita and Meg are feeling as tense and nervous as I am. My stomach gurgles as though trying to harmonize with the water cooler, and the combined effect is so mind-blowing it makes Beethoven's Symphony No. 9 sound rudimentary.

While we sit and wrestle with our bodily functions, my thoughts drift back to Hazel. Despite her wonderful friends and the other people who have her back, I still haven't seen her in school since everything went to hell. As I think about everything she's lost because of one sex tape – her job, her future, her parents' respect – anger spikes in my lungs, and the pressure on our meeting mounts. This has to go well. We owe it to Hazel, and past Izzy, and all the future Hazels and Izzys who will continue to get hurt unless we can put an end to the phenomenon. We need to hold the Dannys and the Bakeheads accountable.

Eventually, after forty-five minutes of waiting and gurgling, a harried assistant bustles into the room and apologizes for the wait. A corporate lunch overran, she explains. We follow her down a corridor, traipsing deeper into the belly of the government building, and it transforms from the sleek and modern annex to the old-fashioned and oak-paneled original structure. Hung on the walls are portraits of old city councilors, and more recent photographs of state visits, all proud handshakes and fluorescent-white politician smiles.

We're let into a small office with an unnecessary number of filing cabinets, and the human equivalent of a banana nib rises behind the desk.

"Hi, girls. Chris Vaughan. Real pleasure to meet you today." His black hair is slicked to the side and bears striking resemblance to an oil spill.

Of course. Of course Ted Vaughan hires his nephews instead of, you know, actual qualified people. Chris, Zachary's cousin, was only a few years ahead of us at Edgewood, and was an immature turd throughout his entire school career. And as a leading expert on both immaturity and feces I know what I'm talking about. [Should I add that to my résumé? Answers on a postcard.]

Forreal, though, one time Chris stole a well-endowed sophomore's bra from the locker room and wore it like a hat all day. The sophomore – a timid, self-conscious girl who abhorred gym class at the best of times – complained to Principal Schumer, but he ruled it "a bit of harmless fun" and nothing more. All because the Vaughans had donated money to the school library the year before.

Long story short, the Vaughan family is, with the possible exception of Zachary, The Actual Literal Worst. And now here Chris stands in an office-slash-hunting-cabin. It's wooden and musty, with deer antlers and rifles mounted on the walls. All it needs is a bear-skin rug and an NRA bumper sticker and the look would be complete. There's an aggressive space heater puffing out hot stale air, which is how I immediately know that Chris Vaughan is, both physiologically and morally, a reptile.

Once the faux-friendly introductions are out the way and Chris asks why we're here, we launch into our spiel with gusto.

Meg takes a deep breath and delivers our opening lines, words cool and clear like a glacier. "Revenge porn – the practice of distributing intimate or explicit photos or video of someone without their consent – has been long been protected by legal loopholes. It still remains fully within the law in this state."

"And yet the phenomenon is so widespread it's practically a pandemic," Ajita continues. With her confident academic demeanor, she now resembles an incredibly hot professor. "A

2016 report from the Data & Society Research Institute, and the Center for Innovative Public Health Research, found that one in twenty-five people in the US have either been victims of revenge porn or have been threatened with the posting of sensitive images. That number jumps to one in ten for young women between the ages of fifteen and twenty-nine."

I allow a beat of a pause before I deliver my line. "I was that one in ten," I say, maintaining intense eye contact with Chris. I want him to feel as uncomfortable as I have for months.

Now I'm supposed to deliver some personal anecdotes about how badly the scandal affected me, how it decimated my self-worth and left me unable to get out of bed. It's supposed to segue into the suicide stats we researched. But as soon as I open my mouth I freeze. Chris stares at me, glazed and semi-expectant. Sweat pools in the small of my back, and the ice-grip on my gut tells me I can't do it. I can't tell this man-lizard about my deepest, darkest moments.

I give Ajita the tiniest headshake, and immediately she understands. She jumps straight in with the suicide statistics, and then Meg talks about a specific fifteen-year-old girl in Kansas who took her own life after her sex tape got out. Finally we end by sharing some of the most effective legislation from other states, which could potentially be adapted for our own.

My final line is delivered with all the am-dram panache I can muster. "I wasn't the first woman in this state to have her nude picture leaked. But with your help I could be the last." [Of course this is factually inaccurate. Hazel has already come after me. But there's no room for pedantics in good speechwriting.]

Chris, whose eyes glassed over several minutes ago, plasters a fake smile on his face. He rises to his feet, clapping his hands together once with an air of finality. "Great. Thanks for coming in, girls."

Wait, what? That's it?

My volcanic mouth erupts once more. "First of all, we're not girls. We're women. If I *were* a girl, my leaked nude would be considered child pornography, and the guy who distributed it would be in prison." I glare at Chris. He looks like he's never cared about anything less in his life. "Secondly we refuse to be fobbed off. This matters. Are you going to take it further?"

"I will pass on your concerns to my seniors." Chris's tone is placid and non-committal.

"Great. When?" Meg demands.

Chris smiles again, more strained this time. "As I'm sure you can appreciate, this is a very busy office."

"And because this issue impacts young women the hardest, it's not worth the effort, right?" Ajita snaps.

"That's not true. We care about all our constituents, and by extension we care about the issues that matter to them. But we have limited time and resources, and –"

"If it was important to the gun-wielding old white men who

voted Vaughan into office, I'm sure you'd find the time and resources." I gesture angrily to the hunting rifle mounted above his desk. I'm getting angry – too angry – but I'm powerless to stop it. The floodgates have opened.

All semblance of pleasantry has now evaporated from his expression. He grits his teeth and says. "You *girls* take care now."

I see red at this point. Literally my entire field of vision is dyed a startling crimson, and a violent impulse rises to the surface. I want to hurt Chris Vaughan. I really do. And that fucking terrifies me.

I manage to bite down the urge to kick him in the teeth, and instead settle for an incredibly mature and professional, "Please fuck all the way off, sir."

Oh, how mistaken I was to imagine the meeting with Vaughan's staffer would be some kind of outlet for my anger. In the end the experience has completed my transformation into human volcano. I recommend steering clear of me unless you'd like to be smothered by a toxic ash cloud.

On the bus home we try to remain positive, despite the sinking feeling of defeat pressing down on us.

"I'm sorry for losing my shit," I mutter, staring out at the gray suburban landscape. I mean it too. I just made Chris all the more likely to trunk our proposal and refuse all future meetings with us. I fucked up. Anger got the better of me, like it has so many times recently, and it's scaring me more and more.

"Don't apologize. You said what we were all thinking." Ajita's smile is taut.

"I mean, he didn't say no," Meg says after a beat, forever the most optimistic of the three of us. "He says he's going to present the issue to his seniors, right? So we follow up next week and demand to know what action he's taken."

We sit in silence for a few blocks, knowing deep down that this is the end of the road.

"This makes me sick to my stomach," I eventually say. "All of it. Part of me thinks it'd be easier to cope with if our senator had a strong moral opposition to what we're proposing. Like the Roe v Wade, pro-life v pro-choice stuff. At least then it'd mean he cared. But their total apathy is soul-destroying."

Tears prickle behind my eyes as the reality of what I'm saying hits home. The powerful people in this country don't care about my suffering, about Hazel's suffering. We're nothing to them.

Ajita stares out the bus window. The sky is heavy with impending rain. "You nailed it when you said that thing about how if it was important to the gun-wielding old white men who voted Vaughan into office, they'd find the time and resources." Her clenched fist raps against the juddering window.

"It's because teenage girls don't have the money to donate to their election campaign," I mutter as the group's official poverty correspondent. "So they don't give a flying erection about our demands."

"Why on earth would an erection be airborne?" Ajita asks sincerely.

"We can't let this beat us, guys," Meg insists as the bus shudders to a halt by the second-to-last stop. An old man carrying a newspaper and a cane steps on, shooting us a cute, friendly old man smile. "Seriously. We just have to keep pushing until they listen. Even if we have to go in there every week and demand they pay attention. In fact, I'm emailing to arrange a follow-up meeting right now."

Despite Meg's relentless chirpiness and the entertaining mental image of a flying penis, I feel flat and hopeless the rest of the ride home. Worse still, I feel like I've let Hazel down with my sharp tongue and my inability to discuss my experiences when it matters. What if sharing my personal story would've made all the difference? Maybe we would've got through to Chris if I'd been able to talk about how it felt to go through it, how much the hatred stung, how I'd considered ending it all.

9.15 p.m.

We commiserate with a pool tournament in Ajita's basement. Prajesh has invited a girl over, who has in turn invited her best friend for moral support, none of whom have said a word in the last half-hour. Anyway, Becca and Addie seem sweet, despite their inability to form words, and Praj is acting all cute and bashful. But, you know, also mute. Oh, how I do not miss being thirteen. [Not that I was a shy thirteen-year-old or anything. I've always been loud and obnoxious. In fact, I was even more prone to verbal diarrhea in my younger years.]

Meg has drawn up a round robin tournament draw, due to her superior knowledge of sports and general organizational prowess, and Ajita is currently playing – and destroying – her brother.

When she pots her third ball in a row Prajesh hisses in her ear, "Come on, sis. Addie's watching. Gimme a break." Ajita opts not to honor his request, and instead proceeds to humiliate him even further. To be fair Addie and Becca are huddled on the couch, whispering behind braces and waaaaay better makeup than I ever had at their age. So they're not exactly paying attention to Prajesh's humbling defeat.

My hand is deep in the M&M bowl when my phone dings. The name on the screen makes me yank my hand away faster than if the M&M's had grown teeth and/or achieved singularity.

Zachary Vaughan.

I read in disbelief.

Hey Izzy. So . . . there's something I think you should know. I stopped by my dad's office earlier, and I heard him talking to Chris about your proposal. They were mocking you guys, and when I walked in Chris was looking at your nudes on his phone, making gross comments and all. Anyway, I'm not sure why I'm telling you this . . . probably because I'm pretty pissed off that my dad couldn't give a shit about

something that affected me too. But yeah, I also just wanted you to know that I'm not like my dad, not at all, and if you ever need anything, I'm fully on your side. :) / :(

After I show the message to Ajita and Meg we're so pissed off and disillusioned that we rant over each other in one long chorus off pissed-off disillusionment.

"How can one family be such a giant festering puke stain on this state?" Ajita snarls.

"I mean . . . maybe not the *whole* family," I say, shocking myself. "That's a pretty decent thing for Zachary to do. Going behind his dad's back like that. He doesn't owe me anything, so . . . I dunno. Pretty cool of him."

Addie and Becca listen in fascination, which I totally get. Eighteen-year-olds are a constant source of awe and terror to thirteen-year-olds, so if you factor in some good old-fashioned political outrage, the effect is quadrupled.

"Maybe Zachary would be willing to do a bit more digging around for us?" Meg suggests. "Like keeping tabs on what his dad's saying about our campaign. It'd be kind of useful to have an inside contact, especially if the office keeps stonewalling us."

"What campaign?" Ajita replies miserably, shoveling M&Ms into her mouth with reckless abandon. "Sounds like it's pretty dead in the water."

Prajesh, who usually stays silent on these matters, says, "Yeah, I hate to say it guys, but Senator Vaughan has this state in the palm of his hand." Addie and Becca gaze in admiration at his political savvy.

Becca nods passionately in agreement. "At least you tried. You guys always were the underdogs."

"Tell me something I don't know," Ajita sulks, M&Ms now just being poured straight into her face directly from the pouch.

"Challenge accepted," I reply in an attempt to lighten the mood, even though part of me doesn't *want* to lighten the mood because I'm so damned frustrated. [My mind is a war zone.] "In the nineteenth century there were some very entertaining slang terms for sex, including 'being among the parsley' and 'fandango de pokum'. I find these both highly entertaining and believe we should incorporate them into our daily vernacular."

Ajita stares at me, purple-painted lips pursed. "Literally what even goes on inside your head? Is it a non-stop acid trip?"

"And what would happen if we *actually* gave you acid?" Prajesh enquires. "Would you be doubly weird? Or would it just kind of . . . cancel out?" Addie and Becca giggle girlishly.

"I think we can still fight this," I mutter, ignoring the jokebait for once in my life. Resolve firms in my gut like concrete. For some reason having guys from school rally around us is super validating. Carson and his teammates defending Hazel, Zachary going against his dad to stand up for something that matters. It makes me feel proud to be a young person. When we rage against the machine together we can be unstoppable.

"How do we fight it, though?" Ajita asks, through a mouthful of masticated chocolate peanuts. [Do you not just think "masticated" is the most hilarious word in the English language?]

"I think we need to show that our votes have the same influence as the gun-wielding old white men," Meg says.

"Exactly," I agree. "Maybe we can't donate to their campaign, and we never would. But come election day we all have one vote. We have the power to vote him out of office. So we have to be loud enough to make Ted Vaughan realize that if he doesn't listen to our demands, he will lose his seat. There are midterm elections this year, right? So we make this a key issue. Get his Democratic opposition on our side. Show how crucial the youth vote can be, you know?"

"For once in your life, you might actually be right." Ajita nods, facing me now, intensity painted on her usually demure features. "What Vaughan is most afraid of is losing his power. Okay, so the midterm elections are several months away, but still. We have to make him and his campaign team believe that this is an election-deciding issue."

Meg looks solemn as she pushes her bangs out of her eyes. "The problem is that right now, it isn't. Not enough people care."

"So we make them care," I insist. "We go at it with everything we've got. We film sketches and skits and make them go viral. We organize protests and rallies. We get all the girls in school behind us. We get high-profile people to support our mission.

We make noise — a lot of it." Ajita and Meg nod vehemently, jaws firm and eyes sparkling. Addie and Becca watch with bated breath. I pause for dramatic effect. "We fight as hard as we can. Because we're bitches, right? And bitches bite back."

Thursday 12 January

4.57 p.m.

As I'm leaving school in my Martha's uniform I spot Danny's mom's car parked outside the school gates, half mounted on the sidewalk. As I get closer I notice the passenger seat is empty. I wave politely at Mrs Wells, but she outright ignores me. Huh. Weird.

Maybe she didn't see me. It's hard to tell which way she's looking, on account of the fact that a) my eyesight is roughly equivalent to that of an elderly bat and b) it's pretty dark outside already. Or maybe Danny has told his parents some twisted version of what went down last fall, and they hate my guts almost as much as he does. That seems a more likely explanation.

Pulling even closer still, I eventually make out the way Mrs Wells clutches the steering wheel with both hands, face pressed against the center, her shoulders shaking as though she's crying. My heart sinks hellward. I may not be friends with Danny anymore, but Mrs Wells was like a surrogate mom to me growing up.

I'm just a few feet away from the car now, and I'm torn. Should I tap on the window and ask if she's okay? Or will she just hate me even more for drawing attention to her sadness? Mrs Wells is a proud woman. Things must be pretty bad for her to publicly break down like this. I remember what Betty said a couple months ago, about Danny's parents being on the brink of divorce. Is that why she's crying in her car at five o'clock on a Friday afternoon, where every high-school kid in the town can see her?

I also tentatively wonder if she's been drinking. She does love her Chardonnay, and the car is parked at a jaunty angle . . .

Before I can decide on whether or not to approach the vehicle, someone shoves past me from behind, and my feet slide out from under me. I land in a heap on the snowy sidewalk, grateful that my puffy jacket broke my fall.

Still, a giant "ooft" escapes my life, and my assailant stops in his tracks to look down at me.

Danny. Because obviously.

Even through his thick glasses I can tell his eyes are swollen and puffy. He's definitely been crying too.

He peers down at me. "Iz? Oh God, I'm sorry. I couldn't see where I was . . . here, let me help you up." He proffers me an arm, and I accept, purely because clambering up by myself on snow-covered sheet ice seems borderline impossible.

"Don't worry," I say, and I actually mean it. For the first time in months hatred is not the only emotion I experience while in his presence. "Is everything okay?"

"Yeah, it's just . . ." he starts, then seems to remember we're no longer friends. He shakes his head. "Yeah. Everything's fine. I'll see you later."

And, with a weak smile, he opens the car door and slides into the passenger seat. As the overhead light illuminates the dashboard I watch as he and his mom share a hug, Mrs Wells sobbing into his shoulder.

My heart splinters. Yes, so we're no longer friends, and yes, he betrayed me pretty badly. But the Wells were like family to me for the longest time, and being unable to comfort them is hard to stomach. I almost consider jumping into the backseat, but a couple things stop me: I don't want to intrude, and my sense of pride is too overpowering. Plus I remember everything he did to me, and it takes me straight back to wanting to flush his head down a public toilet. So I tear my eyes away from the heartbreaking scene in front of me and start walking in the direction of Martha's Diner.

Was it really only a few months ago that Danny, Ajita and I were closer than close, spending our evenings in her basement eating a metric fuck-ton of nachos, playing pool and dreaming up logistically impossible sketch ideas? Is it possible to be nostalgic for the way things were so recently? How is it possible for so much to change so fast?

Is this growing up? Because if it is, I'm going to need instructions on how to make it stop. Peter Pan had the right idea. Does anyone have his phone number so I can create a group chat with Benjamin Button?

Friday 13 January

11.42 a.m.

It's Friday the thirteenth, and as the most superstitious human on the face of this earth Ajita spends the whole morning wearing a scarf of garlic cloves. I am not sure what vampires have to do with Friday the thirteenth exactly, but when I tried to ask her she just started shrieking about my conspiring with the werewolves to bring about the apocalypse. I wish I was joking and/or exaggerating about any of this, but alas Ms Dutta finds all new ways to push the boundaries of lunacy.

Anyway, we're walking back to our lockers after third period when Meg approaches – with none other than Fern Fournier by her side. They're not holding hands or anything, but they do look particularly friendly, giggling and making pretty intense eye contact. Fern is wearing a skater dress and wooly tights with a chunky knitted beanie over long, shiny black hair. Her lipstick is deep purple-black, and her metallic gunmetal eyeshadow is gothy and awesome. She looks killer, I have to admit, but I'm team Ajita forever and always until the day I die. Even then,

I'm totally gonna become a sassy poltergeist and play pranks on anyone who dares mess with my homegirl.

Ajita sees them coming and immediately rips the garlic scarf from her neck before they can see. This makes me weirdly sad. I've never seen her try to hide her bonkers sense of humor before.

"Hey, guys," I say, shooting Ajita a concerned look as she stuffs the pungent bulbs into her satchel. "How goes it?"

"We're good!" Meg says, dabbing at the corner of her once perfectly lined eye, which is smudged from cry-laughing at something Fern said. "Hey, do you guys want to go see a movie this weekend with me and Fern? There's that new Amy Schumer thing we wanted to watch, right?"

"I've already seen it," Ajita snaps, in a very un-Ajita manner. "But have fun."

Fern blinks in confusion. "Didn't it only come out today?"

But it's too late – Ajita is already storming away toward the restroom, stray garlic cloves scattering behind her.

"Previews," I reply helplessly.

Yikes. Subtle my homegirl is not.

1.32 p.m.

Carson and I are strolling to his homeroom after lunch, and it's taking all my earthly willpower not to mention the Ajita/Meg/Fern thing, after what happened last time I flippantly cracked

113

jokes about my best friend's relationship drama. Must. Not. Discuss. Relationship. Drama. Thankfully Carson is mid-diatribe about some kind of televised sportsball game from last night, and doesn't even notice that his girlfriend looks like she's trying to pass a kidney stone right here in Room 106B.

However, one thing that does get his attention is when I pass Zachary in the hallway, and he smiles and says hey. And I smile back and say hey. Apparently this is a completely unfeasible turn of events that defies the space-time continuum.

"What the hell?" Carson says, not shittily but just a little surprisedly. "You guys are friends now?"

I shrug. "He apologized to me. And fed us info from his dad's office. We're cool."

"Really? After what he did to you?"

Try as I might, I can't read his tone. My first instinct is that he's jealous, but that would be pretty off-brand. Still, his words are strung together with something tauter than usual. We slip into homeroom, and for once we're the first ones there. Carson dumps his backpack on a seat on the back row. I flip the light switch on.

"I mean, he didn't technically *do* anything," I say as the classroom flickers and groans back to life after its lunchtime siesta. "It's not like he leaked the pictures."

"Nah, but his dad did pull some messed-up shit. Up there on his soapbox slamming you, and all. And what about that speech Zachary made in the cafeteria?"

"Well, yeah. None of that was great. But people can forgive other people. Like Ajita forgave me."

Carson shifts uncomfortably, his usually loose and relaxed posture stiffening. He rifles in his backpack, not meeting my eye. "Does that mean you're gonna forgive Danny?"

Ah. There it is, the bungee rope pulling his words tight together. How long has he been thinking about that? "What? No! Of course not. Why?"

I flump down into a seat in the next row, and immediately begin picking at the dry skin around my fingernail.

Carson shrugs. "I just don't want him hurting you again, is all."

Is that all this is? Concern for my happiness? He knows Danny had romantic feelings for me, and maybe still does. Does he feel threatened by that? After all, there's a whole bunch of history there, and not all of it bad. That's a weighty thing for a new boyfriend to process.

Still, I don't want to bring it up in case I'm off base – don't want to put the concerns in his head if they aren't there already – so instead I ask, "Do you believe in redemption? Like as a concept."

Carson scoffs, something unreadable flitting across his face. "As a concept, yeah. In practice . . . nah."

I want to know what that fleeting emotion was. Is he thinking about his dad, and the way he abandoned them? His mom's partner? Someone else who fucked up on an epic level? There's still so much I don't know about Carson, and I want to know it all. I want to crawl up inside his brain and have a lengthy rummage around.

Attempting to coax it out of him, I gently say in the most shrink-like manner I can muster, "Why not?"

Suddenly he looks absolutely mortified to be having this conversation, and rolls his eyes elaborately. Scratches behind his ear. "This is kinda intense. Let's talk about somethin' else. What's goin' on with your screenplay?"

Frustration pulses inside me. I want us to move beyond this surface-level stuff, beyond the jokes and the flimsy conversations about sportsball and his pizza co-workers. But it's starting to feel like we'll never get there. That might be an extremely spicy take, considering we've only been together a few months, but I'm a teenager and thus entitled to dramatics.

Seriously, though, it's like having a mirror held up to my own behavior, and unlike when I look in an actual mirror I do not like what I see. Is this how people feel talking to me? When I constantly make jokes instead of properly engaging in conversations?

Because it's really fucking annoying.

8.43 p.m.
Tonight's Bitches Bite Back meeting has a key difference: Hazel Parker joins us.

116

Thanks to my desire not to spend another second in Martha's Diner this weekend, the BBB session is held in Ajita's basement. However, the resulting absence of milkshake joy is not conducive to productivity, so Ajita whizzes up some goodness in her brother's NutriBullet. It's difficult to describe the exact flavor of the resulting goo, but all I can say is that the concoction includes almond milk, peanut butter, frozen banana, chocolate syrup, vanilla ice cream, strawberry fizzy laces, a slice of her dad's birthday cake, peach yoghurt, six (6) spoonfuls of sugar, and a half-chewed taffy Ajita found in a drawer.

It's so sweet I can hear my teeth weeping in protest. You have to admire Hazel's willingness to consume such an abomination in the name of political progress.

After Mrs Dutta crows about the mangled taffy ruining the blender's blade, and Ajita offers to replace it with her mom's razor blade – because "judging by the beard on her chin, it is not currently in use" – we head sheepishly down to the basement. Hazel remarks upon the coziness with its beanbags and beat-up old sofas, pool table and ping-pong corner and an unreasonable quantity of fairy lights. I've spent so much time here in my eighteen years of life that the compliment fills me with pride, even though I deserve little to no credit.

Hazel perches on a beanbag while Ajita sits cross-legged on the floor and Meg nestles into a sofa, I take the fusty armchair that almost definitely moonlights as a termite colony. Hazel wears an oversized Los Angeles Chargers sweater, and has her long creamy-blonde hair swept up in a messy pony. Her eyes are red-rimmed, and there's a fresh breakout of acne spreading up her jawline. Even as the least maternal woman in North America, the urge to wrap her in a huge hug is overwhelming.

"So how are you doing?" Meg asks her in a soft voice.

Hazel looks like she's about to say something, opening her mouth slightly to speak, but she presses her lips shut and shakes her head violently. Her green eyes fill with new tears. My heart actually, literally aches for her. I know that feeling. I know it so well it's like a family member.

"It gets better, Hazel," I say, mimicking Meg's soft tone, which is all new territory for me given my malfunctioning foghorn of a voice box. "It does. I promise."

Tears spilling into her milkshake – in fairness this is a good strategy because the salt may offset some of the sugar – she mumbles, "I feel like I've lost everything. My job. My future. My freedom."

Ajita slurps tactlessly. "Your freedom?"

Hazel shrugs, staring at her pink paper straw. "I used to feel like I could go anywhere, do anything, be anything. It sounds privileged and entitled, I know, but it's true. I felt invincible."

I nod in understanding. "And now you feel completely and utterly vincible."

Ajita shoots me a quizzical look. "Is 'vincible' even a word?"

"Now is not the time for your pedantry, dear pal," I respond matter-of-factly, before turning back to Hazel. She's now sucking the sleeve of her sweater like a toddler. "Have your parents spoken to you about it yet?"

"Only to tell me I'm grounded. And that they'll no longer support me going to college. They don't trust me not to bring even more shame to my family name." This last line brings about a huge hiccup, followed by a fresh deluge of sobs.

"This is where I think having dead parents has its distinct advantages," I deadpan.

Hazel laughs a soggy, snot-filled laugh. "You're so lucky."

"The luckiest," Ajita mutters. She's being pretty snarky and sharp tonight, even with me, and Meg keeps throwing worried glances in her direction. I don't even know if they've spoken since the movie invitation gone wrong.

Hazel lays her milkshake down on the table and tucks her feet up on the beanbag. "I just don't know what to do. I've never felt so powerless in my life. So . . . helpless. Like nothing in the world can make this better apart from going back in time and making sure this never happened." Her teeth grit ferociously. "God, why did I film that tape? It was so fucking stupid of me. So enaive. I'm so furious at myself."

"No!" I say, urgency leaking into my voice. "You are not at fault here, Hazel. You're the victim, not the abuser. You have every right to feel furious. Hell, I do. More now than ever.

But try to direct it outwards – to Bakehead, to society, to the way the world treats teenage girls."

Meg nods emphatically. "And that's why we're here. To hold society accountable. To hold the *world* accountable."

Hazel wipes her tears on her already damp sleeve and sniffs. "Okay. Okay. I'm with you. What do we do? How do we fix this? Because I never want another girl to feel how I feel right now."

I remove my therapist hat and don my political movement hat, eyeing Ajita and Meg for support. Meg nods, smiling encouragingly, but Ajita has a weird, unreadable expression on her face, even when I mime actually changing hats. It's like she's fighting an internal battle. And I'm not a hundred percent sure why, but I think I can hazard a guess.

"I think we should start by looking into Vaughan's Democratic opposition," I say, tucking my feet up underneath me and reaching for the laptop. "If our strategy is going to be to focus on the midterm elections, and to make Vaughan think he might lose if he ignores this issue, we need to know more about who he's going to be up against. They're a potential ally for us, right?"

"Right," Hazel says, looking at me with admiration. It feels good, not just to support her emotionally but to support her on a far grander scale too. "Let's do this."

An hour later, we've learned everything there is to know about Rosa Garcia, the underdog of a newcomer who's running a grassroots campaign in the run-up to the election. Her platform is built on progressive values, and she's been incredibly outspoken about equality and diversity, which hasn't been all that popular since our town does not have a great liberal presence. There are literally more Confederate flags in this state than Democrats. But still, Garcia is unrelenting in her passion and determination, and seems to be building a small but solid fan base online. Also, she has a kitten called Ruth Bader Ginsburg. So she's pretty much a perfect human woman.

We then spend another hour drafting an introductory letter, making sure the tone is absolutely perfect. As well as tailoring the email to include past campaigns of hers that we particularly admire, we also outline our cause in detail – using our stats and including links to the media coverage from my scandal – and say her vocal support would give us a much bigger platform to effect change and push for revenge porn legislation.

I even sign off in a formal manner, as opposed to "catch you on the flip side, my dude". I don't think I've ever typed the words "kind regards" in my entire life, so now I feel like a bona fide professional.

Getting someone like Rosa involved feels like the longest of long shots, but, hey, this girl made it to BuzzFeed. Anything is possible when you're shameless.

Saturday 14 January

10.18 p.m.

When I check my phone after finishing my diner shift – another mercifully busy one, thank the milkshake gods – I see a new email notification and my heart skips in excitement. It's not Rosa Garcia, but it *is* Eliza. Seeing her name nearly makes me jump with joy. Jump! Me! Doing physical activity! It's absurd on the face of it.

> Hi Izzy,
> Thanks for sending over the latest draft of *Love for Hire*.
> I aim to get fully up to date on client reading this weekend, so I'll do one more pass, and if we're both happy with it I'll start making calls and setting up meetings on Monday. How does that sound?
> Please let me know if you have any questions at this stage.
> Eliza

What even. How is this real.

Walking out the back exit of the diner, I hug my phone to my chest, not even caring about the stench of kitchen waste emanating from the dumpsters or the raccoon furiously chewing through the industrial garbage bags. Right now, I feel like I'm strolling down the Hollywood Walk of Fame, and every single star is there for me. [Good grief, Ajita is right. I really am an incredible narcissist.]

It's snowing lightly again, and the night is quiet. And yet there's a buzz in the air, like the low hum of a light bulb, that I swear I could reach out and touch. My excitement is so potent it has an almost-physical presence.

Still high on Eliza's email, I wrap my puffy coat tighter round me and start walking home through the lamplit streets. Seriously, people talk about Hollywood as if it's this cutthroat, dog-eat-dog world, but my experience so far has been nothing like that. Eliza took a chance on me after I got kicked out of a reputable competition, and she's been absolutely awesome and patient with me ever since. Sure, she only makes money by selling scripts, but the fact remains that I've been welcomed with open arms by one of those nasty gatekeepers you hear so many horror stories about.

I fire off a response as I walk, although typing is waaaaaay easier said than done since my thumbs are pretty much frozen to the screen at this point. I may as well be in Narnia, except there's probably better Wi-Fi in Narnia, which is saying a lot.

Eliza asked if I have any questions, so I scan my brain for things I actually do want to know the answer to. [I mean, in terms of screenwriting. There are many questions in life I would like to know the answer to. For example: If man evolved from apes, why do we still have apes? Why does glue not stick to the inside of the bottle? If our knees were backward, what would chairs look like? These are the things that keep me up at night.]

Eventually I settle for a few general questions about the submission process and what I can expect once she's sent my script out into the big bad world. In all seriousness, I have no idea how excited to be about this, and I don't want to let myself get too euphoric in case it comes to nothing.

Please, please don't let it come to nothing.

[Good God, this is a whole new level of melodramatic. Someone fetch me a tiny violin pronto. Or a tiny harp. I've always felt them to be more solemn.]

Sunday 15 January

8.00 a.m.

My ten-hour Sunday shift is an entirely uneventful state of affairs. At one point in the afternoon, when the sun is setting and the clouds are dyed pinky orange, I see Meg and Fern making their way down the street outside, obviously on their way to the movie theater. I wave, but they don't see me. They don't even stop and peer through the diner windows in the hopes of seeing me, even though they know I'm working today. Even though they aren't doing anything wrong, it makes me a bit annoyed on Ajita's behalf.

Right when we're about to cash up for the night, one of our regulars comes in and asks for his usual orange juice and filter coffee. He's around a hundred years old – no word of a lie – and he usually comes in every morning as soon as we open up. Every. Single. Morning. And yet that morning, he was nowhere to be seen. We all exchanged worried glances, convinced something bad had happened to him, on account of the fact he looks like he's about to keel over at any given moment. Bless his pancreas.

[Not that his pancreas is in a particularly poor state. I just believe the heart gets more attention than any other body part in the blessing stakes, and we should really be giving some of the other organs a chance.]

But there he is, eight forty-five at night, wearing his trench coat and carrying a newspaper tucked under his arm, requesting his usual beverages and pulling into his usual booth. Croc Queen nods in his direction, silently instructing me to take his order because she does not give one singular fuck at this point on a Saturday evening. I fight the overwhelming urge to roll my eyes and/or slowly peel every slithery scale off her body one by one.

"Good evening, sir," I say, cheerier than a cheerleading squad during national cheer week, but also inwardly homicidal. "Extra-pulp OJ and a small filter coffee?"

"Right you are, sweetheart," he says, matching my absurd grin. He's kinda cute, in that shriveled fossil sort of way. To the extent where I don't even mind him calling me sweetheart, which usually makes me want to cut out a person's eyeballs and serve them on cocktail sticks like pickled onions. [I really do apologize for the needlessly graphic violence in this scene. You didn't sign up for a slasher horror and yet here we are, mildly discussing the removal of various body parts from the people around me.]

"Coming right up," I say, not even bothering to jot the order down on my notepad.

The nice thing about this old dude is that he's one of the only people in the state who hasn't seen my nudes. Don't ask me how I know this – I just do. You can tell by the look in people's eyes, by the way they talk to you. This guy hasn't seen me naked. And that's a rare thing nowadays.

When I return with his OJ and the jug of filter coffee, now lukewarm at best, I flip his mug over on the saucer and start pouring. "Have you had a nice Saturday, sir?" I ask, completely ignoring the fact I'm sloshing coffee everywhere. I really am a godawful waitress. "We were surprised not to see you this morning."

"Oh, it's been magical." He looks up at me, eyes twinkling. He hasn't even opened his newspaper yet. "My eldest granddaughter came to town. She's just had a baby of her own, you know. A boy. Little Samuel. He has my eyes."

The old man starts shaking with laughter. I have no idea what's funny. Old people have a habit of doing that. Laughing at the sound of their own voice.

"How wonderful," I say, injecting some pep into my already peppy hostess voice.

"It was," he says, still chuckling away to himself. "You know, sometimes I struggle to get out of bed in the morning. I really do. Not just because my knees are made of biscuits, but because there's nothing new anymore. Just the same old faces in the same old town I've lived in my whole life. Do you know, I've

127

only left here once? Vietnam." He shakes his head. "And after that, boy was I glad to get back here. That's maybe why I haven't left since." Another bout of irrational laughter. "Anyway, all's I'm saying is that nothing changes. Same old faces, same old places, day in, day out. But today, seeing this tiny town through my great-grandson's eyes, it felt brand new." A warm smile. "My name's Frank, by the way."

I smile back. "Izzy."

As nice as the whole exchange with Frank is, it gets under my skin a little. Is that what I'm going to be like in sixty years time? Will I still be seeing the same old faces and the same old places, day in, day out? Is that what will become of me if I never leave this town – if I skip college to work in the diner and take care of Betty?

The claustrophobia is like a tight belt round my chest, and the restless niggling in my gut tells me I want something more.

Monday 16 January

9.00 a.m.

I hang out with Carson before school starts. We're chilling in the art studio, his awesome remixed reggae music playing through tinny phone speakers and chatting about his kid sister's latest hilarious outbursts. She's three and the single funniest human being on this planet. She deserves her own YouTube channel. I'm not exaggerating. I would hit that subscribe button so fast I'd give myself finger whiplash.

"So then the little monster points up at the kitchen counter and starts yelling at mom, 'What the fuck! What the fuck!'" Carson snorts as he carefully lines the edges of a new canvas with masking tape. "Mom was trying to cook spaghetti while she was mid-phone interview, so she had the employer on speaker. And there's this three-year-old screeching 'what the fuck!' over and over again in the background." He finishes up with the tape and starts sketching the outline of something in faint gray pencil. "Turns out she was trying to say 'want the fork', but, needless to say, Mom didn't get the job."

Arms elbow-deep in the sink as I wash Carson's paintbrushes I laugh. "That's hilarious. And unfortunate as hell. What was your mom interviewing for? Thought she wouldn't be able to afford childcare if she went back to work?"

Carson's hand dances effortlessly across the canvas, and I start to see the light outline of a couple holding hands take shape. "It was a work-from-home gig. Social media management for an online bingo company. She was never gonna get it anyway – her and technology don't get along – but it opened up a couple other doors for her. Fingers crossed."

Out in the corridor, students gradually start filling the hallways. We still have twenty minutes until first bell, but most of the various sports teams get here early for practice.

"Cyra is hysterical," I say, working soap into a particularly dried-out brush. The feeling of the hard bristles is oddly pleasant on my fingertips. "Remember when she told your neighbor that your mom couldn't come to the door because she had crabs?" I start laughing so hard at the memory I slosh muddied water all over my sweater.

Carson chuckles too, laying down his pencil and examining his handiwork. "Yeah, I doubt my mom will be informing Cyra next time she has cramps. That's how rumors start, yo."

There's a quiet knock on the door and we both look round, confused. Nobody ever knocks, since it's a communal art studio and everyone's free to come and go as they please. To my infinite

130

surprise Ajita's standing on the other side of the glass window. Carson and I both smile and gesture for her to come in.

"Hey, guys," she says brightly, easing the door closed behind her again. "Well gosh darn, isn't this just the cutest scene I ever did see?" Ajita's fake southern belle accent is like a cheese grater on my eardrums and she knows it.

I shoot her a dirty look. "If you use that hillbilly voice one more time, I'll chop you up and stir-fry you over a medium heat until golden brown."

"Bitch, I'm already golden brown," she retorts, dumping her satchel on the table next to Carson's sketch. "And your threats really are becoming very niche these days. Are you getting enough sleep?"

I pull a face. "Not even close. But since Betty's moaning about my limited cooking repertoire, I have been reading more recipes. Sorry, buddy. I promise never to stir-fry you."

Ajita's hair is damp and wavy from the snow, and her cheeks are flushed and shiny. She obviously just got here. It was kinda weird walking into school without her this morning, but I wanted to catch up with Carson since I'm probably not going to see him the rest of the week. Shift clash problems.

She snakes over to me as Carson turns back to his work. Nudging my hip with hers, she lowers her voice. She smells of snow and shampoo. "I got you something."

I frown. Out of her pocket she pulls a small pink envelope

with my name neatly printed on the front. I dry my hands and take it from her, flipping it over and sliding out two new patches to iron onto my satchel. The first is an open mouth with vampish teeth and a droplet of scarlet blood dripping from each canine. Inside the mouth, over the stark red tongue, are the words Bitches Bite Back in black-and-white pop-art style letters. The second patch is simple: #EndRevengePorn written in vivid violet.

They. Are. Incredible.

Ajita grins, gesturing to the identical patches secured on the lapel of her leather jacket. "I got a bunch made. Like a thousand. I'm going to hand them out to every girl in school. Oh, and I got posters printed for our open BBB meetings. Crannon says we're cool to use the theater, so our first one is Wednesday at lunch. You ready? Cos I'm ready."

I throw my arms round my ridiculously awesome best friend. "Thank you," I whisper in her ear.

"Please get off me," she whispers back.

Tuesday 17 January

7.49 a.m.

Last night's shift was so dull I almost slipped into a coma. I'm glad today is my day off, although the smell of fried food is pretty much embedded in my skin at this point, so I'm reminded of the diner everywhere I go. Oh, how I love smelling of old hot dogs.

12.35 p.m.

Meg approaches my locker just as I'm about to head to the cafeteria to meet Ajita for lunch. As she pulls the brakes on her chair she seems a little tired, and stretches out her arms as though they're aching.

"Hey, Meg," I say, smiling warmly. "Many apologies for the frankfurter scent I'm rocking. Please refrain from applying mustard and/or ketchup to my face."

Meg laughs. "Sometimes I worry what the hell I married into when I became your friend."

"It was a questionable decision on your part, dude."

There's an awkward silence, and it's clear she's preparing to ask something. I'm pretty sure I know what. She fumbles with the fingerless gloves sitting in her lap, folding and refolding them. Then: "Hey, so . . . does Ajita hate me?"

Yep, there it is. Ajita has been acting so strange around her, and I'm not surprised Meg has picked up on it.

I have to force myself to meet her gaze. "No, Meg. She doesn't hate you. I promise."

"Okay... if you're sure?" Meg says uncertainly.

Even as I say the words, I wonder whether they're true. Ajita is getting harder to read these days. Okay, so I haven't asked her about her potential feelings for Meg yet, but I know beyond a shadow of a doubt that even if we were alone in her room right now, she'd still put her guard up faster than a Viking shield-maiden.

6.17 p.m.

Betty works all day at the diner while I have the day off, and thanks to all the recipes I've been reading I actually cook a Decent Meal for dinner. Chili con carne! With rice! Betty seems thrilled when she gets home. I mean, it's not a patch on her speciality mac and cheese, but I'm proud of myself nonetheless. Thank you, internet-recipes-so-simple-even-I-can-understand-them.

As we're eating I attempt to tactfully broach the subject of

Danny and his mom. The car-crying scene has gotten under my skin. "So have you heard anything else about Mr and Mrs Wells? Are they still divorcing?"

Chili con carne dribbling down her chin, Betty replies, "I'm not sure if you've noticed this at all, oh granddaughter of mine, but I'm currently working 193 hours a week. Keeping up with the community center gossip has not been high on my list of priorities. In fact, on the scale of things I give a rat's ass about, it falls somewhere between flossing and the wildlife of Papua New Guinea."

"What did the wildlife of Papua New Guinea ever do to you?" I grumble, frustrated that my mining for information has reaped no golden nuggets.

Dumbledore is watching us eat and salivating so intensely that soon there will be no kitchen, no apartment, just a drool lake roughly the size of Alaska, and Betty and I flopping around and wailing like Loch Ness monsters.

It's only then that I notice how quickly Betty is shoveling the chili down her throat, as though it's a matter of national security that she finishes within the minute.

Astonished at the animalistic chowing down, I put down my own fork and say, "Hey, where's the fire, Betty-O?"

She polishes off the final scraps of rice and throws her cutlery down like a kid who wants to go back outside and play with her friends. "Thanks, that was great. Can I borrow your laptop?"

I blink in bafflement. "Do you know even know how to operate a computer? What do you need it for?"

She scoffs. "None of your beeswax."

"It is very much my beeswax, since it's my laptop you're demanding use of," I point out, trying not to spit rice everywhere. Dumbledore squirms in desperation, even though he's just had his own dinner. The dog is a greed machine, I swear. He would just eat and eat and eat until he died, given half the chance. [He and I have that in common.]

"Who raised you, you ungrateful swine?" Betty demands, hoisting herself up from the kitchen table.

"Fair point, well made," I concede, mentally scanning my browser history to make sure there's no porn still on there. Not that Betty has the technical savvy to know how to view my search history, but still. You can never be too careful. "The password is dumbledore0305."

"I know," she says with a horrifying wink.

I try to feel ashamed, but I'm all tapped out. That's the one good thing about sex scandals, I suppose. Your shame stores end up pretty depleted, and you're freed from inconveniences such as embarrassment and regret. [There I go again with my ruthless optimism. Doth mine upbeat nature knoweth no bounds?]

As Betty departs the room with surprising speed and vigor I call after her. "You never told me why you needed it, you old weirdo?"

She's too busy humming the theme tune from a popular porn channel to answer.

Wednesday 18 January

6.46 a.m.

Despite being used to performing on stage in front of hundreds of people, thanks to my regular appearances in school plays, I'm actually pretty nervous for the inaugural open meeting of Bitches Bite Back. I'm not sure why I feel so apprehensive. For one thing, there's a decent chance nobody will turn up besides me, Ajita, Meg and Hazel. But maybe that's *why* I'm so scared. What if nobody cares about this thing we're so passionate about?

Like I say, I'm no stranger to putting myself out there. Whether starring in high-school productions, directing my own sketch comedy or sending my first ever screenplay to a panel of ruthless industry judges, I'm usually comfortable with taking that leap into the public domain. [And humblebragging, evidently.] But I guess that's different, because in all of those areas, I'm hiding behind characters – characters I play, characters I write, characters I boss around. With Bitches Bite Back, it's just me: Izzy O'Neill. Being authentically myself and being open about the issues I care about. GROSS.

It's taken me a lot to reach a point where I'm able to open up to Betty and Ajita about the way I'm feeling. Until a few months ago, I would rather have swallowed a hive of bees than talk about my problems. And now I'm about to waltz into the theater and discuss the most painful experience of my life with a room (hopefully) full of people I barely know.

Weak-willed temptation urges me to call it off, to tell the others I'm sick, to run away to Mexico and work in an iguana sanctuary where I can pretend none of this ever happened.

But I can't run away, not now. The stakes are too high. I have to summon all the world-ending rage I've been feeling for the last few weeks and use it to carry me through this meeting. I need to rally the troops if our campaign is going to be anything resembling a success, and I'll never be able to do that if I can't inspire people with my own story.

People don't care about abstract; they care about what's in front of them. It's that instinct that makes you dive into a lake to save a drowning kid, instead of donating money to a national lifeguard charity. The immediacy and specificity are what tug on your heartstrings, what drive you to action.

Okay, so people might not care about the idea of one in ten young women who fall victim to revenge porn, but they might care about the young woman standing in front of them. I can give them that immediacy in the form of Hazel, give them that personal angle by sharing my own pain. It's going to be hard

– harder than anything I've ever done – but it's the only way to get the ball rolling.

I'm not ready, but I am determined. And for now, that's enough.

1.54 p.m.

Blood roars in my ears as we walk toward the auditorium. This is so personal, and the stakes are so high. This is not some childish sketch, or a beer-fueled party game. This really matters. Hazel looks at me expectantly.

The pressure sits on my chest like a rock. Self-doubt grips every sense, makes my nerve endings feel raw and exposed, makes my bones rattle in my body. For this campaign to really resonate I know I need to open up, need to explain how it feels to fall victim to revenge porn. And yet how can I possibly share my innermost pain with the world, knowing my every word and thought and feeling will be judged? Will I be discussed and picked apart and questioned – again?

The velocity of my heartbeat only increases when I hear the unmistakable silence behind the double doors. And I know right there and then that I can't do it. Somehow, talking intimately to a handful of people is even worse than a packed out theater.

I turn to Ajita, Meg and Hazel. "I can't do this. I can't. Please. I'm sorry."

Ajita shoots me a rare sympathetic look, while Meg

squeezes my shoulder. Ajita whispers, "It's okay, dude. You're human. Want me to do it?"

"Or I could do it," Hazel offers, a steely glint in her gaze. "I have nothing left to lose, right?"

I stare at her in envy and admiration. Why can't I be that strong? "That would be amazing. I . . . thank you, Hazel."

She smiles warmly, squaring her shoulders. "Hey, it's not just for you. It's for me too."

Thursday 19 January

9.54 a.m.

Once the initial paralyzing fear wears off, disappointment lies in its place. It's a new feeling, and one I can't say I'm a huge fan of. Usually my expectations of myself are so low that I can never be disappointed – underachieving for the win! – but I really wanted to nail the speech yesterday. And yet I couldn't even get myself onto the stage.

In the end Hazel did a killer job of talking about the impact the tape had on her, exactly the right mix of emotional and fierce, then Ajita shared the stats we now know by memory, and talked about suicide rates and other stuff. We got away with it because everyone in the room knows either me or Hazel, so they already care about the issue. But still, I'm going to have to get over this if I want any hope of getting complete strangers to emotionally invest in our cause.

I hope to see Carson this morning, partly so I can mope and partly so we can exchange saliva, but there's no sign of him, not even in geography. He must be working. I'm a shitty girlfriend – I should really know when his shifts are. He pays so much attention to me, to every tiny thing going on in my life, and yet my own brain is so full to bursting that I can't retain information about his shift patterns for longer than five minutes. Did he tell me he was working today? My queendom for a more effective brain!

Actually, come to think of it, we've barely spoken all week. Not for my lack of trying either. I've messaged him a few times, but I've barely heard a peep. Have I done something to upset him? At any given moment in time it's fair to assume that I've upset someone. Hell, I didn't even know he was mad about the sex-doll sketch until he explicitly told me.

I fire off a quick text just to make sure.

Hey! Everything okay? Are you in school today? Lemme know if you need me to pick up any assignments for you. I will accept payment in pepperoni pizza and hand jobs. Preferably not at the same time, although I am willing to experiment.

11.18 a.m.
I still haven't anything from Eliza about sending my script to production companies. I keep trying to remind myself how busy she is and how grateful I should be that she's even working with me to begin with, but truthfully I'm disappointed. She told me we'd be pitching by now, and yet she hasn't even gotten back

to me on the edits I did, which she promised to do by first thing Monday.

My paranoid brain is screaming THE SCRIPT IS AWFUL AND YOU ARE AWFUL AND ELIZA IS ONLY JUST REALIZING HOW AWFUL YOU ARE AND ALL OF THIS IS GOING TO BE TAKEN AWAY FROM YOU SO PLEASE PREPARE FOR YOUR IMMINENT HOMELESSNESS, YOU TALENTLESS TOERAG.

My rational brain says: Chill, she's just busy.

Most of the time I'm somewhere between the two.

9.28 p.m.

I get an early finish at the diner tonight, since we serve a grand total of twenty-one customers in the entire time I'm there. I mean, I'm grateful for the chance to get an early night for once, but I could really use the extra hour's wage.

The one good (?) thing about tonight's shift is that Danny comes in for dinner. The sheer relief of seeing him alive and reasonably well is almost enough to offset the usual wave of rage that crashes through me whenever I see him. Almost.

Still. I'm glad he's okay enough to frequent the diner.

At first he's alone, and as he pulls himself into a window booth and stares out onto the dark street I consider sliding onto the bench opposite and forcing him to talk to me about what's going on with him at home. He hasn't spotted me yet, so I study him from a safe distance, figuring out my best move. He looks less sad than last time I saw him, but also less . . . everything. He looks utterly numb.

I'm just about to bite the bullet and go over when the bell over the doorway chimes again, and Sharon walks in. She's the deadpan girl from theater group who starred in one of our sketches last year – and who turned on me the instant the sex scandal broke. I feel a surge of rage when I lay eyes on her, like I did for the first month or so after it all went to hell. I wonder if this anger will ever go away. I wonder if I even want it to.

Sharon strides confidently over to Danny and right into the spot opposite him. His face brightens when he sees her, but not much.

I briefly wonder whether they're on a date. Then I wonder why I care. As Betty would say, the wildlife of Papua New Guinea is of more interest.

Plastering my hostess smile onto my face, I grab a couple menus and march over to their booth, even though they're not in my section. The other waitress Lola – who has epic pink hair and an undercut – frowns over me stealing her table, then shrugs when she figures out that it's less work for her and pulls her phone out of her back pocket. Croc Queen isn't around to yell.

"Hey, guys!" I say chirpily, plonking the two menus down in front of them. Danny almost jumps out of his skin. "Can I getcha anything to drink?"

"Yeah, two orange sodas," Sharon answers, colder than an ice bath in the Arctic. No please, no thank you. She doesn't even look at me. I'm just a waitress to her now. A slutty, overweight one if her mean comments on social media are anything to go by.

I resist the urge to slap her with a wet haddock and turn to her date. "Danny?" I ask, partly to ask whether he wants anything else and partly to see whether he's going to chide Sharon for her rudeness, but neither occurs. He just shakes his head, still gazing up at me as though he's never seen such a stunning sight in his entire life.

Then I realize: He had no idea I worked here until now. Why would he?

The strangeness of the situation hits me as I stroll back to the kitchen in a daze. My former best friend has no idea what's going on in my life, and I have no idea what's going on in his. His mom could be dying for all I know. This new distance is painful and strange. And I realize with a sharp pang that I don't want it to be this way.

As I pour their orange sodas I ask myself: Do I . . . miss Danny? Even after everything he's done?

Memories of him, the old him, flood through my brain. The seaside road trip his mom took us on when we were both six or seven; he found a perfectly symmetrical shell and gave me it as a gift with the most bashful look on his face. The time we went to the pet store together to spend his five dollars of pocket money; he bought a goldfish, named it Steve, and gave it to me. Betty and I had that thing for six years before it eventually committed suicide by jumping out of its tank and into Dumbledore's water bowl. Without being too graphic, you can imagine what Steve looked like after being partially digested by a wiener dog. Not great.

My chest aches. There are so many memories I have of Danny before he fell in love with me. Or has he always felt that way? Come to think of it, most of my stories involve Danny doing something nice for me, giving me something he thought would cheer me up, telling a funny story or pulling a stupid face. He got real good at that after my parents died. There was a lot of cheering up to be done, and he took to the task like a Steve to water.

And yet he ruined my life, or at least tried to. He fucked up so badly. And right now, I'm just so damn mad at him for that. Not just because of the thing itself, but because the thing itself led to the loss of a great friendship. All I want is for him to never have done it. I want so much for us to still be friends, and yet how can we be? It's too much to forgive.

Or am I being too harsh? Have I always been too harsh on him? I mean, obviously he was an enormous bucket of dicks for leaking my nude and performing all the associated douchebaggery. That's not what I'm having a change of heart over. But in the events leading up to that — when I knew he was into me and trying to buy my love — did I jump the gun in judging him for it?

Should I have been more lenient, more understanding?

I used to be so sure of myself, but lately I've been second-guessing a lot of stuff. Maybe that's what happens when the entire world turns on you.

But then I start remembering all the comments on the Izzy O'Neill: World Class Whore website. All right, so he didn't write them all himself. But he still made the website. He still provided the trolls with a platform for their hate. And whether it was a moment of weakness or a well-thought out scheme, he still fucking did it. How can that ever be forgiven?

It's so damn frustrating. I don't want to have to cut him out of my life; I just want him to have not messed up to begin with. I miss the tripod, I miss our conversations, I miss having him there through the good times and the bad. I would love to tell him about my agent and my screenplay ideas, to commiserate over the impending midterm exams, to chat about new YouTube channels we're into. But how can we ever go back to that after everything he's done?

The simple answer is: we can't.

11.15 p.m.
When I get back I take another shower. I know it's not the responsible thing to do, not when we're trying to keep our bills as low as possible, but I'm so cold from the walk home, and the inside of our apartment is barely warmer than it is outside, that

I'll do anything to warm back up. As I reach for my towel, which is still damp from my earlier shower [$^0/_{10}$ do not recommend], I catch sight of myself in the mirror, realizing with a start that I haven't really looked at myself naked since the nude pictures leaked. Since I used to check myself out daily, the thought makes me kind of sad.

I force myself to look; properly look. And it's almost impossible to do so without also seeing the nude photo, burned into my psyche forever. In the same way that the nude doesn't exist without my body, it's like my body doesn't exist without the nude. My body *is* the nude. They are one and the same. Neither can live while the other survives. That kind of thing. [That's another *Order of the Phoenix* reference, FYI. I'm not *completely* insane. Ahem.]

I can't look at my naked self the same way knowing thousands if not millions of other people have done the same. They've studied me from behind the comfort of their smartphone screens, free to linger as long as they like. There isn't one inch of me left that's mine and mine alone.

Danny did this. Danny did this. Danny did this. How could I ever even consider forgiving him?

11.54 p.m.
Betty is snoring so loudly it's like the *Millennium Falcon* is launching next door. How severe do we think the punishment

would be if I smothered her to death using Dumbledore's robes? I think I'd be willing to serve up to three years in prison for involuntary manslaughter. At least then I might actually get a decent night's rest.

Friday 20 January

7.28 p.m.

Ajita and Meg swing by the diner after school for some shakes, and since it's pretty quiet all round every time I stop by their table to take their order or pick up empties we tackle another item on our Bitches Bite Back meeting agenda.

When I deposit their peppermint mocha shakes, for example, Meg announces: "So some members have been requesting informative videos as well as sketches, which I think is an awesome idea. Any suggestions for conversation topics to get us started?"

"What life would be like if the dinosaurs still walked among us?" Ajita suggests, stirring her sludgy shake.

Meg laughs. "I was thinking more along the lines of feminism."

As subtly as I can I study the vibe between Ajita and Meg, attempting to detect any trace of a crush on either of their parts. But while Ajita seems slightly tense, Meg is her usual sweet, earnest self. It's impossible to read the situation, so I give up trying.

"Who's to say the dinos weren't super feminist, Meg?" I

object, picking up their empty glasses at a snail's pace. "The velociraptors definitely had an agenda. There's no way they were neutral on gender issues."

"All right, all right," Meg concedes. "The first topic of conversation will be dinosaurs. All those in favor say aye?"

"Aye, strongly in favor," Ajita and I both say at once.

11.05 p.m.

Texting Zachary about the campaign, and not hating it as much as one would expect when dealing with the direct descendant of a lizard king. He messages me first:

Hey. How's the campaign going? Haven't heard Dad talking about it lately.

I decide to sugarcoat the truth somewhat.

Howdy! It's going good. Recruited a bunch of people at school, and we're making a ton of content. Early stages :)

That's cool. I'm so glad you're pushing back. My dad bullies way too many people. It's nice that he's not gonna get away with it this time. Hey, have you talked to Rosa Garcia? She's running an election campaign and really cares about this stuff. Plus she's angling hard for the youth vote, so it'd make sense for her to get on board with something teens care so much about.

This reassures me somewhat, that our brains are working in similar ways. He's spent his life surrounded by political scheming, so if he thinks getting Rosa on side is a strong strategy, he's probably right.

Yeah! We emailed her last week, but she hasn't got back to us yet. Fingers crossed.

Sweet. That'll definitely work. Besides, Dad hates strong women almost as much as he hates weak men, lol. This is, like, the best way to get under his skin.

I send him a long row of bicep emojis, then:

You sound like you're pretty pissed at your dad right now. As a tragic orphan I have zero clue how that feels, but still. Here if you wanna vent.

He waits a while before texting again. I brush my teeth, take off my makeup and get into bed, snuggling into Dumbledore, much to his disgust. My phone buzzes just as I'm drifting off to sleep.

It's just pretty shitty knowing your dad is not a great guy.

Monday 23 January

9.36 a.m.

Thanks to Ajita, the hallways are a sea of Bitches Bite Back patches. #EndRevengePorn is ironed onto every cheerleader uniform in school. Ajita has pinned posters on every noticeboard, and the more awesome teachers have let her stick them up in classrooms too.

Ahead of this week's BBB meeting, Meg and Ajita film Hazel talking about her experiences and post it to YouTube. Every new BBB member shares it on social media, emails it to friends and family, comments and likes and retweets until there's no escaping it. And though it doesn't go viral like my nude picture did, by sheer force of will the video gets over a thousand views within the first twelve hours, and it drives a whole lot of traffic to our website – where our mission statement takes center stage.

As I watch the video, I'm awed by Hazel's courage. The openness with which she tells her story. She talks to the camera as though it's her best friend, unfaltering in her delivery. She shows the authenticity of her emotions in such an unselfconscious way that I cannot help but envy her. I know it's what I need to do too – it's what everyone *expects* me to do, the loud-mouthed figurehead of a major scandal – but watching Hazel doesn't inspire me to do so. It just makes it seem so much harder.

9.19 p.m.
After my evening shift at the diner, I finally hear back from my agent!

> **Hi Izzy,**
> **I read your revised script this past weekend, and I think you've done an amazing job. I just have a couple more minor notes (see attached doc) and then we're ready to start pitching.**
> **If you could make those two changes tonight – they should only take you a half-hour, tops – then I'll get on the phone first thing tomorrow and start setting up some meetings.**
> **Best,**
> **Eliza**

Shit, she emailed me hours ago and I haven't responded yet, let alone actioned her edit notes. No fear, though – soon as I'm home, I shall roll up my sleeves and get stuck in.

I'm gonna need alllllll the coffee, and the most obnoxiously flavored creamer money can buy. I once found matcha green tea flavor in a health food store, no word of a lie. Because who doesn't want their coffee to look and smell like a nuclear swamp? [If you are wondering why I was in a health food store, it's because I was forced there against my will.]

11.57 p.m.

When I get in from work Betty is once again inexplicably hogging the laptop, but once I wrestle it back off her I manage to make the changes to the screenplay and send it back to Eliza before the clock strikes midnight. I feel like Cinderella, if Cinderella smelled like deep fried chicken and hadn't washed her hair for a week.

Wednesday 25 January

7.00 a.m.

Over the last few days, it's been all systems go, firing on all cylinders, etc., etc. As you know, this is not my natural state, since I prefer to be in a state of extreme relaxation at all times. If I could spend my entire life sitting in a comfortable chair and getting drunk with Ajita, I would absolutely do that. But alas, I have recently discovered the existence of ambition somewhere within my deeply lazy soul, so some compromises must be made. Please just know that if I ever do make it to the red carpet, I shall be bringing along both Ajita and a comfortable chair.

Anyway, despite me working a ton of diner shifts, Eliza and I finally finished up my first screenplay and it's now out on submission with production companies in LA! Eliza spent all of yesterday calling up hotshots who might be interested in my script. It's a very surreal feeling knowing that such a high caliber of producers might actually consider reading my work.

At this point that's my main hope. Selling a movie still seems a little far-fetched for a nobody screenwriter like me, but even imagining a professional producer casting their eyes over my words is validation enough. I'm pretty happy, you guys. Pretty darn happy.

7.34 a.m.
Breakfast. Waffles, coffee, Betty. Need I say more?

Dumbledore just barked aggressively at my elbow, so apparently yes. He's obviously reading over my shoulder. Just to make it clear, my hormonal dachshund is also present at breakfast.

"What's going on today, kiddo?" Betty asks, scooshing whipped cream all over the world's fluffiest waffles and handing the plate to me. Stomach gurgling with hunger, I take to it with the bottle of chocolate syrup and immediately tuck in.

"Oh, the usual," I say through a mouthful of waffle. [That sounds dirty. All of the lols.] "Politicians will continue to make a mockery of this country. Billionaires will continue to be billionaires. The Earth will travel round the sun exactly once."

Betty frowns, flumping down in the chair opposite me. "I don't think that's right," she says as Dumbledore leaps up onto her lap and starts wriggling up underneath her shirt. She doesn't look even vaguely concerned as he reappears out her neck hole and proceeds to steal the first bite of waffle from her fork. She rolls her eyes, abandoning the dog-drooled fork and picking up the entire waffle with her bare hands.

"Since when did you stick up for the politicians and the billionaires?" I demand haughtily. My laptop sits on the counter playing a livestream of the morning news. As if to prove my point, a billionaire is currently waxing lyrical about how all corporation tax should be abolished.

"No, the sun thing," Betty says. "I think when the Earth goes round the sun once, that's a year, not a day."

Although she could be lying to me and I'd have no idea, this does ring true. I snort at my own idiocy. A waffle crumb ejects from my nostril. Dumbledore almost has a fit trying to leap over the table and snaffle it. "And once again I have proven that education is pointless, and my brain is no more likely to retain information about the workings of the solar system than it is to cure cancer."

Betty takes a sip of scalding coffee, not flinching as it steams up her glasses. "Yeah, yeah. You'll miss it when you leave."

Normally I'd throw some snark about how I would never miss Bunsen burners or pathetic fallacy or Mr Wong's wooden ruler in a millions years, but this morning I stop short. After everything I've been worrying about over the last few weeks, I suddenly realize that for once, Betty is right. I *will* miss it when I leave. And if I don't find something to fill the void, maybe I'll spend the rest of my half-lived life missing it. Can I really go through the next six or seven decades without ever studying Shakespeare or solving another mathematical formula? Or having some purpose other than serving milkshakes six days a week for the rest of my own eternity?

A funny thing has happened since I landed my agent. Every second I spend relaxing, whether in a comfortable chair, or with Ajita, or otherwise . . . I feel a little guilty. Like every second that I don't spend working on my writing is a second further behind my competitors I'm falling. Logically I know there's no rush, and I have my whole life ahead of me to forge and establish a career for myself. But the masochistic part of my brain that loves to torture itself keeps convincing the rest of me that if I don't keep writing and writing and writing until my fingers bleed and my eyes cave in, I'll be stuck working in the diner forever.

And that's a weird thing to be afraid of, because until very recently I thought that's the kind of future I'd be content with. Working in the diner, writing on my days off, hanging out with Betty and Dumbledore. Yet lately, I keep thinking about Frank, and the way he talked about being stuck in this town since he came back from Nam. Sure, he has a nice life, full of OJ and newspapers and pleasant walks down the street with no real worries. But what was it he said? "*Sometimes I struggle to get out of bed in the morning. I really do. . . . there's nothing new anymore. Just the same old faces in the same old town I've lived in my whole life.*"

I remember the hollowness of the words as they left his mouth, so stark in contrast to the joy when he was talking about his grandson. There was definite regret as he told me how he'd only left once, for the war, and never again since. Deep down, I know I'd feel the same if I followed the same path.

Before Eliza, I'd convinced myself that Frank's path was my only path too. But with that fateful email offering me representation she offered me a glimmer of hope. Just a glimmer, and yet so much more than I'd ever had before. Not a door, but a window. And it's impossible to resist looking through.

So I guess that's why I'm working myself so hard, firing on all cylinders even though my cylinders protest so vehemently. Because we all know girls like me, people like me, have to work so much harder than the privileged if we ever want to make it big.

I'm scared, though. What if I'm not working hard enough? What if I fall short? What if I become Frank?

Betty senses the shift in mood, probably because my face is so expressive I can't even have a sexual fantasy about the shower head without her noticing. And also because I've been silent for about twenty minutes. So she quickly moves the conversation along.

"Speaking of politicians, how's everything going with Bitches Bite Back?" she asks. "Have you bitten Ted Vaughan yet? Personally I'd like to see you take his hand clean off."

I dab at my syrup-covered nose with my sweater sleeve, wishing for the millionth time that I had Ajita's freakishly long tongue. "I dunno. Things are going well, but I'm having problems with speeches. Talking about my experiences and whatnot. Right now, for example, I would rather poop my pants every day for the rest of my life than talk to you about my insecurities."

"Fair enough. For what it's worth, kiddo, I still think you'd make a much better politician than Vaughan and his ilk."

"May I remind you that I recently believed the Earth hurtled round the sun on a daily basis."

"Not your finest moment," she admits gravely.

10.23 a.m.

Ms Castillo spends the entirety of first-period English impressing on us the importance of our upcoming midterm exams, and while I usually tune out at this stage, today I'm filled with doubt and apprehension.

Up until now, I've just accepted my academic ambivalence as fact. A personality quirk. Something that wouldn't matter in the long run, because I wasn't going to college anyway, so what do grades matter? Besides, you don't need a diploma in order to be funny.

But what if I'm just shooting myself in the foot even more by shunning formal study? I'm already behind the majority of other aspiring comedy writers because I don't live in LA, and I can't go to a fancy college and join a famous improv troupe, and I definitely cannot afford to enter competitions or attend workshops and conferences. My high-school grades are one of the few things I *can* control, and I'm choosing not to put in any effort. Is this beyond stupid and short-sighted?

Logic tells me I'd be better off spending my time honing my craft and getting as good at writing jokes as possible. Realistically that's what agents and producers and all the other gatekeepers care about. And yet I'm doubting myself more and more these days. Because if the comedy-writing thing doesn't pan out, which is highly likely, I truly have nothing to fall back on. No life raft, no safety net. Nothing.

Yikes. This is why I so often choose to sit in a comfortable chair and relax. Y'all see the trouble you cause when you start to think things through? It's only ever an exercise in frustration and futility. So it's best not to think at all, and conserve all your energy for the important things, like sex and laughing.

I really am one of the great philosophers of our time. Like Socrates but more into nachos.

2.25 p.m.

After our Bitches Bite Back meeting at lunchtime, I am more fired up than, I don't know, a firing squad. Except, you know, less murdery.

Since Hazel's speech gathered so much social media steam, the group size has more than doubled in the seven days since we last met. In the front row I'm super excited to see Bella, a trans girl and incredible activist from our school, who also has the coolest fashion sense in the actual world – all floaty blouses and vintage cowboy boots. [Do not tell Ajita I like another girl's style more than hers. You understand her penchant for flaying by now.] Anyway, Bella is a big deal online. Her blog about trans issues is always being covered in *Huffington Post* and *Teen Vogue*. The fact that Bella thinks Bitches Bite Back is worthy of her time is incredibly validating.

I dump my faux-leather jacket on the front row, next to where Ajita and Meg sit and chatter enthusiastically about the fresh order of patches Ajita has already had to place, and clamber to the stage in my stompy Docs. I'm still nauseous with fear, but this time I've told myself that I don't need to go personal. I just need to actually talk, using my mouth, which I didn't manage to do last time round. Baby steps.

"Less than two weeks ago," I start, projecting clarity and purpose as best I can despite the tremble in my throat, "we met with a political staffer from Ted Vaughan's office to discuss the current lack of legislation surrounding revenge porn. That staffer, like the senator who represents us, gave precisely zero fucks about the pain of teenage girls. Especially teenage girls like us: poor, and brown, and disabled." My eyes blur with familiar anger as they dance over the crowd. "We have to make the Vaughans – and the world – see that if they don't listen to our demands, if they don't start to care about our suffering, they will

164

lose support, and as a result elections. They will lose respect."

Meg does a sassy finger snap, and a bunch of people laugh. It eases some of the tension in the room.

"The best way to send this message is through a good old-fashioned protest," I continue. "And so we've decided to hold an End Revenge Porn rally. We'll seek the support of local businesses and Vaughan's political rivals, we'll get influential journalists and bloggers and YouTubers on board, and we will make ourselves heard. We will make change happen. And in a little over a month we'll start by taking to the streets — and showing just how powerful bitches can be."

Once the cheering subsides, we spend the rest of the session brainstorming ideas for the rally, from witty slogans to influencers we should approach to appear at the march. Meg gives a brief talk on the Bitches Bite Back website, announcing plans to set up a media kit section where users can download images, badges and social media statements to share in support of the cause.

Once the meeting is over and everyone is filing out the auditorium, babbling and buzzing from the excitement of their new quest, Bella approaches Ajita, Meg and me in the front row, where we're gathering up notes and discussing Ajita's idea for quirky T-shirts promoting the march.

"Hey!" I say, beaming at Bella like some kind of maniacal clown. "Thank you so much for coming. I adore your blog.

Basically I'm a huge fangirl of yours. Forgive my nerding out."

"All nerding out is henceforth forgiven," she says, laughing and tucking her braided black hair behind her ear. She wears gold, sparkly eyeliner, which complements her dark brown skin like whoa. "Anyway, I have a proposition for you."

"We become best friends and take over the world?"

"Erm, rude," Ajita objects.

"Sorry," I correct myself. "Second best friends."

"Erm, rude," Meg chimes in.

I roll my eyes. "Fine. Top ten best friends. But world domination is still on the cards, if you're game."

"Always." Bella laughs again. "What I actually wanted to suggest, though, was that I become a guest columnist for the BBB website. I admire what you're doing, but it's very cis-centric. What about a new blog section exploring slut-shaming from a trans perspective? It wouldn't take over the revenge porn campaign, but it would definitely feed into it. I could explore trans issues in the context of revenge porn, and interview trans girls and women who've been victims of it."

"I love that idea!" I reply, fighting the burning shame that I hadn't even thought about it from that angle before. "Seriously. Yes. Thank you."

"Awesome!" Bella beams, shifting her slouchy leather purse from the crook of her elbow to her shoulder. "I've done a lot of digging around online, and there's very little writing on the intersection between slut-shaming and trans sexuality. And it would be super positive for the Bitches Bite Back movement to start conversations around this stuff."

"Definitely!" I say. "Not least because I want to learn more about it myself. In fact, why are you still talking to a maniacal clown of a person instead of writing?"

"You're right," Bella says, nodding. "I'll rectify the situation immediately. Toodles!"

"That girl," I say earnestly to Ajita, watching Bella walk away, "is so cool she can pull off using the word 'toodles'. How is that physically possible?"

7.18 p.m.

I haven't seen Carson in a while, so I decide to head over to his place after school to make sure everything's okay. I'll take him a copy of our needlessly complicated math homework from Friday so he doesn't think I'm clingy. Not that my clinginess is a great secret, but still.

The night air is bitter and stings my face as I walk, hands shoved into my puffy jacket pockets. I miss being able to cycle everywhere, but the ceaseless snowfall makes it impossible.

Three-year-old Cyra answers the door in her *T. rex* PJs. "S'Izzy! S'Izzy, s'Izzy, s'Izzy!" She leaps around ecstatically, which makes me grin forreals, and hugs my leg as though it's a life raft. "Car-kin! Car'kin!" she yells frantically back into the house. She's always had trouble saying Carson's name. I have no idea where the "K" comes from. Kids make zero sense.

"Who's there, Cyra?" Annaliese shouts from the kitchen, where I can hear her chopping veggies as her two youngest boys play toy trains round her feet.

"It's me, Annaliese!" I call back. "Is Carson around?"

Before she can answer, Carson himself thuds down the final few stairs and lands in the hallway.

"Hey," he says, climbing over a plethora of toys and books to get to the door. Instead of kissing me, he bends down and scoops Cyra up into his arms. I try not to feel affronted, or jealous of a three-year-old, which is the height of pettiness and yet totally on-brand for me. "What brings you here?"

I go to pull the math homework out from under my arm, then realize I left it on the kitchen table. "Uh, I was bringing you an assignment. But I left it at home, because my brain cells appear to be dying in their thousands at the moment. Can't figure out whether it's an epidemic or a mass suicide."

"You got a lot going on. We both do." Cyra blows a raspberry into his ear, bursting into a fit of giggles. "Wanna come in?"

"Absolutely."

As he puts Cyra down so she can run back inside, I notice his hands are covered in paint: candy pink and lime green. Not his usual palette, which is a strange thing to think, and yet it jumps out at me like a neon sign.

168

"Hey, what are you working on right now?" I ask as we slip into the hallway. Cyra's toys are everywhere. And I mean everywhere – hanging from the lights, shoved under rugs, piled up in heaps. Navigating them is like an assault course, and as we all know I am not so great at the whole physical activity thing. So an impromptu workout is an unwelcome addition to my visit.

"What? Oh, nothin', man, nothin'." He shoves his paint-streaked hands into his pockets. "You want a drink?"

We head to the kitchen and each grab a glass of chocolate milk. Carson drinks roughly nine gallons a day, and is something of a connoisseur on the subject. He has very strong opinions on whether it should be made with chocolate ice cream or milk and chocolate syrup. I forget what said opinions are, but still.

Annaliese is in the kitchen making dinner – a giant brisket, which smells ridiculously rich and delicious, like it's been cooking since New Year's. I fill them both in on the rally, and on how Ted Vaughan is even more of a douchebag than previously thought. Annaliese agrees vehemently – the dude axed a program that provided low-income kids with free breakfast at school each morning, which hit the Manning clan hard. We also talk about how the next month is going to be pretty intense, what with midterm exams and protest prep to think about, but that I feel optimistic. I feel like we can really make a difference.

"You need help with anything?" Carson asks. "Like with the rally and all. Need me to makes signs or whatever?"

For a moment I consider asking him to paint Ajita, Meg and me onto a sign, standing hand in hand as we face the patriarchy head-on. How awesome would that be? But then I remember how much work he has to do, both at the pizza place and at home, and I don't want to burden him. So instead I say, "No, I'm good. Thank you, though. You're sweet for asking."

"I gotta say, Izzy, you impress the hell outta me," Annaliese says, mashing potatoes in a saucepan. Her sinewy arms ripple with muscle as she works. "You turned a crappy situation into . . . this. You're an amazing woman, y'know that?" She smiles warmly.

"Thanks, Annaliese," I say, grinning back. "That means a lot. It's kind of wild how much it's all taking off. I definitely don't feel anywhere near old enough to handle it. I have zero clue what I'm doing."

Carson and I are leaning back against the counter, and he nudges my shoulder with his. I turn to face him, and he's got the sweetest proud boyfriend look on his face. All dimples and sparkly eyes. He kisses me softly on the cheek, and Annaliese watches us and smiles.

I want to bottle this moment. The rich brisket smell, the buttery potatoes, the steam in the kitchen fogging up the cold windows. The sweet taste of chocolate milk, made the right way, whatever the right way may be. The happiness I feel when I'm around Carson and his family – warm and safe and loved.

Friday 27 January

5.15 p.m.

Today's another snow day, but there's no work for me at the diner. I spend my morning making sure I'm up to date on school assignments and cooking a batch of meals for the freezer using some nearly bad veg I picked up for nine cents. There is every chance Betty and I will immediately die from extreme food poisoning, thanks to my heavily improvized recipes, but it's the thought that counts. [That's a valid defense against manslaughter charges, right?]

Then, because I have been tasked with handling the PR for the End Revenge Porn Rally [yes, the PR for the ERPR – try saying that without setting your mouth on fire], I get to work emailing every single one of the local and national journalists who reached out to me at the height of the scandal. Back then, I ignored every single request for comment that landed in my inbox, but now my job is to recapture their attention. To pique their interest once more.

Instead of sending a blanket email to the hundreds of contacts

I have in my account, I take the time to research each one, look into the kind of story they cover, and tailor my approach accordingly. I include some personal insights from the scandal to lure them in, laying it on thick with the emotional angle [easier when typing than talking, it turns out], then go in for the kill and explain how we hope to turn the horrific story of what happened to me into actual political change. It's time-consuming, but I get into a good rhythm, and come late afternoon I've replied to over half of the journalists in my inbox.

By the time I head over to Ajita's I feel like I deserve the break. Studying for midterms can wait. I'm beat.

Meg is already chilling in the basement by the time I get there, which means I can't talk to Ajita about her romantic feelings, and somehow it doesn't seem like the kinda thing I can just text her about. Like: "Hey, dude, quick question, I know we've barely acknowledged the fact you're gay, but are you in love with Meg?" No. Even I have more tact than that. Most of the time.

Plus, I'm not sure I should even address it with Ajita at all. It took her an eternity to tell me about Carlie, and even then it was only because I accidentally found out through inadvertent laptop snooping. And, y'know, accidentally told Carson, who had his phone hacked, by a person who very deliberately revealed this info to the entire world. When that came out Ajita denied the rumors to everyone except me. Her family and tight-knit Hindu community still have zero idea.

Ajita and I have barely discussed it since. Up until now, I've been kinda leaving it for her to decide when she wants to talk about it in more depth, if she ever does. I'll be here for her as soon as she's ready. It shouldn't be a big deal, but it super, super is in our current world. And I want to support her through it.

So part of me thinks I need to give her the opportunity to tell me about this on her own terms, this time.

As I flump into the love seat in Ajita's basement and help myself to a handful of extra jalapeño nachos I feel like I'm right back where I belong. I've missed it.

"How's Praj getting on with his running?" I ask Ajita, who's channel-flipping in search of something we've all seen before and thus don't have to focus on in order to follow. "Is he still the next Usain Bolt by all accounts?"

"I dunno, dude, but the smell coming from his laundry basket is borderline criminal. Like, I actually think I could have him arrested for attempted murder." She settles on a weird British sketch show and leans back into the beanbag, grabbing herself the most toppings-heavy tortilla chip in the nacho bowl. "Imagine all the sweaty socks in the world were fermented into a fine paste and used to wallpaper a bedroom. That's what it smells like."

I screw up my nose. "Delightful."

Ajita wrinkles her lips, before diving back into the nacho bowl. I follow suit, as does Meg, until we're all fighting over the same chip. It has the perfect ratio of salsa to guac, and none of us are willing to give it up. Eventually Meg emerges triumphant.

Then, with absolutely no warning whatsoever, all of a sudden I'm filled with painful nostalgia. I remember Danny, Ajita and me hanging out down here throughout our teenage years, without having jobs, national sex scandals or big questions about the future to worry about. And I miss it.

Why? Why do I miss it?

Don't get me wrong, Meg is awesome. What we're doing with Bitches Bite Back is awesome. But still I miss my old life so much it sits in my stomach like a stone. It's like, grief, in a way. When Danny ruined my life, I lost something forever.

My phone sits on the floor beside me, repeatedly vibrating and lighting up from all the email notifications I'm getting. They make it impossible to forget how much things have changed. Gone are the days of only ever getting wonky text messages from Betty and vegetable emojis in my group chat with Ajita and Danny. Oh, how I long for the easy reading of an aggressively purple eggplant.

Ajita clears her throat. "So, Iz . . . Meg and I got you something." They exchange conspiratorial smiles. I irrationally bristle at their scheming, feeling left out once again, because as we have established I am still a twelve-year-old at heart.

"Ready?" Meg says, wiping her brow on her forearm. Her bracelets and wristwatch jangle together.

Ajita reaches down by the side of the beanbag and pulls out a paper bag from the local drugstore. "Okay, so this might be the dumbest idea ever, and if you're not up for it don't worry at all, 'kay? We kept the receipt." She looks to Meg, like this is a rehearsed routine, and again I beat down the ostracized sensation of being on the outside looking in.

"We've seen the way you admire Lola's hair," Meg blurts out in excitement. "And we got you some pink hair dye!"

Ajita jumps right in before I can express my astonishment. "It's wash-in, wash-out," she adds hastily. "If you hate it, it's not a drama. Just a quick shampoo and condish and you're good. And obviously if you don't want to do it at all, it's not a problem – like I say, we kept the receipt."

Then she pulls the dye out the bag, and I have to admit it's the most gorgeous color. It's not quite the bright bubblegum pink of Lola's hair; it's paler, dustier. The model on the box has her hair all messed up, like I always wear mine, and it looks AMAZING.

When Meg first said the words "hair dye", I was initially, like, oh hell no. But now I'm looking at it, and I'm thinking about how at odds with my body I've been feeling, and suddenly there's nothing I want to do more in the world than reclaim the way I look.

I feel the grin spreading across my face, feel my eyes twinkle like they always used to when Ajita dared me to do something.

"Fuck it. Let's do it."

175

10.48 p.m.

Coloring my hair pink is the best thing I've done this entire year. We settle for an ombré dip-dye type situation, which basically involves me sitting on the basement floor Buddha-style while Ajita and Meg work their witchcraft with tinfoil and hair grips. On several occasions we all have to stop for intense laughing breaks, so hilarious is the sketch show in the background, and it's generally a deeply entertaining forty-five minutes.

Then I take a shower in Ajita's bathroom, which is the height of luxury let me tell you. Her parents have one of those elaborate rain shower setups, and I spend a decent portion of my time pretending I'm in a shampoo commercial. In any case, it's just nice to shower for as long as I like without worrying about a water bill, and stepping out into a warm bathroom with underfloor heating. I don't often wish I was rich, because fantasizing is an exercise in futility and a pointless waste of energy, but this is one of those times. If I could have one awesome room in my house, it would be a bathroom like this.

After the most needlessly indulgent shower of all time, I blow-dry my hair to the best of my ability. I feel like people underplay how strenuous drying your hair is. It's up there with changing your duvet covers in terms of getting your heart rate up to an uncomfortable figure. Like is this a beauty regimen or an intense arm workout? Is it normal for your biceps to tremble and cry while holding what is essentially a household appliance above your head for an extended period of time? Or am I just super unfit? [Probably that one.]

Before I leave the bathroom I study myself in the mirror once again. This time I feel different, in the best possible way. My hair – half dirty blonde, half soft pink – brings my blue eyes to life. I didn't really notice last time, but my new birth control and free diner food have made me even curvier than I was before; fuller boobs, softer tummy, wider hips. I look like a woman, not the girl from the nude photo. And I like it. I really do. I look so undeniably . . . me.

My friends are awesome. They knew what I needed before I did.

When I finally emerge, like a butterfly from a cocoon [or something that makes me sound like less of a dickhead], Ajita and Meg are working on a giant protest sign shaped like a pair of boobs. As I walk down the stairs they squeal girlishly and clap their hands together like performing monkeys. And I'll give it to them . . . I feel awesome.

What's more, I feel normal. Like a normal teenage girl, having a normal night in with her pals. Coloring our hair, gossiping about boys, watching TV. As great as all the Bitches Bite Back stuff is, and as passionately as I feel about it, just being a regular eighteen-year-old instead of an inadvertent political figure is super refreshing.

And it's selfish, so selfish, but part of me prays neither of them go away to college. Because if they do? I'll be left in this town alone, knowing the world is moving on without me.

Monday 30 January

6.00 a.m.

My phone has some kind of emotional breakdown from the sheer volume of notifications, so I peel one eye open at this ungodly hour and check to see what the Dickens is going on.

Emails. So many emails. Email responses from over a dozen journalists, all of whom want to cover the story in some way or another. Yes! YESSSS!

One local radio station wants to chat to me on the phone so they can do a short news segment on the rally. Another regional journalist tells me to pick up tomorrow's newspaper, as they've written a two-page piece about the rally and the background behind it. And a national newspaper wants to write an article about revenge porn laws state by state, using my story as a hook.

Holy. Crap.

A writer from a BuzzFeed-style viral news site called Clickbait wants to write a listicle called 'Twelve Reasons We Should All Support Izzy O'Neill.' Her name is George Washington [no, really] and her email is so touching and heartfelt it almost brings me to tears – for more reasons than one.

Because she rightfully points out that if her editor approves the story and they go live with it, I'm likely to start receiving a bunch of fresh media attention. Which means my nude pictures will too. George offers to give me a day or two to think it over, to decide whether I'm prepared for that to happen again. At first I'm all "bitch I'm tough enough to handle this, how dare" but then I start thinking about it, really thinking about it, and the realization of what this means makes my bones feel like lead.

I remember the feeling of being an ant under a magnifying glass, roasting under the gaze of my peers and the rest of the population. I remember feeling like I was in front of a one-sided mirror, where everyone could see me but I couldn't see them. I remember the stares and the whispers and the taunts, the social media outcry and the graffiti on the bathroom walls. The wandering gaze of my teachers and the sympathetic head tilts of my friends. I remember scrubbing and scrubbing and scrubbing, and never feeling truly clean.

Can I go through all that again?

7.16 a.m.

I have to. There's so much at stake.

Besides, this time around, it's different. Last time, I suffered for no real gain. It just . . . hurt. And there was no reason for it.

But now there's a greater purpose to focus on: change. Change that would mean no other girl ever has to feel the way I did.

And this time it's on my terms. I'm choosing to put myself out there like this. The decision is mine, and I can own it. I can hold my head high and know that a leaked nude doesn't make me a shitty person. It makes me a really, really strong one.

I've already weathered this storm. I can weather it again.

3.15 p.m.

School finally reopens after a billion snow days, and it's pretty strange being back. Everyone has a sort of dazed and confused look about them, as though they have recently emerged from a coma, and the reality of midterm exams starting in a couple weeks is beginning to hit.

Obviously there has been some kind of divine intervention because I'm not in work at all today, so can actually devote myself to the art of learning. Only the art of learning is not what I ultimately end up committing myself to.

At lunch I grab myself a corndog and make my way over to the table Carson is sitting at with a couple other members of the basketball team. At least half of his teammates are in the library studying for midterms – lots of them have grades to uphold in order to fill their scholarship requirements – so the atmosphere is generally much calmer and less "banterful" than usual. I mean this in a positive way. Nothing makes me want to disembowel myself with Mr Wong's wooden ruler more than "locker-room talk". [Once again, allow me to remind you that wooden ruler is not a euphemism, otherwise that sentence becomes even more despicable and horrific than my usual fare.]

I slide along the bench next to Carson. "Hey," he says through a mouthful of corndog. "Come sit." I find this sentiment redundant on account of the fact I'm literally already sitting down, but I appreciate his approval nonetheless.

Damn, he looks good today. Like, the goodest. As he takes a slurp of iced tea all I want to do is hold the remnants of his corndog hostage until he tells me why he's wearing that dark red sweater when he knows perfectly well I always want to jump his bones every time he does so.

It's only just occurring to me how long it's been since we've had sex, since we mainly see each other in school and not even I am gung ho enough to be humped in homeroom. Like, I don't think we've had sex at all in January. No wonder I'm up a height about everything all the time, like a dog on heat. All I need is to get laid. [I don't imagine Ted Vaughan's office would agree somehow, but it's nice imagining a world in which sex is the only answer I need.]

"Nice hair," he says, eyeing the dusty pink color. "Suits you."

"Thanks," I say, beaming. It's mostly faded already, but I absolutely adore it so Ajita has promised to buy a semi-permanent box dye and top it up for me. "I'm pretty into it. Is it possible to be attracted to yourself? You of all people must know."

"You crack me up," he says, shoving so much corndog in his mouth that it's borderline impossible not to crack a joke about mouth play. "How's the rally prep comin'?"

I fill him in on all the journalist stuff, including the fact that George Washington him/herself is directly invested in the outcome of all this nonsense. I skim over the agonizing decision-making on my part, mainly because his jock brethren appear to be listening in on what I'm saying as opposed to their preferred activity of flinging their own feces at each other.

I finish by telling Carson how I did a phone interview this morning while I should've been in class, and the radio segment will air tomorrow. They've also set up a page on their website about the march, with a ton of info on how listeners can get involved if they so wish. Plus they're including a link to the fundraising page Ajita set up to help with rally-related costs — banner printing, klaxon-purchasing, etc.

Carson listens to all of this, then stares at me in wonder. "Damn. My girl's good, y'all. Didn't you only decide to march, like, five days ago or somethin'? You're killin' the game."

"Thanks. Hey, wanna hang out after school?" I ask, already knowing what his answer will be. I take a giant bite of my own corndog so I'm not just staring intensely at him awaiting a response. I cannot let him know how thirsty I am for his flesh. [Not in, like, a cannibal way.]

"Sorry, can't. Picked up a shift." He wipes his hands on his jeans and takes another sip of iced tea. "Tomorrow?"

I'm about to say yes, yes, a thousand times yes, for I cannot wait to hump you, when I remember I have diner shifts of my own to contend with. My face falls. "I'm sorry. I would love that, but I'm working."

"Wanna go shoot some hoops, Manning, my man?" one of Carson's teammates asks, slapping him heartily on the back.

"Uh, yeah, sure. Gimme one sec." Carson turns to me apologetically, rubbing his jaw with a paint-stained hand. "Is it cool if I go? I've barely made it to practice these last few weeks. Don't wanna get cut, y'know?"

I swallow my objections. The stupid insecure teenager inside me is all, BUT WHAT IF WE DON'T SPEND ENOUGH TIME TOGETHER AND/OR PARTICIPATE IN ADEQUATE HUMPING, AND YOU FORGET ABOUT ME AND/OR LEAVE ME FOR A FELLOW ARTISTE!!!??? But the rational part of me, which very rarely wins but on this occasion pips my paranoia to the post, says, "Course it is. Go have fun."

"You're the best." He pulls on his beanie and picks up his tray, making his way to follow the rest of the guys.

My heart sinks. Seriously, when will I next see him? I despise admitting how much I miss him, but I do. And also, sex. Remember sex? I do not.

He makes it a few feet, then turns round and says, "Hey."

"Yeah?"

"We're gonna hang out soon. And it's gonna be good. A'ight?"

I grin back. "A'ight."

He bursts into laughter, spluttering everywhere. "I mean . . . as long as you never say 'a'ight' again. Cos, damn, that was white."

6.36 p.m.

!!!!!!!!!!!!!!!!!!!!!!!!!!!!!!!!!!!!!

I'm sitting cross-legged in the basement, having my hair recolored by Ajita and Meg, when an email notification pings through on my phone. Fumbling around on the ground around me, I find a discarded jalapeño and several peanut butter cup wrappers before making contact with the offending device. I bring it right up to my face so I can read it without disturbing their flow.

Hi Izzy,

So I just got off the phone with South Street Productions based here in LA. They love the sound of your script and want to meet you! I pitched it as Pretty Woman meets Magic Mike, which piqued their interest immediately.

I know flying out to California is a big ask, so they're happy to talk via Skype. Does that sound good to you? Let me know if so and I can schedule a video-call. Happy to

jump in on conference mode if it'll make you more comfortable to have me there.

Best,

Eliza

I just immediately start screaming, like not even just excited screaming, but actual oh-my-God-I-am-being-murdered-somebody-help screaming. Ajita nearly flings the pot of dye everywhere in sheer fright, which Meg thinks is the funniest thing she's ever witnessed in her life, so there we are, me screaming, Ajita flailing and Meg laughing, and none of us having the vaguest idea what is going on.

Still maintaining a piercing pitch only dogs can hear, I hand the phone to Meg who reads out the email to Ajita. Then we are all screaming at each other, and the whole world is screaming, and I swear to God I hear Dumbledore screaming back from several miles away, and I might never stop screaming for the rest of my days.

Tuesday 31 January

6.58 a.m.

My segment aired on the local radio station, and a couple other articles went live, and holy hell our donations page has exploded. We've smashed our fundraising goal of $5,000, and have upped it to $10,000 so we can scale up even more. God only knows what'll happen when George Washington hits post on the Clickbait listicle. Perhaps NASA will name a rocket after us, for example, or we'll have our faces carved into Mount Rushmore. You just don't know.

Forreal, though, it's completely bananas how much this is all escalating. I'm completely overwhelmed and in a constant state of resisting the urge to curl up in the fetal position.

Using our new pot of cash, Ajita has put in orders for a couple hundred BBB hoodies and lanyards, so all the official Bitches can uniform up on the day itself, plus she's paid to have an ad placed on the giant billboard outside city hall. It's stark fuchsia and impossible to miss. The entire town is going to know exactly what's going down.

And thanks to the radio segment or the billboard or

possibly both, Rosa Garcia finally got back to us! This was her email response:

> **Hi Izzy, Ajita and Meg,**
> **It's so great to hear from you guys! I listened to Izzy on the radio this morning and I'm so impressed with how well you're pulling your campaign together. It's such an important issue and one that affects so many young women. It truly gives me so much heart to see what you're doing right now.**
> **As you know I'm very busy with my own campaigning, but rest assured I'm going to do everything I can to march alongside you in a couple weeks. There's nothing more important than getting out there on the ground and engaging with real people and real movements – this is what I live for!**
> **xRosa**

Okay, so it's not the in-person meeting we originally asked for, or a public endorsement – yet. But it's still acknowledgment. It still makes me feel like this matters, and that important people are watching and listening. Besides, it's more than we ever got from Ted Vaughan.

The buzz in my veins is becoming a permanent fixture. And I kind of love it.

2.15 p.m.

I'm dying of cuteness. When Meg tries on her fuchsia hoodie for the first time, expertly matching the color to a new lipstick shade, Ajita accidentally makes her romantic feelings known with the following:

"You look beautiful. I mean, you always look beautiful. I mean, not that I notice. I mean . . . Oh God."

And Meg bashfully bites her lip but the grin escapes anyway, and suddenly neither of them are looking at each other, and then after a few long seconds they lift their gaze at the same time and their eyes meet in the bathroom mirror, and honestly it's like I don't even exist in that moment.

Nawwwwwwww. But also, rude.

4.34 p.m.

Carson walks with me to the diner after school, and I excitedly fill him in on the new developments in my screenwriting world. While he manages to refrain from screaming, he does do an adorable little hop in his walk, like an excited puppy, and asks a billion questions about the company and what the call will entail. It's such a fun conversation. I love talking about creative work, no matter how boring that makes me.

But then I make the mistake of trying to talk about the future, about what this new development means, and about Frank, the cute but vaguely depressed diner veteran. I tell him about how it's making me question what I want from life, and how the answer changes with every passing day.

"Do you ever feel like that?" I ask, tucking my chin into my coat for warmth. It's bitterly freezing out. "Just kind of . . . lost and confused about what comes next?"

But as usual he just shrugs, the adorable little hop vanishing from his step. "Nah. I try not to think about it much."

Blahhhhh. It seems like he's becoming even more closed off with every passing day. I swear we used to discuss this kind of stuff, albeit lightheartedly, and yet now anything that goes beyond surface level is pretty much verboten.

Is it me? Am I the problem? Is he getting sick of me? Are these barriers being thrown up intentionally to keep me from getting too attached?

Izzy O'Neill: jumping to dramatic conclusions since always.

10.17 p.m.
My shift passes by in a haze of sore feet, shitty customers and a chronic case of defiant optimism from yours truly. Things are happening. Good things. The rally is gathering steam, and I HAVE A CALL WITH A MOVIE PRODUCER OH MY GOD. Every crappy complaint about slow service and too-cold milkshakes washes right over me, and even my anxiety over Carson's stonewalling is no match for my excitement. I go over and over and over that email from my agent, learning it by heart,

committing it to memory, knowing I will never forget the euphoria [read: screaming] that came along with it.

Everything starts to wind down in the diner after nine, so I spend my final hour in the kitchens, helping the chefs clean up. Lola divvies up the tips from the last month, and I walk away with nearly ninety bucks. I feel like Richard Branson at this point.

I intend to harangue Croc Queen about swapping some shifts next week so I can work on the campaign, but she slips away early as she has done every day for the last week. Perhaps her alligator overlord has summoned all the croc-skinned super villains in the state for their annual Croc Clan Conference.

11.34 p.m.

Betty is sitting in the kitchen when I get home, cradling a mug of tea in one hand and typing furiously on my laptop with the other. Dumbledore is passed out at her feet, tiny paws twitching manically. He must be running somewhere awesome in his dream.

For a few seconds Betty doesn't notice my entrance. It's only when I clink my keys into the bowl on the counter and start unzipping my puffy jacket that she slams the laptop shut so aggressively it's like Croc Queen's head is inside.

"All right, Betty-O," I say firmly. "What are you keeping from me? Out with it. What the hell are you doing with my laptop every night? Because I cleaned out all the good porn."

I pull out the other kitchen chair and flump down into it, only just realizing how exhausted my feet and legs are. For the millionth time in the last month I have all new respect for how Betty deals with diner work despite her bunions and other ailments. The woman is a rockstar. [I mean, the world's worst rockstar. But a rockstar nonetheless.]

"I've said it before and I'll say it again," she answers, holding her chin high like a proud child. "It is none of your damn beeswax."

"For the love of nachos," I say with a sigh. I don't want her to know how crazy this is driving me, and yet sheer curiosity destroys any semblance of chill I may have possessed in the past. "Woman, I am not above waterboarding you. You know this. Remember when you didn't want to shell out for Wi-Fi? And I strapped you to this very kitchen table and wrapped a towel round your mouth? Do you really want a repeat of that?" Dumbledore sleep-yelps under the table.

Betty is absolutely loving the attention. She smirks mischievously. "I'll tell you if – and only if – you'll talk to me about college."

This catches me off-guard as I unlace my Docs. "College? What about it?"

"Where you're going to apply, what you're going to study. That kind of thing."

Carefully avoiding her gaze, I fumble around removing my

thrift-store wristwatch. "What are you talking about, you old loon? I'm not going to college. You know this." Even as I say the words my lungs feel heavy.

"Like hell you aren't," Betty says, draining the last of her tea, thunking the mug down and folding her arms. "So. Where ya going? What ya studying? Tell Aunt Betty."

Honestly. What is happening right now? As I rub my feet with my thumbs I ask, "Are you drunk? High? Possessed by a strangely eloquent demon spirit?"

Betty just gives me a death stare, providing further evidence to back up the demon spirit hypothesis, and waits for my responses to her earlier questions.

I lean back in my chair, tempted to make myself a cup of tea but also too broken to put in the necessary work. "Grandma —"

"Don't you dare."

"Dare what?"

"Call me grandma, like I'm a hundred years old. Betty-O will suffice. Continue."

Instead of pointing out that she is, in fact, a hundred years old, and also my grandma, I roll my eyes. "Whatever, Betty-O. Point is, I'm not going to college and leaving you here alone. Did you miss the whole part where colleges started charging a million dollars a semester? Or did that pass you by as you scoured my porn collection every waking minute of the day?"

Betty holds up a finger to silence me. Dumbledore emits

another cute little yelp. I wonder what he's barking at in his dream. Or is he too possessed by a demonic presence? It's anyone's guess.

She presses aggressively onward. This demon is nothing if not persistent. "You're going to go to college, and you're going to love it, and you're not going to worry about your cuckoo old grandma back home who's perfectly happy cohabiting with her canine pal, okay?"

"You really are cuckoo," I mutter, shaking my head. "Do you have any concept of how expensive college is? You'd have to quadruple your annual salary to get anywhere close to how much tuition fees are, and that's forgetting the sky-high living costs in most college towns. And I know you've missed most parent-teacher evenings for the last four years, and I know I tend to burn my report cards over a scented candle before you can ever read them, but spoiler alert: I am no straight-A student. Short of getting a scholarship for achievement in sarcasm, I think that one's a dead end."

"So what are you gonna do?" Betty asks more forcefully than usual. "Work for Croc Queen the rest of your life? I won't let you waste your talent like that. Nuh-uh."

"I'm not wasting it!" I retort, getting a little irate now. What the hell's gotten into her? Has she won the lottery and just forgotten to mention it to me? College has never been an option for me, and now she's acting all holier than thou because I have no plans to apply. "Didn't you hear what I told you last night? I have a call with a production company next week. I can still make things happen while staying here with you. Plus I'm something of a political icon now. We have this rally coming up. We're going to change things for the better. I'm not wasting anything, all right?"

"Okay, okay," she concedes. Easing off a little, she shifts in her chair, then starts to unwrap a packet of crackers she has stashed in her fluffy bathrobes. From nowhere she also pulls out a pat of butter and a knife, and merrily prepares herself a late-night snack. "So you can make things happen from here. It's still going to be a hindrance, not being based in LA, right? And from what I understand about the movie industry, competition is fierce. Are you sure it's not putting you at a massive disadvantage to be degree-less and living in the ass end of nowhere?"

"Of course it is!" I snap, hating myself for getting angry with her. "It's easy for you to sit and preach this shit when *you* never had to make these decisions. You never made anything of yourself, so why the fuck are you pressuring me to?"

No, no, no. Stop. Please stop. Why am I doing this? I know she's only trying to help, but she's just raising my hopes, making me think college is possible when it's not.

Thankfully my grandmother is a better human than me, and she merely says, "Because I know it's what you want."

Breathing deeply, I mutter, "So what do you suggest? We

borrow cash from a loan shark and have our kneecaps smashed in when we can't even pay back the first thousand bucks?"

"We'll figure it out," Betty says, smoothing a thick layer of butter over her third cracker and shoving it all in her mouth. "We always do."

Overcome with frustration, I drop my head into my hands and bite my thumbs to keep from screaming. Because I want it. I want all these things she's dangling in front of me. I've never truly admitted it to myself until now, but the force of the realization hits me like a truck. I stifle a sob. "Betty, we can't. I can't. So just stop, okay?"

Give her her due, she stops.

Wednesday 1 February

8.00 a.m.

I wake up feeling terrible for losing my patience with Betty last night, so before I head to work I walk and feed Dumbledore, tidy the kitchen and living room, then make her a bacon sandwich and sugary coffee. When I deliver them to her in bed she smiles as though nothing bad has ever happened between us in the entire eighteen years we've known each other.

"Love you, Betty-O," I whisper, planting a kiss on her forehead despite the fact she smells like a dead vole.

11.00 a.m.

As I depart the theater after first period Danny happens to walk through the entrance at the exact same time I'm walking out. The predictable surge of anger crashes through my gut, followed by something else.

For a hot second he looks like he's about to smile and wave, then remembers everything that's happened and his face visibly falls. [I mean, not literally. He's not just standing in the doorway with a gaping hole where his face used to be.]

Then, a few minutes later, he corners me by my locker, as I'm rummaging around for any stray peanut butter cups I may have neglected. "Can we talk?"

On second glance I think he's actually got a haircut for the first time in senior year – it's significantly less matted than usual.

"*Can* we talk?" I reply, not looking up from my snack quest. "Yes. *Should* we talk? That's another question."

"Please." He sounds desperate and frail. It makes me hate him. Makes me angrier than I thought I could ever be.

"Why?" I slam the locker shut, unsuccessful in my Reese's mission. The sound reverberates in my skull, mingling with the rage in spinning fury. "So you can attack me for trying to make a positive change in this damn state?"

The Clickbait feature went live this morning and has already gone wild with shares and comments. I should've known he'd be hunting me down with such immediacy.

"No. I won't. I promise." God, he looks tired.

My first instinct is to storm away, to leave his misery behind. After what he did to me I should never have to share that load ever again. But an entrenched affection rears its ugly head, a relic of on old, deep friendship. It reminds me of the image of Mrs Wells hunched over her steering wheel, sobbing into the stitched leather. Of Danny climbing into the car, tears streaming down his face. Of the devastated hug they shared as I watched from the sidewalk.

"Fine. But make it quick. I have another phone interview in twenty minutes."

We dive into an empty chemistry classroom, benches lined with Bunsen burners and shelves stacked with beakers and test tubes. There's a vague chemical smell I should probably be able to identify, as a student of chemistry, and yet it could be napalm for all I know.

As Danny pulls back a squeaky chair and sinks into it, unraveling a thick scarf from round his chickeny neck, neither of us says a word. There's too much hanging between us. Small talk seems impossible, but so does jumping right in.

"Thank you for agreeing to talk to me," he starts, not looking at me, but not looking anywhere else either. His eyes are glazed and entranced, like he's on a cocktail of medication that's left him drowsy and lost. Maybe he is. "You didn't have to do that."

"Actually, I did. Your mom's holding Betty hostage. The police are in negotiations as we speak. They asked me to keep you talking."

He laughs weakly, a hollow bark of a sound. "Always with the jokes. I miss it."

I shut down his attempt at evoking emotion in me. "What did you want to talk about?"

"I'm . . . having a crappy time."

"Okay."

He swallows hard. "My parents are getting divorced."

No surprises there. "Shit. I'm sorry."

"And my grandpa . . . he's not doing so great. Cancer. They think . . . Well, it's going to be any day now. We already said our goodbyes."

Ah. That explains the desperately sad hug he shared with his mom. Now his eyes glisten and threaten to spill over. Like a phantom limb, the remnants of the affection I once held for him twitch somewhere inside me, railing against seeing him so hurt. If this was the Danny of six months ago, I would reach out and take his arm, gently coaxing him into looking at me, murmuring soft platitudes until he calmed down enough to talk to me.

But this is not the Danny of six months ago. This Danny has used me and manipulated me. This Danny ruined my life, and I'm only just starting to pick up the pieces again.

"Danny, I'm sorry about your parents," I start, measuring my words so they betray no emotion. "And about your grandpa. That sucks, and I'm sorry. I know how much you love him, and how much he loves you. But I don't know what you want from me. I really don't." I feel harsh and cruel and cold, but it's the truth. "Because when I look at you, when I talk to you, all I can think about is that website. Izzy O'Neill: World Class Whore. You did that to me, Danny. And so I really, really don't know what you want from me right now."

He flips a gas tap on and off, the low hiss filling the room before abruptly stopping again. "I don't think I even expected you to agree to talk to me. I thought you would just shut me out." I can barely hear him, his voice is so muffled. "And you had every right to do that. I was awful to you. I was scum. I *am* scum."

"Stop it." My voice sounds empty, because that's exactly how I feel. Hollowed out. "You're just saying that so I'll jump in and correct you. So I'll tell you that you *aren't* scum. So I'll make you feel better despite everything you've done. It doesn't work like that, Danny. It doesn't fucking work like that."

"I'm sorry. I'm so sorry, Izzy." He sniffs so severely that I fear his nostrils have just folded in on themselves.

Seriously, why is he offloading on me? After everything that's happened between us, what does he truly expect from me? And then it dawns on me. I gape at him in horror, disgusted by how low he's repeatedly willing to stoop just to get his own way. "Wait . . . are you . . .? Are you telling me all this just so I'll call off the march?"

"What? No! I just . . ." He stares into his lap. "I don't have anyone else to talk to."

Whose fault is that, dickweed?

I breathe smoothly, deeply, summoning patience when all I want to do is unleash this violent anger on him. "What about Prajesh?"

A strange pfft noise. "Guys don't talk to each other about emotions and shit."

"Okay." I fold my arms defiantly. "Well, that's not on me." The bell rings, signaling the start or end of some class. I don't know; I'm losing track of school these days.

He breathes out long and hard in a shaky, vulnerable sigh, then peers up at me through damp eyelashes. [Why are boys blessed with such great eyelashes? It's the height of injustice.] "I know. I'm just asking for some mercy. Things are hard enough."

I'd kind of expected his rage to hit DEFCON 1 MILLION once he found out what we're doing. [Which makes zero sense as a metaphor since DEFCON 1 is the highest level, and thus DEFCON 1 million is actually a very minor incident, like a conker falling from a tree and killing an ant. But alas, I am not known for making sense, so why start now?] But this? This I was not expecting.

Mercy. He wants my mercy. He wants me to abandon my pain just to alleviate his own. He wants me to do what women have been forced to do for millennia: bury their own hopes and ambitions so the men can chase theirs. And I won't do it. I won't.

Turning to leave the room, so unbelievably done with this conversation, I don't even look back as I say, "I'm not canceling the rally, Danny."

I reach the door. He speaks again, low and hoarse and sad. "Do you know how hard it is to turn on the news and hear your name over and over again? To have everyone in town think you're some evil villain who deserves to be punished?"

*Insert GIF of me looking directly at the camera like I'm on *The Office*.*

I mean, really. He practically wins the argument for me. I don't have to do anything except wait for him to load up the unregulated assault rifle and shoot himself in the foot.

"Are you seriously fucking asking me that? Of course I know how that feels, Danny. That's the entire fucking problem."

1.45 p.m.

As if to spite Mr Daniel Wells the Bitches Bite Back meeting is one of our most productive yet.

Bella is coordinating a massive social media campaign for the rally, as well as guest-posting on the BBB website. She's managed to get almost every girl in school posting with the hashtag EndRevengePorn, and now she's working on reaching out to big feminist accounts to ask for their support. Oh, and she's made a bunch of killer graphics, sharing stats and facts about revenge porn, as well as interviewing other victims and posting images alongside their stories like that Humans of New York account everyone was obsessed with for a while.

Meg has been working her butt off on the website, making sure our server has enough capacity to host our significant increase in users, and the forums are now up and running with moderators and whatnot. The landing page now displays our mission statement in all its glory, so you can't access the Bitches

Bite Back website without clocking eyes with the End Revenge Porn campaign. We've made it abundantly clear that we will not rest until new laws are set in motion.

She's also created a new press section, next to the media kit, gathering together all the media coverage we've gotten in the past few weeks. New articles and news segments appear every day, and though Ted Vaughan has yet to comment the longer he goes without addressing the movement, the worse he looks to his constituents. All right, so most of said constituents are gun-wielding, Confederate flag-waving white dudes with little to no interest in the issue, but still. We're starting to make enough noise that it's going to be impossible for Vaughan's office to ignore without compromising their polling numbers.

Thanks to the Clickbait coverage – which I'm deftly avoiding making direct eye contact with, lest I unwittingly read some of the trollish comments it's inevitably garnering – our monetary donations are topping twelve grand, so we're able to take out even more ads and put in orders for more banners, badges and T-shirts. Then we up the goal to twenty K, vowing to use any further funds to rent out the equipment we need to make this the powerful protest it is: speakers, amps and potentially a basic stage set so I can address the crowds and fire them up with another speech – the thought of which makes my chest twinge with dread.

As I watch the auditorium full of amazing young women work I'm filled with pride and a deep sense of purpose. All right, so there are still a few weeks to go until the rally. But, like the members of a passionate orgy, everyone is working hard and coming together. [Sorry.]

8.23 p.m.
I whizz through my diner shift with as much enthusiasm as I can muster for minimum wage. It's pretty quiet all evening – so much so that I actually get to stand and chat with Frank, who makes the big decision to branch out from OJ and coffee and actually order something from the food menu. I mean, he still has the OJ and coffee. Let's not go crazy or anything.

As I'm pouring his coffee he peruses the menu with so much excitement it warms my cockles. [Does anyone actually know what cockles are, because I do not. Anyway, they were warmed. Moving on.]

"What burger can you recommend, miss?" he asks in his hoarse old person voice. [Seriously, what happens to your voice box as you age? Does it just shrivel up like a sun-dried tomato?]

"I actually have never had a burger here, sir," I admit, laying down the pot of coffee and pulling my notepad out of my apron pocket. "But I hear the Tex Mex is top-notch."

He looks up at me, aghast. "Never had a burger? Are you one of those vegetarians they have now?"

I have no idea who "they" are, but I laugh anyway. "No, sir. I'm a povotarian. Can't afford fancy burgers."

"Well, I'll be sure to leave you a decent tip today." His smile is both warm and haunting, on account of the fact he possesses no more than one and a half teeth.

Thursday 2 February

7.48 p.m.

Meg is out of state at a college interview today – she's applying for
a scholarship to study business and entrepreneurship in Missouri.
I meet up with Ajita after school to exchange assignments and talk
through a game plan for our upcoming midterm exams.

I'm grateful for the night alone with Ajita because I finally
have the chance to subtly prompt her about what's going on
between her and Meg. If she doesn't want to respond she doesn't
have to, but at least I've given her the space to do so. It seems
like a good compromise between letting her tell me about it on
her own terms and ignoring the situation entirely.

After we've eaten our bodyweight in Mrs Dutta's famous
cardamom curry, Ajita and I head down to the basement with
bowlfuls of milk balls– a delicious Nepali dessert called rasbari
– and go over our notes for biology and chemistry. I fire
off a quick text to Carson asking if he'd like a copy of our
plans, but he doesn't reply. He must be working, or helping his
mom cook dinner.

We're about to crack onward with American literature – we're studying *The Grapes of Wrath* because Miss Castillo is a sadist and a psychopath – when a lull in school-based conversation allows me the room to bring up the subject I really care about.

"So," I start in my trademark eloquent Izzy manner. "Meg."

Ajita bites her bottom lip and stares intently at the hand-drawn study schedule she's neatly filling in. "What about her?"

"We don't have to talk about it," I assure her, rearranging my stack of notecards just to give my hands something to do. "I just . . . wanted you to know that you can. And it won't be weird. I promise."

Still chewing her lip, Ajita lays down her highlighter and looks me in the eye. "No . . . I want to. I should."

I nod once, sagely, like a Dumbledore or Yoda type figure. I have always fancied myself as a wise spiritual leader. It seems like much less work than being the Chosen One. You just tell the Chosen One what to do and enjoy a significant portion of the credit when it all works out in the end. A great setup, if you ask me.

"I like her," Ajita says after a moment's hesitation. I'm impressed by how steady her voice sounds. This is a big deal for her to talk about – and a big deal for me to listen to. "I like her a lot. As more than friends. But . . ."

When she doesn't elaborate I say, "But what?"

I also choose this exact moment to eat a spoonful of milk

ball, because I'm never not thinking about my appetite.

Ajita follows my lead, taking a bite of creamy deliciousness. "But Fern. Fern seems super into Meg. She's always texting her, always asking to hang out, and Meg's too polite to say no. So she just lets it happen. And I don't know whether she feels something for Fern too, you know? Because Fern is . . . Well, she's a fucking supermodel, there's no two ways around it. And I'm . . ."

"A fucking supermodel," I finish, staring defiantly at her as though daring her to argue. "Have you asked Meg how she feels about Fern?"

Ajita shakes her head vehemently. "Have you met me? I'm the most awkward homo sapien on Planet Earth. Like, they should actually make documentaries about how awkward I am. I imagine social psychologists would be fascinated to study me."

"You're right," I concur, scraping the last of the milk balls out of my bowl and sucking the spoon in a highly unattractive fashion. "It is a much better approach to just bury your head in the sand and not address your feelings at all."

Gaping at me indignantly, Ajita says, "Are you, Izzy O'Neill, of all people, really taking the piss out of me for not talking about emotions? *Really??* The sheer arrogance and hypocrisy! Maybe you should be a politician after all."

"Fair point, well made," I agree. "Kids in glasshouses, and all that. Anyway, all I know is that whoever you end up with? They're going to be the luckiest woman in the world."

"That," Ajita announces, harrumphing elaborately, "is gross. I preferred heartless Izzy. You know, the one who would rather inject herself with rat poison than have a heartfelt conversation. Where did she go?"

Good question.

Friday 3 February

1.45 p.m.

Ajita and Meg just went outside to "get some fresh air". Since Ajita shares my aversion to the outdoors in general, I know this is a euphemism, I'm just not sure what for. Are they hashing out their mystery conflict? Locking tongues? Talking about how much they hate me and plotting the demise of the tripod? There's just no way of knowing.

9.53 p.m.

Zachary messages me asking to meet up because he has something to tell me about the campaign, so I tell him to come to the diner before my evening shift starts. We sit in the corner booth so minimal people can overhear us, and he orders us both hot chocolate with extra whipped cream since it's roughly -8,000 degrees out. Like literally my nipples are in danger of shredding my uniform any second now.

Zachary stirs a packet of sugar into his already heavily sweetened cocoa, which makes me respect him all the more. "So it seems like the campaign is getting a bunch of traction in the press."

"Yeah," I say. "I shamelessly exploited all the journalists who reached out last fall."

"Hey, why the hell not? You're giving them what they want – a story – and getting PR for the rally. It's a win-win."

I wink and point a finger gun at him. "Exactamundo, my friend."

"Did you just call me your friend?" he asks, faux-astounded.

"It was an accident. Don't let it get to your head."

He chuckles. "Fair enough."

"So what were you going to tell me?" I ask, watching Lola carry three precarious stacks of pancakes to a nearby table. The customers don't even thank her when she lays them down. We exchange eye rolls, then I turn back to Zachary. "Surely he's seen the coverage by now."

He winces as he sips the scalding cocoa. "Uh, yeah. That's kinda why I wanted to meet."

"Well, yes. I didn't think you'd had an aneurism and suddenly enjoyed my company."

"It would take much more than an aneurism." He grins, cream 'tache in full effect.

I clutch a hand to my chest. "Rude."

"I learned from the best. Anyway, yeah, I heard Dad on video-call to his campaign manager. He was all, do I need to address this, and Iannucci – the manager – told him he didn't think it was relevant to their core demographic, and that his loyal voters

212

wouldn't care about something this, I quote, 'trivial'."

"For the love of all fuckery, 'trivial'?? Is he for real? How is an issue that affects many young women trivial?"

He holds up his palms. "Hey, you know I'm on your side here. I know how shitty it feels, remember?"

I scoff, popping a mini marshmallow in my mouth. "You do?"

"Are you forgetting the fact my nude was leaked too?"

"Well, no, but it's not like anyone cared about that."

"Maybe not in the same way they cared about yours, but, trust me, the amount of shit I got from the team for it. Small dick, bendy dick, all that crap." His eyes drop to the table, and his brow furrows. "Not to mention how apeshit my family went."

And I can sense the genuine hurt in his voice, even though it's buried below several layers of faked apathy. I've used that exact tone myself.

"Yikes. I'm sorry, I had no idea." I feel kinda bad for my assumptions that he got off easy. I mean, sure he did in the media, but I can't imagine having Betty turn on me the way his own family did.

He shrugs tightly. "Why would you? It's not cool for guys to let shit like this get to them. Gotta laugh along, right? All just banter."

Using a superhuman amount of willpower, I manage to refrain from rolling my eyes. "If I haven't said it before, dude culture is *awesome*."

"Yeah."

I remember what he said in the hallway a few weeks back: *"I hope this Hazel thing isn't bringing it all back for you?"* Is it bringing it back for *him*? Does the embarrassment and shame still eat away at him the way it does for me? A few months ago I'd have said no way, not a chance. But now I'm not so sure.

He clears his throat, takes another sip, presses his lips together. "So last night Mom and Dad were talking about the rally as if I weren't even there. Saying, like, there's no reason revenge porn should be illegal; you have to learn that there are consequences for your actions; if you don't want naked stuff out there in the world, you shouldn't send nudes or make sex tapes; all about taking responsibility; yadda yadda yadda."

Anger starts to flare in my gut, not yet lava but still something that simmers and spits. "Ah, that old chestnut."

Zachary grimaces. "And then my mom got on her soapbox about how young women have no class these days; she wishes we could go back to the 1950s when women were respectable housewives and didn't run around drinking and wearing hotpants and having one-night stands. And the whole time my dad was just nodding along." He frowns as though in concentration. "God, I hate him."

I let the statement stand, and mull over what he's just told me. At first I thought it was apathy we were dealing with – they just didn't care enough about this issue – and Iannucci's advice confirms that. But there's something worse running through that office, something misogynistic and bigoted, that I have no idea how to tackle. If I did, the whole country would be a much better place.

Try as I might to fend it off, I feel flat and defeated. This is all hopeless. It would take far more than a group of riled-up teenagers to take down the misogyny and bigotry that's been at the heart of society for thousands of years.

"We're never going to win, are we?" I mutter miserably. "Your dad's office holds all the power, and this is how they feel about it. We're fighting a losing battle."

Zachary meets my eye in a rare exception to his trademarked shifty-drug-dealer mannerisms. "You always knew that. It's still worth fighting anyway."

Monday 6 February

7.24 a.m.

The media coverage of the rally slows slightly over the weekend, so while there are a bunch of segment reruns and shares of online articles, there's nothing new being pushed out.

To be honest it's kind of nice to take the opportunity to catch my breath. By catch my breath, I obviously mean serve syrup-and-spit-drenched pancakes to ill-mannered diners at Martha's. [If you are a health and safety officer reading this, please know I am joking about the spit thing. If you are not a health and safety officer, congratulations on your life choices.]

Croc Queen also gives me my first paycheck! Huzzah! Despite all the excitement and world-changing going on in my wider life, it's actually really nice to earn a basic wage from doing a basic job. The money is modest but guaranteed, unlike the lottery of the screenwriting industry or the unpredictability of a bigoted senator's whims. Being handed that envelope at the end of a long greasy shift felt pleasant in its normality.

It's immediately tempting to blow my hard-earned cash on

something ridiculous, like a hoverboard or an iPad, or to be noble and selfless and donate it to the Bitches Bite Back campaign. Or to be sensible and use it to buy groceries and cleaning supplies like I did with the tips I brought home the other day.

And yet a selfish part of me wants to keep this money just for me, for my future. To start a tiny college fund, no matter how small, to represent the idea of possibility. So I open up an online savings account and transfer most of the salary straight there. I'll probably never go to college, but it's nice to imagine that I might.

Carson works all weekend too, and Ajita travels upstate for a college tour. The thought of her moving away really is too painful for words, so I am attempting to banish said thought as best I can. But alas, every now and then I'm struck by a lightning bolt of dread, and it's all I can do not to cycle over to her house and chain her to the basement wall.

Dammit, now I'm thinking about it again. I knew I should've bought those hardcore steel manacles that came up on my sponsored posts yesterday. [You have to wonder what kind of porn Betty is watching for the cookies to start recommending handcuffs. In fact, I really rather would not wonder.]

3.17 p.m.
I fill Carson in on Zachary's updates as we're walking his kid brother to soccer practice. He's silent as he listens, hands tucked

into black jean pockets, purple beanie pulled low over his ears. At first I think he's just absorbing what I'm telling him about Iannucci and Zachary's mom, but he's staring pretty hard at the back of Callum's tiny head as he kicks the ball down the sidewalk in front of us.

When I finish he purses his lips, then says, "I just don't get why you trust him so much, man. Why would he be helping you with this?"

Irritation prickles beneath my skin – has he even been listening? "We talked. The nudes affected him too, Carson. They really did. I didn't realize how much. And honestly, he doesn't believe in a lot of what his dad does."

A pffffft noise escapes his lips, which does nothing to alleviate my annoyance. "So why didn't he defend you at the time?"

"I don't know," I say, trying to tamp down the irritation. Lashing out at Carson is the last thing I want to do. Breathe in, breathe out. "Maybe that's what this is about," I speculate. "Righting a past wrong."

"I dunno, man," he mutters, stooping to pick up his brother's ball from where it's gotten lodged under a parked car. "Something about this doesn't feel good."

"Could we maybe not do the jealous boyfriend trope right now?" I snap, hating myself the second I do, but still completely unable to bite my tongue. "Just, you know, if it's not too much of an inconvenience for you."

I already regret it, losing my temper at this sweet angel who's only looking out for me, but I can't help it. My blood feels like lava. Tears of frustration prickle behind my eyes.

"I ain't jealous, a'ight?" Carson says, patting his brother on the back as he runs off again. "All I'm sayin' is that last time a guy went above and beyond for you, it's ecos he was massively in love with you. And look how that turned out." A shrug. He kicks a stone. "I just don't wanna see you get hurt again."

I start crying for zero reason whatsoever. All control over my own emotions seems to be lost. "No, Carson, you just don't trust me to hang out with other guys. Why? Because I have a past? A sex drive? Because I'm not the Virgin fucking Mary? And what, you think I'm gonna jump his bones the second he does something nice for me?" I practically spit. I'm hysterical now, hiccuping with sobs. An elderly woman across the street stops her stroll and watches my meltdown in concern, but even the shame of that isn't enough to stop my tirade. "That's what you really think of me, isn't it, Carson? Go on, call me a slut. The rest of the world already has."

He should walk away. He should leave me on the sidewalk, hissing and crying. He's too good to be treated like this, I know he is, and he doesn't deserve to be on the receiving end of my detonated emotions. But that's not what he does.

He takes me in his arms, pressing my tear-drenched face into his hoodie. "Look, I know you're goin' through a lot right now.

And I know you got a whole bunch of anger inside you ecos of it. But don't take it out on me, okay? We're not about that. We never have been."

I sniffle pathetically, gripping him so tight I must be cutting off some kind of air supply. "Yeah. I know."

We stand like that for an age, my tears slowing, my heart rate returning to normal, and I've never felt so grateful to have such a patient boyfriend.

Still, it doesn't stem the flow of self-loathing that's gathering speed inside me. Who have I become?

5.45 p.m.
So some good things have finally happened. Gather round, gather round, and I shall tell ye the tale of . . . Okay, no, I am too damn excited to maintain this ludicrous narrative voice. Normal sweary service is henceforth resumed.

1) Just when everything felt beyond hope Rosa Garcia has publicly endorsed the End Revenge Porn campaign! She appeared at a press conference and gave an emotive speech about her two teenage daughters, and how she wants to fight for a better world for them. The idea of them falling victim to revenge porn is too much for her to bear, and she won't stop until the laws are changed. Oh, and she called Ted Vaughan a "coward to end all cowards". So that was cool. It should only be a matter of

time now until he's forced to respond. Whether or not he listens to our demands is another question, but he will have to acknowledge us, at the very least, otherwise Garcia's accusations will ring truer than they already do. As little as gun-wielding, Confederate flag-waving white dudes care about this issue, they don't want to be seen voting for a coward who backs down from a fight. Especially against A Woman, God forbid!

2) In part due to the steadily escalating media coverage but mostly thanks to Garcia's statement, I've been asked to appear on a local TV station and discuss the rally??? Me. Izzy O'Neill. Impoverished orphan, slut extraordinaire. Appearing on live television to talk about politics. It's absurd at the face of it.

In all seriousness I almost vomited with sheer nerves and terror when the email landed in my inbox. Live. Television. Like, live. As it happens. What if I swear? Or stress-fart? Or lose the power of speech? All of these are equally viable.

My appearance is this Saturday, which gives me five days to a) drag a brush through my hair, b) develop a sarcasm filter, c) borrow some fancy clothes from Meg, d) beg Fern to apply makeup in my favored Crazed Sex Doll style, e) pretend to understand politics, and f) change my entire personality.

[Let's start with the stress-fart references. They should probably go.]

Tuesday 7 February

6.41 a.m.

It's the day of my Skype with the South Street Productions, the company interested in *Love for Hire*, and I've already been to the toilet in excess of eighteen times this morning. I really wish I was exaggerating for comic effect, but alas, the state of my bowels is very sorry indeed.

I manage to swap my evening shift for a day shift, which, while not great for my academic career, is necessary if I'm going to be home in time for the 5.30 p.m. call. Although I am cutting things a little fine – if Croc Queen keeps me behind for even an extra fifteen minutes, I'm gonna be in trouble. It would've made things much easier if I'd asked Eliza to push the call back by a half-hour, but as an eighteen-year-old writer with no qualifications and no experience I don't feel like I have the bargaining power just yet.

To make sure everything is ready to go the second I get back home, I lay out a change of clothes for me to wear, since I don't think pancake batter-covered shirts are really a professional look outside of the diner setting, plus a can of dry shampoo and a tube of nudey pink lipstick that perfectly matches my hair. It's not perfect, but it'll have to do.

I'm as ready as I'll ever be.

Then the panic ensues. Where am I going to take the video-call? I can't be sitting cross-legged on my bed, which is where I do all my typing, otherwise they will know instantly that I am a fraud and an imposter. I don't have a desk, and the kitchen is in a perpetual state of disarray. Even if it weren't, I feel stupidly embarrassed about the outdated decor and cluttered countertops. These hotshot producers probably have sleek, modern studio apartments in West Hollywood, all clean white lines and hardwood flooring, whereas our kitchen looks like something out of communist East Berlin. Actually, worse. Two of the cupboard doors are hanging off their hinges, and there's a permanent scorch mark on the back wall from Betty's keys-in-the-toaster incident.

I normally don't notice any of this. It's just home. But when I'm looking at it through the potential eyes of millionaire producers it suddenly feels like a dirty little secret I'll do anything to hide.

Think, O'Neill. Where can you go that has free Wi-Fi, minimal background noise and not-hideous decor? The library? No, it closes at 4 p.m. due to budget cuts. School? The Wi-Fi is ropey at best.

Shit shit shit shit shit. Would it be too weird to ask Ajita if I can do it in her basement?

But that won't work either. Ajita lives in the fancy neighborhood, and it would take way too long to get from the diner to her place.

It's going to have to be here. Guess I better get started now if I want to get the kitchen looking as acceptable as possible before this evening.

7.59 a.m.

Deep-cleaned the whole place to within an inch of its life. I superglued the broken cupboards shut, which is admittedly quite a short-sighted solution, and yet right now I'm desperate enough not to care.

Before I leave for work I close the kitchen door and pin a note for Betty on the outside:

Dearest Betty-O,

Please enter the kitchen at thine own risk. Have rigged a booby trap above the door, and if you open it even a millimeter, a kitchen knife will swing down from the ceiling, attached to a two-liter soda bottle, and stab you in the chest. I saw this on a show about bailiffs. Some dude couldn't pay his mortgage, so he just killed the bailiff and buried him out back. I would suggest this as a solution to our own issues, but as you know we have no backyard.

(Seriously, though. Please don't go in the kitchen. I have filled up Dumbledore's water bowl, so if you are really thirsty just drink from there.)

Love, Iz-on-your-face

5.06 p.m.

It's after five and I'm still in the diner. Fuck fuck fuck fuck fuck. I can't leave until Lola gets here to take over the evening shift.

Please, Lola. Please hurry.

10.23 p.m.

I've been crying solidly for over three hours now. Betty tries to console me with a steady stream of hot cocoa and forehead kisses, now that the booby traps in the kitchen have been disabled, but it's no use. I'm beyond devastated.

Here's what happened.

I don't get to leave the diner until nearly five fifteen. There's still a lot of ice on the ground, but thankfully the sidewalks have been well gritted enough that I was able to cycle to work this morning. So the second Lola arrives I sprint out the back door of the diner, jump on my bike and pedal as hard as I can in the direction of home.

My appearance doesn't matter. The grease-stained shirt doesn't matter. Just as long as I'm home in time to take this call.

Of course, pedaling as hard as you can comes with its own dangers, and when I'm about a hundred yards from the gates of my housing community, I skid on a patch of black ice and collide with a trash can, which sends me careening sideways off the bike and landing on the cold hard sidewalk with an oomph.

Grazed hands aside, I'm relatively unscathed, but the accident wastes time I simply do not have. It's nearly five thirty by the time I make it home and fly through the gates, panting like a mad woman. Betty calls hello from the living room, but I'm too breathless, too stressed to greet her back. What if they've already phoned? What if I missed it?

I make it to my room and wrench my laptop open, double-clicking the Skype app as I pull my shirt off over my head without even undoing the buttons. I tug the fresh one on, hissing as it brushes my grazed palm, in the time it takes to load the app.

No missed calls.

I almost burst into tears with relief. I allow myself thirty seconds of perching on the edge of my bed, head in my hands, desperately trying to get my breath back. Then I dab my sweaty forehead on my duvet cover, pull my hair out of its topknot and shake it out, spraying a metric fuck-ton of dry shampoo onto the roots. Thank God the pink still looks kickass.

Glancing back at my laptop, I see it's now 5.31 p.m. No missed calls. I make sure the volume is turned way up, so I don't miss it, then smear a coating of pink lipstick onto my chapped lips. One look in the mirror tells me some lip liner is desperately needed, but this will have to do for now. I even have time to pat some matte powder into my skin so I look slightly less like I've just competed in an Iron Man.

At 5.34 p.m. I relocate to the kitchen. Mercifully Betty has obeyed my threatening note and not used the kitchen all day – or if she has, she hasn't left a trace of her presence – so it still looks slightly less horrifying than usual. I set myself up in a chair, back to the wall, so that the producers are unlikely to see the kitchen at all. I place my stack of notes next to the keyboard, and wait, barely believing that I managed to get here on time.

It's not until around 5.45 p.m. that I start to wonder if something's gone wrong. Have they forgotten? Did I get the wrong day? Did I give them the wrong number?

Panicking that the latter reason is to blame, I open up my email provider and hit "get mail".

No internet connection found.

My stomach drops. No. No. This can't be happening. No.

"Betty?" I yell. "Is the Wi-Fi down?"

"I don't know, is it?" she calls back so unhelpfully I regret taking the knife-bottle contraption down.

"Looks like it!" I shout, manically hitting refresh on the connection wizard. Still nothing.

"Oh, crap," Betty shouts back. "I forgot to pay the broadband bill! Shit! Sorry, kid! I'll do that first thing tomorrow."

"BUT I NEED IT NOW!" I wail like a child who didn't get dessert. Dashing back to my room, I grab my phone out of my bag and refresh my emails using mobile data.

Inbox (1).

Hi Izzy,

South Street just called me — they're having difficulty getting through to you on the number you provided. Is there a problem?

Let me know ASAP. These aren't the kind of people you want to keep waiting.

Best,

Eliza

A wave of panic surges through me. I check the number I gave Eliza and it's correct — my only issue is the lack of Wi-Fi. I fire off a quick reply.

Eliza,

Sorry, having internet connectivity issues. Give me five minutes?

Izzy

After all my preparations this morning, I feel like the epitome of unprofessionalism. What am I going to do? I asked for five minutes, but what's that going to achieve? Unless . . .

"Betty, can you call the internet provider now and pay the bill?" I yell, voice trembling. "You can use my card, I have about twenty bucks on there. Will that cover it?"

"No problem, I got it." A few minutes of silence pass by achingly slowly, during which I refresh my emails a dozen times and consider taking the video-call on my cell phone, which would look beyond amateurish and yet I have no other option. Then: "I'm on hold, kid. They say it's going to be a fifteen-minute wait."

"Fuuuuuuuuckkkkk," I moan, flumping down onto my bed. There's not enough time to get to Ajita's, and even school is a twenty-minute walk away. Dumbledore pads up to me and starts sucking my ankle in his creepily comforting way.

It's 5.52 p.m. I pull my phone out from under me, gulping down my panicking breaths; my only chance to sell this screenplay and solve our problems is slipping through my fingers.

Eliza,
On the phone to the internet provider – can you buy me
fifteen minutes?
So sorry.
Izzy

I cross my fingers, toes, ears and boobs that Eliza can get me more time. I can't let this opportunity go to waste. Before it even sends, though, a reply to my first email pings through.

They've moved on to their next meeting now, and I don't imagine they'll be willing to reschedule.

Eliza

The tears come instantly, flowing faster than the River Nile in mascara-filled streams down my face. Dumbledore increases the intensity of his ankle sucking.

Betty yells through the paper-thin walls. "Still on hold, kid. Don't worry, we'll get this fixed."

"It's too late!" I call back feebly. Then, quieter, into my pillow. "It's . . . it's too late."

A half-hour later, the Wi-Fi is back on. I wipe my snotty nose on my sleeve and retrieve the laptop from the kitchen. The sight of the immaculate kitchen, of my neatly stacked notes and freshly printed screenplay send me into another crying fit. Past me was so hopeful, so prepared. And it didn't fucking matter.

Curled back up in my bed, pink lipstick and pristine shirt somehow still intact, I type out a painstaking, lie-filled response to Eliza.

Eliza,

I cannot apologize enough. Our Wi-Fi went down because

of the snow, and we tried everything to get it back up but I couldn't do it in time. I'm so sorry. The last thing I wanted was to mess South Street – or you – around.

I understand if it's not possible to reschedule the meeting, but I promise that next time I'll get set up in the library to ensure this doesn't happen again.

Izzy

I watch it send with a hollow hole in my heart where my hope used to live. [Good lord this is dramatic. Gotta love that teenage angst. I think you're supposed to get over it when you're, like, sixteen, but alas, I am still as fond of melodrama as ever.]

After a while Betty comes through with a bowl of mac and cheese for me. I've never been allowed to eat dinner in my room – it's always been a formal affair at the kitchen table, with no TV in the background. But the old bird is making an exception today, and I appreciate it a hell of a lot.

Refreshing almost constantly, I wait with bated breath for Eliza to reply, but she never does. Was this my one shot? Have I destroyed my only hope of success?

Okay, so it was Betty who forgot to pay the internet provider, but I should have double-checked. Triple-checked. Knowing I had the most important Skype call of my career, I should not have left a damn thing to chance.

I'll never understand those people who can't eat when

they're sad. Food is literally the only thing that makes my life worth living at times. Although after my fifth portion of mac and cheese, I'm starting to question my life choices. Not enough to stop eating, of course, but enough to give me pause for thought.

Still weeping ceaselessly, I take a shower and scrub my face clean of sweat, tears and congealed makeup, and immediately feel forty-two percent better. I wish I was in Ajita's bathroom so I could slather myself in fancy lotions, but my drugstore moisturizer will have to suffice.

When I eventually make it back to my room, still wrapped in just a towel, I'm surprised to see someone perched on my bed, which is essentially a mangled crying den at this point.

Carson.

"Betty told me what happened," he says gently, standing up and wrapping me in his arms. "I'm sorry, Iz. It wasn't your fault."

"I know," I say, even though I don't. It feels like everything is my fault, these days. I always used to be a stubborn asshole when it came to admitting fault. Then the sex scandal happened and I went too far the other way.

He strokes my hair, even though it's damp and tangled, and kisses my forehead. He smells of the cold outside. Beads of water run down my back, and I shiver. He hugs me tighter, rubbing the small of my back to warm me up, and just like that my inner sex demon is awakened. [What? It's been a while. And I'm traumatized. Give me a break.]

I press my body flat to his, and place my free hand on his jaw, pulling him down to kiss me. Just a peck, then another, then I nibble his bottom lip. At first he frowns, then visibly throws caution to the wind and kisses me back. Hard.

Carson pushes me back against the wall and I moan softly. My towel drops to the floor as I grab the bottom of his sweater and pull it up over his head. For a moment we just look at each other – me naked, him shirtless – and grin goofily. And then we're kissing again.

He kisses my neck, my shoulders, my collarbones, first gently and then more deeply, hungrily. I run my hands over the hard planes of his body before tucking my thumb into the black waistband of his boxers. He quirks an eyebrow at me. I nod.

And we proceed to fandango de pokum.

11.19 p.m.

While we're lying together on my single bed, naked and tangled in my duvet, I lace my fingers through his. They're stained blue and purple from painting.

His chest rises and falls beneath my cheek as he swallows. "It's going to work out, Iz. You're going to have more shots than this. You're only eighteen. There's a whole career ahead of you, you know? There's no rush."

I sit up slightly, pulling the duvet up to my chin. "But there is."

He frowns. "Why?"

"Because if I could sell my screenplay, I could go to college."

The confession sits heavily in the air between us.

"I didn't know you wanted that," he says slowly, measuredly.

I shrug. "I tried to talk to you about it. About being confused about my future and all. But you kind of shut it down."

He frowns again. "Me not wanting to talk about my future doesn't mean you can't talk about yours."

Shrugging again, I nestle even further into him, inhaling the smell of paint and fresh air. "It's hard to have a one-sided conversation, though."

"Yeah, I get that. I'm sorry." He runs a hand through my hair, which is incredibly brave of him. "So college, huh? What's changed? I thought you wanted to stay here. Look after Betty."

"I'm starting to think maybe I only wanted that because I didn't truly believe I had any other options." And it's true. Ever since Betty confronted me about it the other night, the possibilities – or lack thereof – have weighed heavily on my mind, and I've been wondering what I would want if I had the luxury of deciding.

"I get it," he murmurs, kissing me on the forehead. And I know he does. He gets it like nobody else does. "The world sucks sometimes."

I retort with my usual classy clap-back: "Your face sucks sometimes." This is categorically untrue. It is my own face that sucks, in the context of being among the parsley.

Seriously, though, why am I like this? I finally got him to be open to a decent conversation, and my humor reflex killed the moment. I am the actual literal worst, and a hypocrite beyond all comprehension.

Carson groans, rubbing his face with his hands. "Always with the 'your face' jokes. Some things never change, huh?"

"You wouldn't have me any other way." I wink in a gangstery way. [We've been through this before, O'Neill. Gangsters are not known for their winking prowess.]

"No," he says, suddenly all serious. He leans over and cups my face in his palm, gazing right into my eyes as though there's nothing else in the world. Right now, there isn't. "I wouldn't."

Yet paranoia kicks in despite the tenderness of the moment, and I read between the lines of his words. Does he only like the funny, confident, unemotional version of me? The me he first met, cracking jokes about the Fritzls and laughing off a humiliating sex scandal without outwardly showing any kind of hurt? Now that I'm showing him my softer parts, my hopes and fears and the colossal grief chasm in my chest, will he have second thoughts?

Everyone knows that being in love means loving every single version of another person. What if this version of me makes him realize that he doesn't love me after all?

Thursday 9 February

4.35 p.m.

I'm two days into midterm exams, and they're going as terribly as you might expect. Math, chemistry and biology are all spectacularly difficult, and I'll be lucky to scrape Cs in those. I spend last night studying with Ajita and Meg, and they do a fairly good job of calming me down about the impending TV appearance. We post some stuff on the Bitches Bite Back social media accounts, research funny slogans to paint onto banners, and give quotes to a fresh wave of journalists who land in our new shared inbox.

At one point, though, I leave the room to go for a whiz, and when I come back Ajita and Meg are muttering in hushed tones about their college tours and interviews. I get back just in time to hear the tail end, and it makes me feel like dirt. Not just because I'm jealous that they get to go to college at all, which I am, but because they feel like they can't even talk about it when I'm around. Like I'll just expire right there and then of fatal bitterness. To be fair, they're probably right.

I still haven't told them about my disastrous failure re South Street – just fobbed them off with vague answers when they asked. I'm not sure why? Probably because telling them would make it real, and I can't bear the fact that it's real. It truly feels like I've blown my first real shot, and I'm waiting on tenterhooks for Eliza to drop me as a client. Is she regretting her decision to take on an inexperienced, immature asshole with no money or professional skills whatsoever? I wouldn't blame her if she was.

This morning I wake up early to go through my history notes before my morning exam, and despite the IV of coffee I instantly hook myself up to, nothing sinks in. I read the same passage on Henry VIII at least forty-seven times, but can I remember the names of his wives? Can I hell. All I know is that there was an improbable number of Catherines.

Betty and I haven't spoken much since the Wi-Fi fiasco. She's almost constantly on my laptop, which leads me to think she's immersing herself in the online dating world and/or making a quiet fortune on sex chat rooms. At this point either would be a win, providing her new beau is flush with cash and willing to whisk us both out of poverty and find Dumbledore a canine companion named Grindelwald.

Speaking of the devil, Dumbledore seems to sense my failure-inspired helplessness and melancholy, because he is now sucking my unshaven legs almost twenty-four hours a day. Even when I haven't been at the diner and I don't taste of delicious fried chicken grease. Bless him.

Since our epic parsley-fest, Carson has texted me roughly once a minute that everything is going to be fine, even though it clearly and categorically is not going to be fine.

BECAUSE I HAVE TO APPEAR ON LIVE TV. And despite my best efforts my personality remains absolutely unchanged.

Saturday 11 February

5.16 a.m.

Every other senior at Edgewood High will probably spend this weekend in a state of euphoria now that midterm exams are over, and we're only one more set of assignments and exams away from graduating come summer. Plus it's still a few weeks until results are available, so right now we all exist in that blissful limbo in which you've neither flown nor flunked. Well, blissful unless you're me. Because I'm about to appear on live TV.

My call sheet arrives with an obscenely early arrival time. Like, I have to be at the studio for three thirty in the morning to go live at six. Should I be offended that they think they need that much time to make me presentable? Or just grateful for the amount of help they're willing to throw my way? I opt for the latter.

Once a makeup artist with severe contouring finishes applying 9,000 products to my face with a trowel, a hair stylist works my frizzy tangles into smooth, glossy waves. This is an incredibly painful experience. Forgot thumbscrews – if you need information out of someone, just come at them with a comb after they haven't brushed their hair for months. [This paragraph is clear evidence I should never be trusted with state secrets. Not that I would be, but still. If Donald Trump can become president, I can be a double agent, no?]

The whole time this is happening, my nervous stomach is gurgling like a wildcat drowning in oatmeal. At one point it's so aggressive that the MUA jumps and drops a lipliner into her soy latte. I try to helpfully tell her that since the name of the color is Magic Mocha, it's adding some authenticity to proceedings, but she doesn't look overly impressed by my input.

9.27 a.m.

Fucking fuck fuck fuck. Why did I go on live TV? Surely a crown of thorns and/or crucifixion would've been the less painful option?

It starts out okay. I was so worried that I'd get on air and freeze up when the host, Kirstin Destefano, asked me the first question, but I'm surprised how calm and composed I am. Right up until we go live, I'm a nervous wreck, and almost throw up in a wastebasket. But the moment the interview starts, it's like being in the eye of the storm. My hands stop shaking and my voice box relaxes, and my am-dram pedigree truly kicks in.

In the first few minutes Kirstin definitely shoots for the sob-story angle, which is exactly what I don't want to happen on account of my inability to talk about my emotions. But I keep in control of the conversation, for the most part. I make sure the rally is the focus, outlining the changes we want to see, sharing those infamous statistics, and issuing a call to action to viewers all over the state. I can tell Kirstin is getting a little frustrated that I won't talk about how it all made me feel, and at one point she definitely glazes over as the producer says something in her ear mic. And that's when it all starts falling apart.

The screen between us suddenly illuminates with the garden-bench photo, explicit parts blurred over, and Kirstin gives me an overly sympathetic head tilt. Then says, "So how does it feel when you see this picture now? Do you have any regrets?"

Regrets. That loaded word. That loathsome, victim-blaming word.

I snap. "No, I don't have any regrets. The entire fucking point –"

"May I remind you that this is live television, and we do ask you not to curse."

Chest thudding painfully, I take a deep breath. "The entire point of our campaign is to challenge the victim-blaming culture around revenge porn. The perpetrator should face consequences, not the victim."

"So you feel like a victim?" Kirstin asks simperingly. I want to punch her in her smug fucking face.

"In a lot of other states, I would be considered the victim of a crime, yes."

"Is that how you feel?" she repeats, a dog with a bone.

It's a trap. I know if I say I feel like a victim, the Ted Vaughans of this world will destroy me. They'll say I brought it on myself, they'll say I need to show some self-respect, they'll inexplicably bring The Troops into it.

But if I deny feeling like a victim, it'll undermine the entire point of the campaign. It's a lose-lose.

"I don't want to answer that question," I mutter, sending murmurs through the audience as Kirstin raises her palms in mock defeat.

"And yet it's something you must feel strongly about, right? To go to all this trouble?"

"Yes. I don't want any other girl to have to suffer what I went through."

"Can you describe that suffering for me?"

I do freeze then. Tears spring into my eyes before I can stop them, and I start shaking my head manically. I want to scream at the producers to turn the cameras off. I want to run from the stage. I want to leave this all behind. I can't do it I can't do it I can't do it. I can't relive this again and again, knowing that it's going to make fuck all difference.

Struggling to catch my breath, I've been silent for so many moments, ignoring Kirstin's follow-up questions, that she eventually gives in to the producer in her ear and introduces the next guest.

Rosa Garcia.

Oh my god. She's here! Yes!!

The next ten minutes are a blur. Rosa hugs me on stage, and I'm shaking like a leaf as she gently ushers me back down onto the sofa next to her. She smells of vanilla perfume and freshly steamed pantsuit.

She talks eloquently and passionately about the issue, covering a lot of the same ground I did, but coming at it from an even more political stance – talking about other states that have effective legislation, walking Kirstin through the process of tabling a law change like this. She takes the opportunity to talk through some similar issues she's been building her platform on. And I just sit there the entire time trying not to let my eyeballs leak as violently as they want to.

Even as I hear her talk, I know we need more. It all sounds so dry, so abstract. If I had been able to talk about the emotional decimation I went through, it would give much-needed context to this info dump. If I could've got the audience and viewers on my side, given them insight into how much psychological damage revenge porn does, Rosa's passionate debating would've actually resonated.

But as the segment ends and we're ushered off stage I know it's too late. I missed my chance – maybe the last real shot I'll ever have at making this change happen.

I try to talk to Rosa after the show, but she's already being whirled away for a meeting, and she's gone by the time I even get to her dressing room.

2.05 p.m.

Despite my catastrophic TV performance, Rosa's debating skills have clearly had some kind of an impact, because our donations have just topped $20,000. The total is ticking up by the minute, and with every extra cent the potential of the rally gets bigger and bigger. Now we can afford the loudspeakers, and the stage, and microphones and amps.

Of course with the increased exposure comes increased criticism. Social media is a chaotic hellscape of conservative horror and disgust. Lots of amateur political commentators dub the rally a waste of taxpayer money, which is hilarious since not one penny of taxpayer money is being used to fund the protest, and yet right-wingers super enjoy being up in arms about that kind of thing. Like, God forbid our taxes are used for the betterment of society.

On Twitter, a dude named Brandon3141992, whose avatar is inexplicably a shiny red race car, denounces the cause as: "Recreational outrage for misandrist feminists. Absolution and promotion of slutty behavior." We are very happy with this turn of phrase and vow to include it in all promotional materials henceforth.

Most predictably of all, my nude pictures are making the rounds all over again. My bare tits and foofer are splashed all over social media, and the fantastic photograph of Zachary and me on a garden bench is being shown as part of the rally's press coverage. Which, why. Okay, yeah, it's backstory to the rally's origins, but is it really necessary to dredge up the exact thing we're campaigning against?

After we leave the studio, Ajita and her mom take Betty and me out for lunch in the city, and I try to avoid looking at my phone the whole time we're chowing down on delicious teppanyaki. The chef does a cool trick, flipping an egg into his hat, but my laughter and delight is hollow even to my own ears. Knowing that everything is blowing up all over again and being powerless to stop it leaves me feeling vulnerable and small.

Again I feel like I'm irreparably bound to Those Photos, like I do not exist without them. Like everything I am and everything I want to be, everything I do and say and feel, is forever tethered to one mass of incriminating pixels. Even if I win an Emmy or end revenge porn or change the world in whatever way I can, there will always be people who say, "Oh, hey, isn't that the girl with the lopsided boobs and the questionable cowgirl technique?"

2.14 p.m.
Suddenly I'm overcome with the urge to run: run out the

restaurant, away from this town, to a far-flung place in another city or country or universe. A place where nobody knows my name or my body.

And so I run.

2.39 p.m.

Turns out I ate too much teppanyaki, and my cardiovascular fitness is almost nil, so I only make it to the end of the street before collapsing into a heap of sorrow and frustration.

Ajita follows me while her mom and Betty settle the check. Because she's a good friend she sinks onto the sidewalk beside me, despite the overflowing dumpster and evil-eyed raccoon staring us down, and says, "Talk."

I slump back against the brick wall. It's freezing even through my sweater, like leaning against an iceberg. "I can't do this."

She shimmies closer and leans back against the wall, so we're sitting side by side, then rests her head on my shoulder. She smells of green apple shampoo. "You can. We can."

"It's easy for you to say," I mutter. "Your naked pictures aren't forever tied to this cause."

"Would it make you feel better if they were?"

"What?" The raccoon eyes us with interest.

"Seriously," she says. [Ajita, not the raccoon.] "I will take a nude selfie and distribute it to the entire world if it'll make you feel less alone."

This makes me laugh, but also makes my chest twinge in gratitude. Because I know she would. She really would. "I love you, but don't be ridiculous. I'm just . . . I'm sick of this." I sigh, tilting my neck so my head is resting on hers. "I want to move on. I know they're calling me the face of change, but I don't *want* to be. I want the world to already be good without my input."

"Uh, yeah. That's not unique to you, dude. Every single person who strives for social progress feels that way. You think Martin Luther King, Jr. wanted to be a revolutionary? No, he wanted racism not to exist to begin with. He wanted to be able to have dreams about other things, like a nice porch, or a sailboat. Things he wanted for himself, or *would* want if the world were already good. But the world is not good. And someone's gotta force it to be."

Comparing me to MLK feels like a stretch, but the point hits home. Nobody *wants* to be a social justice warrior. They just want shit not to be so broken.

"Why does that someone have to be me?" I whisper. The raccoon, realizing we're not smuggling anything edible, returns to its rummage through the trash bags. "I want to be a normal teenage girl, with a normal life and normal problems." Then, heavily: "A normal future."

Ajita exhales, a puff of condensation appearing in the frosty air. It really is fucking freezing. "It . . . doesn't have to be you. You know that, right? You have a choice here. You don't have to be the face of anything, if you don't want to be."

The words breathe levity into my heart, but the momentary relief is fleeting. "It kind of feels like I do."

"I know." She unloops the chunky purple pashmina from round her neck and spreads it over both of us like a blanket. "You're under a lot of pressure, and you *can* walk away, okay? Nobody would think any less of you if you did, least of all me. But just know that you'd be walking away from Hazel. Away from yourself. Away from every other girl, past, present or future, who's going through the same thing you are."

We sit there in silence for a few minutes before Betty and Mrs Dutta find us. In that time the cold, hard pressure weighs heavy on my chest.

If I walk away, I'm letting everyone down. I'm giving into the world, into the patriarchy, into Ted Vaughan and Danny and every other entitled dickhead out there. But if I persevere, it's going to be excruciating. It might bury any hope I have of a future.

It's the world, or myself. And I'm ashamed to admit that it's a much more difficult choice than it should be. Because while everyone likes to imagine themselves as a world-changer, the reality is so much tougher. It involves sacrifice and martyrdom. It involves going against the self-preservation that's wired so deeply inside you it's impossible to remove.

But every cause needs a face. Everyone knows that. There has to be a symbol, an icon, a Katniss. A martyr. A Chosen One.

I guess the thing I never realized about the Chosen Ones is that most of the time, they'd rather just be normal. And let's be real, most Chosen Ones don't have to save the world while naked.

"I don't know what to do," I murmur, a tear rolling down my cheek and into Ajita's wooly hat. I think of all the people discovering my nudes for the first time, forming snap judgments about who I am, mocking me with their friends at dinner parties, laughing at all the parts that make me human. It stings no less now than it did back in the fall.

"I know," Ajita replies. Betty and Mrs Dutta walk slowly down the street toward us, not even slightly fazed by the sight of us sitting in the gutter. "But I'll be here while you figure it out."

11.48 p.m.
I've become that girl who fails whenever the stakes are high. I fuck up important Skype calls and I fuck up TV interviews and I fuck up. I just fuck up over and over again.

Never in my life have I felt this insecure, this vulnerable, this unsure of myself. Honestly? I feel very, very eighteen.

Sunday 12 February

9.00 a.m.

Betty and I are having breakfast, each in our standard uniform of two fluffy bathrobes over our Martha's shirts and a pair of obnoxious novelty slippers on our feet, when the intercom buzzes. Instead of troubling myself by walking over to the device and answering, I peer out the window and see who's at the gate. Danny.

To be fair we are overdue a confrontation according to his weekly schedule, but rather than being a normal Gen Z dude and calling me out via strongly worded text message, he actually shows up at my front door to talk face to face. Like, who does this in this day and age? It's like people who call you on the phone when a simple text would do. Just why? [Don't even get me started on video-calls. If I ever meet the sadist that invented FaceTime, I will personally crush their spine in a trash compactor.]

Betty is about to leave for work – the chefs start earlier than the hostesses so they can prep for the day – so she gifts me her two bathrobes. I layer them both over the two I'm already wearing to add size and stature to my silhouette, and hopefully intimidate my arch nemesis into submission. I'm just trying to locate some stilts to add height when Danny knocks aggressively on the door.

So spherical that I bear striking resemblance to BB-8, I swing the door open like a queen about to address my empire. Like, bow down bitches. Your orb ruler is present.

You know how Danny doesn't flush with anger, but rather gets paler and paler until he becomes translucent? Total Moaning Myrtle vibes. Anyway, today he's essentially just a floating ghost carcass. It's a strong look.

Even though he's undoubtedly prepared for his outburst, and probably ran lines the whole way here, my appearance throws him off kilter and renders him temporarily mute. To be fair, I am now so round, and the hallway is so narrow, that I actually touch both walls at once with my new girth. Dumbledore perches on my humungous shoulder like a parrot, giving Danny his very best stink eye while also sucking my earlobe.

Summoning all my queenly eloquence, I politely enquire, "May we help you, Daniel?"

He opens his mouth to speak, but no sound comes out, assumedly through the sheer shock of my appearance. Dumbledore wriggles on my shoulder, having tired of my earlobe, and I lower him to the ground. He eyes Danny's feet as though contemplating pissing all over them.

Danny looks down at Dumbledore, then back up at me, vaguely dazed and confused like he has no idea how he got here. "You were great on TV yesterday. Thanks for not mentioning my name."

Anger bristles, but I tamp it down. "I might've, if I hadn't frozen like, I don't know, a margarita."

As though finally registering my outfit he bursts out laughing, though it's a hollow, unhappy sound. Then, as abruptly as he started, he stops, face crumpling. "I'm sorry. I'm so sorry." He dumps his backpack on the ground and covers his eyes with an arched hand. "I miss you so much, Izzy. You and Ajita. I would do anything for you to forgive me."

That annoying phantom affection for him twinges, and as he breaks down in tears all I want to do is throw my arms round him. Dumbledore, confused over where we stand on Danny now, nuzzles his shin. Danny stoops down to pet him, sobbing into his fur as he does.

"I don't think it can happen, Danny," I barely whisper, tightening my fuzzy robe belt. I suddenly feel extremely, deeply sad. "Almost every moment of pain I've had in the last few months has been because of you. If you'd murdered my parents in a van while intoxicated, you would have the full house."

He sniffs, wiping his nose on his jacket sleeve and staring at Dumbledore as though this tiny canine holds the key to the universe. "I know. I don't understand myself. It's like . . .

I feel everything too deeply. I drive myself crazy."

"Maybe you should talk to someone," I say. "A professional, I mean. You've got a lot going on, with your parents and your grandpa and all, and some unresolved anger issues for sure. It might help. Gotta be worth a try, right? You can't go on like this."

Silence settles between us, the only sounds Dumbledore's wagging tail and Danny's occasional sniveling. Snow starts falling quietly outside, muffling the distant sound of street traffic. Despite my 9,000 bathrobes, I shiver, the frost settling in my chest.

Forgiveness. Redemption. They're peculiar beasts. Because as much as you want to believe in them, it's so fucking hard. It's so fucking hard to be a good enough person to implement them.

And yet we have to keep believing in them, now more than ever. We live in a time where our mistakes exist in perpetuity in a cloud in the sky. Our nude pictures, our outing of our best friend, our very darkest acts . . . they live forever, thanks to technology. And if there's truly no way to atone for them, life would be so beyond unbearable. None of us would ever leave the house again. We have to believe there's a way back from the absolute worst versions of ourselves, because wouldn't the world be so much worse if we didn't even bother to try?

But it's hard. God, is it hard.

"We'll never be us again, Danny," I say, leaning against the doorframe. "You have to understand that. But if you want to start fixing some of the damage you did? If you want to begin the long road toward redemption?" He looks up at me expectantly. "March with us next weekend."

Danny nods slowly, like he's in a trance. "I . . . yeah. Okay. I will. Thank you."

As gently as I can muster I say, "Bye, Danny."

As he walks away I find myself really, really hoping my ex best friend seeks the help he needs. Although our relationship is forever broken, I still don't want to see him this sad. Because the truth is he's sad to his bones, and he was practically a brother to me, and . . . I don't know. While I will never forgive him, and I will never forget what he did, we both need a clean break from this. We need closure. But right now he's clinging to his despair like I'm clinging to my anger. And closure has never felt further away.

3.06 p.m.

We spend in excess of forty-five minutes at the diner trying to find Frank's misplaced dentures, only to eventually track them down to the deep fryer, delightfully battered and golden brown.

1.43 a.m.

Just like I did at the height of my scandal-based anxiety, I decide the correct course of action is to self-flagellate by looking at the online backlash to my thoughts, feelings and general antics.

A quick scroll through social media shows me that the

reaction to my nudes is just the same old recycled horseshit. Namely comprising of a slew of whore/slut/scum-based insults, descriptions of the kind of brutal sex they would like to subject me to, and, more whimsically but still not awesomely, rating my pierced, lopsided boobs out of a hundred. [Currently averaging a 4.37, in case you were wondering. Yes, out of a hundred.]

Strangely, reading rape fantasies about myself does nothing to alleviate my bad mood. If anything, it only adds another concern to the agonizing "should I go ahead with this rally?" debate. Am I putting myself in real, physical danger by doing this? How can I tell whether the graphic and disgusting comments online are the work of a keyboard warrior thousands of miles away in outer Siberia, or real threats from guys in my hometown? The thought temporarily paralyzes me with fear so potent my blood and muscles and organs freeze solid.

After I get the feeling back in my limbs, and I've quadruple-checked that the front door is definitely locked, and also practiced rapidly typing 911 into my phone in case I need to dial at any given moment, I decide to abandon social media in lieu of reading the media coverage of the rally. Hopefully trained journalists will have more rational opinions of this political movement we're attempting to start than your average online troll/rapist. I mean, hopefully. I'm not holding my breath.

The split between favorable and non-favorable coverage is

roughly fifty-fifty. The journalists fighting in my corner just *get* the point of the protest. They understand that it's not just an attempt to promote and celebrate teenage promiscuity, like their rivals seem to think. It's about consent and shame and bodily autonomy, the right to choose and the right to privacy. It's about violence against young women. It's about life and death. [Think I'm exaggerating? Google the hundreds of young women who've taken their own lives after their nude picture was leaked.]

And yet my critics don't get this. They say there are more important issues to worry about – carbon emissions and animal cruelty and poverty and human trafficking and the war in the Middle East – than teenage girls who get drunk and send nude pictures and then complain when that picture is shared around. They share fake images of me burning the American flag and tearing up the Constitution. They write think pieces on the absence of Good Christian Values™ in today's southern youths, they draw false equivalencies between revenge porn laws and sex education and teen pregnancy, distorting facts and bending truths just to push their agendas. However they dress up their views, what it comes down to is this: these people believe teenage girls These Days are sluts, and deserve to be punished accordingly.

Tiredness hits me like a brick wall and I slump back onto my pillow, laptop sliding to the floor with a thud. I can't do this.

This fight is too hard, the deck stacked against me in every conceivable way. The mountain is too high to climb. So why bother climbing at all?

Monday 13 February

7.32 a.m.

Since Hazel no longer has cheer practice first thing Monday morning, and since it's roughly -11,000 degrees out, she offers me a ride to school in her beat-up old car, which looks like it's been through a trash compactor six times then had four wheels tacked on the bottom. Still, the shelter from the freezing gales is much appreciated, as is the chance to catch up with Hazel about how she's doing.

"Despite everyone's campaigning, it doesn't look like I'm getting my job back anytime soon," she mutters, stuffing gum in her mouth as we pull up to a set of traffic lights. "So once this tank of gas runs out, I'm screwed. My parents have cut me off, money-wise, and I doubt anyone in town will hire me now."

"That's not true," I say, trying to do damage control on my smudged eyeliner in the rear-view mirror. "I got a job at the diner a few weeks back. It dies down, I promise."

"Does it, though?" Hazel asks, staring out the window at an

elderly couple holding hands as they cross the street. "I mean, really, does it?"

"Well, to the outside world it does." I smother my wind-chapped lips in drugstore balm. "Internally . . . that takes a little longer, I guess. Even when it's no longer news, you still feel . . . broken, I guess."

Vocalizing this aloud – the fact I'm still struggling – doesn't even feel weird. In fact, it's kind of nice having someone to talk about it with who totally and utterly *gets* it.

"I know what you mean." Hazel sighs. "All the shitty external consequences were pretty immediate. The first few weeks? Sheer hell. And now it's like I can feel everyone moving on, losing interest – except my family, that is . . . and yet it's still as raw inside me as it was when the tape first leaked."

"It's still all you can think about," I murmur. "Still all you see when you look in the mirror."

Hazel's eyes glisten as she nods, and kinship hums wordlessly between us. And for once I don't feel so alone in this very specific hell.

10.47 a.m.

Zachary messages asking to meet me in the woods before school. I tell him I can't, that there's no point, that we can't win this, but he insists it's important. Important enough that we have to meet in absolute private. Thankfully our gym teacher/CrossFit douchebag is not there scaling trees while yodeling naked, so we must consider this a win.

"So do you want the good news or the bad news first?" Zachary asks, brushing a layer of powdery snow off a tree stump and taking a seat. He's wearing one of those waxy green hunting jackets all rich people have.

"Good news, always," I say, leaning back again a tree, praying the branches above don't tremble in the next few minutes. It would be just like me to get a concussion from falling snow. "Also if you could find a way to spin the bad news into more good news, that would be excellent."

"I'll try my best. Okay, so good news, my dad is starting to pay attention to the campaign. The TV appearance from Rosa Garcia got under his skin. So apathy is a thing of the past."

Well, that's something at least. "And I'm guessing the bad news has something to do with the response he has planned?"

Zachary shrugs, compacting a patch of snow beneath his stompy winter boots. "Maybe, maybe not. Okay, so before I tell you this, I need you to know that I'm not a hundred percent sure on what I heard. I may be putting two and two together and getting ninety-one."

"That's my kind of math."

"I'm sure midterms are going to go swimmingly for you. Anyway, so last night he was video-calling Iannucci, and I was listening at the door, because I'm getting pretty into snitch life."

I nod. "It suits you. May I recommend a career in the FBI?"

He half smiles. "You laugh, but if this law thing doesn't work out, I'm considering it."

"You should. So what did Iannucci say?"

"It was both of them really. They were talking in super-low voices, but it sounded like they were organizing a counter protest."

"What? Why?"

"I dunno. Maybe they're thinking that if it gets violent and out of control, it might turn the press against you, and snuff out your momentum pretty quick. And it would give them a solid reason not to table your proposal."

This feels as cold and bitter in my chest as the February wind. "Yikes. Are they allowed to do that?"

"I'm not sure. I think it depends on whether they pay the counter protesters. If they do, and they use taxpayer money, they're in serious hot water."

I mull this over for a minute, trying to figure out how we can use this to our advantage. Eventually I say, "If they did that, and we had proof . . . would we be able to use that as leverage? Get them to push the legislation forward?"

He looks up from his snow-stomping, eyebrows raised. "You . . . know that's blackmail, yes?"

"Ah. That rings a bell."

"So maybe not quite the right tactic at this point."

I sigh, running my hands over the frozen tree bark. "Maybe

not. But it's your job to spin this as good news, so go. What's our play here?"

He swallows, and takes his time answering. Starts making a face in the compacted snow with twigs and stones. Stops just shy of a full mouth and clenches his fist. "If I can get evidence? We take it to the authorities."

For a second I think I misheard him. Can he really be suggesting this?

"You would do that? Turn over your own father? I mean, I don't have much experience with fathers, so maybe that's a completely normal thing to do."

He shrugs stiffly. "It's not. But I'd do it."

And then suddenly I fear everything Carson told me is true. Why is Zachary doing this? Am I barreling head first into another Danny situation? A guy doing nice things for me just so I'll fall in love with him and/or suck his penis? Is he just in this for a repeat of the garden-bench escapades?

"Why?" I ask, voice small.

Another tense shrug as he stabs a final twig into the snow face. "I don't believe corruption should go unpunished."

"Well, yeah. And I don't believe in shoplifting. Doesn't mean I turned Betty in when we were so broke we had to lift bags of rice from Walmart."

"Betty isn't my dad."

"Do you really hate him that much?" As the words leave

my mouth I already know what his answer will be. Almost every single interaction I've ever had with Zachary has been shaped by his hatred of his father, from our first real conversation on the fateful garden bench to the way he freaked out when the nudes leaked.

"Yeah. Yeah, I really do."

Tuesday 14 February

4.14 p.m.

It's Valentine's Day! Carson and I are both working tonight, but we hang out at the diner for a while before my shift starts, because romance. Admittedly this is rather like hanging out at school before class begins, or hanging out in a juvenile detention facility before you've committed the crime, but since Croc Queen isn't working today and Lola promised to swing us free cream sodas, we were powerless to resist the lure of sweet, delicious beverages.

We're sitting on the same side of my favorite booth right in the outer corner of the restaurant, surrounded by glass on two sides. The windows have steamed up as usual, and coupled with the frosty snow outside and the fairy lights against the sunset, there's kind of a magical wintry glow about the place. And, you know, the smell of the meat-brains-sawdust combo the chefs use to make cheeseburgers. But mainly the magical wintry glow thing.

I have every intention of having a relaxed mini-date with my nice and hilarious boyfriend to celebrate V-day, but the instant he asks me how things are going with the rally I spill my guts everywhere. He drinks his entire cream soda as I talk about the TV appearance and the backlash and Danny, and feeling scared and angry and vulnerable, and how I don't know if I can do this. The words tumble out in a garble, but thankfully Carson is used to my double-speed rants, so he's able to keep up with most of it.

"It's just . . . so many people hate me for what I'm doing. For what I stand for." I sigh, fiddling with the end of my straw. It's paper, because we have to save the environment and all that, but I've been toying with it for so long that it's starting to disintegrate into a soggy clump. "And it's overwhelming, you know? How am I ever going to change their minds?"

Carson considers this for a moment. He pulls the zipper of his green hoodie all the way up to his chin, then drags it back down to his chest. Repeats. Then: "One at a time, yo. One at a damn time."

"That sounds slow, and also unachievable."

"Why, man? You changed mine."

I look up from staring at his beautiful pecs. [I am very sorry for the constant objectifying I perform while Carson is around. Trust me, I hate myself for it, but have you seen the guy? Yes. Exactly.] "I did? Does that mean you once considered me a slut who should hang like a witch for my sexual appetite and/or piercing kink?"

265

I'm pretty sure they burned witches, not hanged them, but thankfully since my boyfriend is not a relentless pedant à la Danny Wells he lets it slide.

Carson's eyes widen. "Hell no! Dude. Of course not. I ain't ever thought that. But like . . . a'ight, so you know you said some of the journalists think there's more important things to worry about, and all that? I guess I kinda . . . I don't know, man. I kinda get it. The stuff my community's fighting for, Black Lives Matter and whatnot, it just seemed way more critical, you feel? More life and death. But that's before I knew you and saw what you went through, and listened to you talkin' about it all. Like puttin' it into context and all. I had no idea girls killed themselves over this stuff, man. I really didn't. So I guess you made me see it's all life and death, and just because you care deeply about one issue don't mean other issues can't matter too."

Carson usually employs his passionate voice only when he's talking about me, or about social justice, so the combination of the two is hiking the intensity level up several notches. I can almost see the smoke billowing from his ears. It's hot, in every sense of the word.

I nod, letting his words sink in. "Okay, so . . . maybe people's apathy I can overcome. But what about the ones who hate me? I mean, really, truly hate me?"

In painstaking, gut-clenching detail, I tell him about the online rape threats, and his fist clenches so hard round his cream soda glass that I'm amazed it doesn't shatter. Then I talk about how last night, after I read those comments, I checked the doors over and over, and practiced typing 911 at great speed. At this he shakes his head in disbelief.

"Man, I can't even imagine practicing calling the cops to make yourself feel safe. Like, that would make me feel the exact opposite of safe. Having a cop turn up." He shakes his head, rubbing at the stubble on his jaw. "Shit makes me angry, man."

My anger rises to meet his, until I'm fairly sure we're just sitting in our own personal cloud of smoke at this point.

"How do you deal with the anger?" I ask. "I mean, you've been dealing with this your whole life, which is just . . . there are no words for how much that sucks. But I'm pretty new to the all-consuming rage. How do you stop it from, like . . . It's like acid, you know? It's burning my insides away. And I can't seem to make it stop."

After a momentary pause without music, the loudspeakers start up again, this time playing the first non-Christmas song of the year. A half-hearted cheer, initiated by Derp Elf, ripples around the diner. Carson smiles at the sight, then turns his serious face back on as he picks up a pack of artificial sweetener and rolls it between his fingers.

"Honestly? There's no stopping it. Not completely. The anger, it . . . pulses. It's just there, always, and you can't even imagine it not being there." He shrugs. "But there's shit you can do to manage it."

"Like what?"

"Helps to have an outlet. That's why I paint."

I nod. "Writing comedy is like that for me."

Carson's eyes meet mine, deep and dark and meaningful. After a few moments of eye contact, I break gaze and turn to stare out the window. My own pale reflection looks back at me, young and tired and scared. I roll this conversation around in my head. Carson's hand finds my knee and gives it a squeeze. I turn back to him, and when I do, the embers inside me spark. Not the embers of anger I'm so used to burning, but the embers of hope I thought were long extinguished.

"I need to do the rally, don't I? Not just to effect change, but . . . as an outlet. For myself."

He nods, pressing his forehead to mine. His skin is soft and warm. "Yeah, Iz. You need to do the rally."

His lips brush mine, and I lean into the kiss. My lips are chapped and gross, but his taste of sweet, creamy soda. We press our bodies together in the booth. With one hand I tuck a finger into his waistband, and with the other I cup his jaw in my palm.

And a new surge of emotion rises to the surface, not as heady as arousal, but deeper somehow, more visceral, more everything. I know what it is, but I'm scared to call it by its name.

"This was the best Valentine's gift I could ever have asked for," I murmur, pulling away only a millimeter.

"What's that?"

I peck another kiss on his lips. "Renewed faith in my cause," I say softly. "In myself."

He chuckles. "Oh. I thought you meant my boner."

"That too, babe. That too."

10.54 p.m.

I have to walk home from my shift since it's too snowy to cycle, and the darkness makes me paranoid. Every shifting shadow, every patter of footsteps, every passing person with their hood pulled up makes me think of those violent sexual comments.

My fear sensors tingle, like they've recently been plugged into an electric socket. With every step I get more and more worked up, convinced one of my potential assaulters is lurking round a dark corner ready to pounce.

Should I even be out walking alone right now? Knowing there are people out there who think those things about me?

I mean, I'm a young woman. Of course there's always a low-level layer of fear whenever I walk anywhere alone, especially in the dark. Usually I just bury it, refusing to let that constant low-level fear control my life.

But now it's very, very high level. My heart gallops in my chest, and my vision swims. My breathing grows faster and more shallow, and I'm almost in tears by the time I reach the gates to my housing community.

It takes almost half an hour in the shower and a cathartic crying session to alleviate the feeling, and even then it's impossible to let go of completely. Because when you're a young woman this is how you experience the world. It just is.

Familiar anger rises in my overworked chest, and yet this time, instead of allowing it to roil inside me, claiming my body as its own, I pick up a paintbrush.

1.32 a.m.
By the time I'm done the protest banner reads BEWARE OF THE ~~DOG~~ BITCHES, and the anger in my chest has been dulled to a whisper.

Wednesday 15 February

6.32 a.m.

Let me tell you, there is no greater pleasure in this world than drawing nipples on beige, pink, yellow and brown balloons with your elderly grandmother. Especially when said aged grandmother accuses you of being ageist and lets half the air out of the pink ones when you're not looking.

4.02 p.m.

Despite a renewed sense of purpose and commitment to the rally, I'm still feeling a little flat and helpless, since I've managed to screw up my screenwriting career before it even started. I'm in desperate need of a mood boost. So the plan this evening is to meet in Ajita's basement for a mountain of nachos and another hair-coloring session – I want to top up the pink, and Meg wants to take the plunge with some turquoise, so Ajita and I are making it our mission to give her the perfect Cinderella moment. Our hair's gotta look on point while we're changing the world, right? Then we'll go through the schedule for Saturday with a fine-tooth comb, and prepare for the Bitches Bite Back meeting tomorrow lunchtime – the final one before the march – and figure out what we need every single one of our hundred volunteers to do over the next few days.

As much as I'm excited for tonight, it's getting to the point in the academic year where every girls' night is laced with sadness. I know our days are numbered, and once they both go off to college I'll only see them in the summer and over the holidays. What started as an abstract fear in the back of my mind – the fear of being left behind – is becoming more and more real with every passing minute.

The thing about the future is that nobody tells you how quickly it comes round. [This is a lie. Literally every adult tells you this. But it's, like, a basic requirement of being a teenager not to listen.]

8.46 p.m.

Heyyyyyy, internet. I regret to announce that I am typing this blog post while under the influence of substances widely considered unsuitable for individuals below the age of 21. Who am I kidding? I regret nothing. Beer is great.

My evening was nothing short of magical. Literally how did I get so lucky, friendship wise? Skipping over the fact one of my two lifelong best friends betrayed me to the entire world, I really have been extremely #blessed in the pal department.

So we're sitting on Ajita's basement floor surrounded by peanut butter cup wrappers, each of us rocking freshly applied hair dye in very professional foil contraptions. I've opted for a pink ombré top-up, Meg has gone all-over turquoise, and Ajita went with a violet toner to give her deep brown hair a purple sheen. I've brought Dumbledore with me since Betty is working late and there's every chance I'll crash at Ajita's after a few beveraginos. He's currently sucking my big toe with a vaguely sexual expression on his face, strange little creature that he is.

"So how are you feeling about the screenplay thing?" Ajita asks as tentatively as though embarking on hostage negotiations.

My stomach grips at the memory. I've been trying so hard to forget everything that happened with the missed Skype call and Eliza's subsequent disappointment, and with the rally as a distraction it's been working for the most part. But I know I need to come to terms with it, and to formulate a game plan going forward. I guess there's no better people to formulate a game plan with than my two best friends who have my back no matter what. [This is untrue. Industry professionals are far more qualified to offer career advice. But also not as much fun, so.]

"God, the whole thing sucks," I admit, draining my second bottle of beer and reaching for a third. I remove the cap with my teeth, and can almost hear my dentist screaming into the night.

"So does your face," Ajita says matter-of-factly.

"Yes, very good," I reply patiently. "Honestly, though, I'm

273

too embarrassed to even email Eliza and ask what happens now."

"Maybe the shame of your fuckup has driven her to the Canadian Rockies, where she will live forever with the wolf people."

"Are there even wolves in the Rockies?" Meg asks.

"I am not sure," I admit, "because like most people with better things to do my mountain wildlife knowledge is limited."

"Is Eliza still pitching the screenplay around elsewhere?" Meg asks. "Sorry if that's a dumb question. I have no idea how all this works."

"Dude, neither do I," I confess. "Like I say, I'm scared to ask. Maybe she's still talking to production companies, or maybe she's given up on me altogether. Either way, we clearly haven't had any interest, otherwise she would've emailed. It's been radio silence ever since the Skype fandango."

"So what do you do now?" Ajita asks, leaning back against the sofa and stretching her legs out in front of her. As she does she edges a tiny bit closer to Meg, who looks at the new proximity out the corner of her eye and smiles. I stifle a smirk. "Are you working on something else?"

"Nope. I know I should be, but honestly my confidence has taken a knock."

"Thank God for that," Meg deadpans. "You really were becoming an incredible narcissist."

Ajita and I gape at her in astonishment. This is the first time she's shit-talked to me, and she does it with such perfect delivery that Ajita begins a slow-clap. I join in. Even Dumbledore looks up from chewing my toenail, clearly enjoying the moment.

"Well played, my friend." I nod sagely. "Well played. But I do hope you know the floodgates have now opened, and I fully intend to take the ever-loving piss out of you from this moment on. Cool?"

"Cool." Meg grins, turquoise-covered hair plastered to her head with wet dye.

"Good to hear," I say. "I'm tempted by some kind of alien-type joke on account of the fact your hair makes you look like ET, but kids in glasshouses, and all that."

"Yeah," Ajita agrees. "You're better than that, O'Neill."

In the most perfect comedic timing ever Meg chooses that precise moment to let rip with an almighty burp. She giggles and looks expectantly at me, as does Ajita, stifling what looks like an epic witch cackle.

After a few beats, I splutter and snort. "I'm sorry, I got nothing. My sense of humor is poached in beer. There is nothing I could possibly say to make that moment funnier than it already was."

"So you don't have any new screenplay ideas cooking up?" Meg asks after we've all recovered from the hysteria, shoving another Reese's in her mouth.

Suddenly I stare at the floor, as though fascinated by the Britain-shaped wee stain from when Ajita laughed so hard she wet herself. "Um, yeah. I guess I do have one idea. I'm just . . . not sure I'm ready to write it yet."

"Is it a story about a young woman whose life is destroyed by the leaking of her nude photo?" Ajita asks.

I snap my head up. "How did you know?"

She rolls her eyes, stroking Dumbledore's upturned tummy. "I mean, it's pretty obvious dude. You're not that hard to read. Okay, so what's holding you back? Why aren't you ready to write it?"

"You may have noticed this, dear friend, but I'm not that great at talking about my feelings and emotions. In the last few weeks I've had a spot of difficulty reliving the entire shitshow in front of my peers and countrymen. So the thought of spending months on end trying to get it all down on paper is mildly horrifying."

"But isn't this the best time to try and write it?" Meg says, slurring slightly. Her eyes are a little glazed after her two beers, but in a happy, sparkly way. Her cheeks glow warmly. "Like, maybe this is the thing that'll make you more comfortable talking about it – if you explore it through fiction. I really think you should do it, Izzy. It could be so great. And it would speak to so many people."

Meg's words ring in my ears like bells. Exploring my pain through fiction. That could be the key to everything.

Her words are getting me all fired up, as is the beer/sugar

combo, and determination begins to prickle in my gut. "Maybe I should. Maybe after all the rally stuff has –"

"No, dude," Ajita interrupts. "Email Eliza now. Like right now. You've been scared to reach out, right? So use this as a reason. Say you have a new idea and wanted to hear her thoughts."

Long story short: I'm now sitting on Ajita's bathroom floor, having waited way too long to wash off the pink dye, because I just emailed Eliza a pitch for my new screenplay: *SLUT*.

Oh God. If Eliza hates the idea, she basically hates *me* as a concept. And if she likes the idea, I have to relive the experience all over again in order to write it. Wait, why did I do this again?

11.53 p.m.

I arrive back in the basement with shocking pink hair, and find Ajita giving Meg honest-to-God French braids. She sits on the sofa while Meg sits on the floor, and deftly weaves segments of seafoam green hair as Meg shows her a puppy video on her phone. They both make "awww"ing noises, Ajita leaning in so close she's probably breathing directly into Meg's ear. Meg does not seem perturbed by this.

"That's adorable," Ajita says, squeeing at the screen. Her deep-violet hair looks glossy and awesome. She's blow-dried it into soft waves, and honestly it's like a shampoo commercial in here. You know, minus the dachshund humping a beanbag.

"Right? Fern sent me a bunch of them. Hang on, let me find the one of a baby St Bernard . . ."

At the mention of Fern's name Ajita immediately sits up rigidly and proceeds to plait the rest of Meg's hair with all the precision and affection of a German engineer at an F1 pitstop. Meg winces as Ajita yanks slightly too tight. She shows Ajita another video to which Ajita merely says, "nice". Still neither of them seem to have noticed my arrival.

I clear my throat. "Ahem. May I have thine attention please? Eliza doth has responded."

Squinting at my phone screen through beer-fuzzed eyes, I read the email aloud: "*Okay, so I love your idea for SLUT, and the fact that it's something you've been through yourself is such a strong hook. Definitely start working on it when you get the chance!*"

As Ajita and Meg congratulate me there's a strange ringing in my ears. Not just because of the alcohol – at least, probably not – but also because of the weird, spiky adrenaline flooding through me. I'm genuinely afraid of writing this screenplay. I'm scared of digging back into the darkest hours of my slut-shaming experience. But that's exactly why I need to do this.

Friday 17 February

8.48 p.m.

What. A. Week.

I'd planned to update this blog every day to keep track of our rally progress and how everything is taking shape, but it's just been too wildly busy. To give you some indication of just how busy, I have not washed my hair in eleven days. Betty is threatening to put me in quarantine lest I doth washeth my mane.

Dumbledore whimpers whenever I enter the room. This may sound like an overreaction, but you forget the poor devil has a much more powerful sense of smell than we mere mortals. I basically could be locked up for animal cruelty at this point.

Anyway, here's a small fraction of what the last few days have entailed. Hopefully it will make you judge me slightly less about the hair washing/animal cruelty thing.

• I do more than a dozen interviews for an all manner of media outlets: radio, TV, newspapers, podcasts, YouTube channels, and what I unfortunately suspect to be a low-budget porno e-zine, because those are apparently a thing now. I suddenly have much more sympathy for celebrities who have to do eighty press junkets every day for months on end when they're promoting their latest movie. It basically involves repeating yourself over and over and over again, and thinking surely they'll all be bored of hearing the same set of answers every time I open my mouth, but alas the same questions keep coming. This works out for the best, since I've got the art of answering these questions in a non-personal way down to a tee, and I manage to avoid another talk show-style disaster.

• I'll be honest, I never thought this was possible, but I think I genuinely might have grown tired of the sound of my own voice. [I know. As the most narcissistic little bitch on this planet I'm as shocked as you are.]

• Betty even does an interview! A regional radio station thought it'd be interesting to hear her take on the situation, and to be fair the old bird knocks it out of the park. She talks about raising a granddaughter in the social media age, generational differences in the way young women are treated now versus when she grew up, why she thinks it's so crucial that we fight this issue, even though there are undeniably bigger problems in the world. Then she issues the most powerful and moving call to action I've ever heard, aimed not at teenage girls but at their parents and grandparents, urging them to rise up and fight alongside us instead of judging us for having different moral codes. She also briefly discusses how proud my own mother would be of me, but I could barely hear what she said over the sound of my wracking sobs, so there you go.

• We round the troops and take care of every single logistical detail of the rally, and then some. We plan for every possible eventuality, including but not limited to: alien invasions, plague outbreaks, mega tornadoes.

• But also we make sure the more sensible elements are all in hand – the tech crew from the school theater are going to handle setting up the stage and sound system with the companies providing them, while the Bitches Bite Back gang are going to be leading the march, making sure everyone follows the pre-planned route around town, and nobody gets crushed by stampeders and/or alien invaders.

• And! The rally has received so much interest, thanks to the media coverage, that our fundraising even covered the cost of arranging twenty private buses to ferry people from the big nearby city to our tiny inconsequential town for free. They all got booked up within twenty minutes. So we have a confirmed

1,440 people traveling for an hour each way to attend the rally. Cool cool cool cool cool.

• Hazel Parker, who's been channeling her anger into acting as business liaison for the event, has convinced a bunch of local restaurants to donate refreshments to marchers. So far we have a waffle stand from Martha's Diner, a pizza stand from Carson's workplace, a noodle bar from the fancy Chinese restaurant, hot cocoa and coffee from a cute indie coffee house downtown, a burger truck from an Italian-American guy who is almost definitely in the mafia, and a giant lemonade stall funded and run by the teachers, parents and pupils of two middle schools in the area. Unfortunately we were not able to secure free bottles of water, because the local plant is owned by a rich Vaughan relative, but still. It's precisely zero degrees out, so sunstroke and heat exhaustion are even less likely than mega tornadoes on our risk assessment analysis.

1. I have no idea what witchcraft Hazel performed to get all of these entrepreneurs to support us, and I'm briefly concerned that she's participated in some sort of sinister blood magic in order to make it happen, but this business liaison thing is a stroke of genius. Ted Vaughan definitely considers his key demographics to be a) salt-of-the-earth folks hit hard by mine closures, b) assault rifle collectors, and c) business owners who want to pay

less corporation tax. The fact that so many of the latter business owners are openly supporting this cause *has* to make him sit up and pay attention.

2. All I'm saying is that if I find out Hazel has been blackmailing all of these entrepreneur types into cooperating, I won't be all that mad at her. The end justifies the means, etc.

3. Oh God. I have become an evil dictator blinded by my cause.

4. Strangely I am okay with this. Any of you who doth object shalt be flogged and taken to the gallows. Now someone bring me some mead.

5. [I don't know why it's my default to become a medieval person in any and all improvization scenarios.]

Oh, and Carson arrives after his Friday-night late shift to wish me luck for tomorrow, offer me leftover pizza, which I gratefully accept, and ask if there's anything I need from him. The conversation goes like this:

Carson: D'you need help with anything, my man?
Me: No, I think we're good! But thank you.
Carson: Really? There ain't anything?

Me: I don't think so? We've been flat out all week preparing, and I think everything is in place. But you're the best boyfriend for asking.

Carson: Man, I wish you'd've let me help out this week. I could've, I dunno, lifted some boxes or somethin'.

Me: Firstly that is highly rude and offensive. Women are, on occasion, also capable of lifting boxes. That may sound wild, but it is true. I have seen it with my own two eyes. Secondly I knew how busy you were. How many shifts have you worked this week? Four? Five?

Carson: Still. I want to help.

Me: Okay. You know what the absolute best thing you could do for me would be?

Carson: Name it.

Me: Be there tomorrow. Preferably carrying a banner and wearing that beanie hat that makes me want to jump your bones.

Carson: [long pause] Will there be cops there?

Me: I . . . yeah. Yeah, I think the station is sending some. Not in riot gear or anything, just to keep an eye out for trouble.

Carson: You know what their favorite definition of trouble is? Black people protesting shit.

Me: Yeah. I wish it wasn't like this.

Carson: Me too. Me fucking too.

So who knows whether Carson will be there tomorrow. I left the ball in his court. Of course his support would mean the world, but at the same time I don't want him to feel uncomfortable or in danger at my expense. Still, his concerns are real. We have a lot of black supporters attending tomorrow, thanks to the viral intersectionality video. What if the cops *do* rock up in riot gear? Will everyone be safe?

8.17 p.m.
Nerves. Oh God, the nerves.

After I announce I am going for a jog to alleviate some of the midterms-and-TV-appearance stress, and then make it precisely 100 meters before promptly remembering why I do not jog, Betty presents me with a whisky-spiked hot cocoa. We've been laying off the liquor lately, on account of Betty's attempts to lower her blood pressure/cholesterol/yadda yadda, but this feels like a whisky situation if I ever saw one. She also tops my cocoa with an Everest-sized peak of whipped cream and enough marshmallows to sink a submarine. [This is not a great metaphor due to the fact submarines are literally designed to sink, but I am distraught. Get off my back for once in your life.]

"Okay, first off, you need to take a big old gulp of that cocoa," she says. "I don't care if you give yourself third-degree burns in the process. You need whisky more than oxygen right now."

I do as I'm told. The hot cocoa scalds my tongue and the whisky burns my throat for good measure, but it feels strangely good in a painful sort of way.

Betty throws a mini marshmallow up in the air and fails to

catch it. Dumbledore has a seizure with excitement, swallows it whole, then nanoseconds later develops a severe case of the zoomies, which is what we call it when he sprints aimlessly around the apartment like a chinchilla on crack. Maybe we could make some extra cash by renting him out to a circus of some sort?

She dunks a pinkie in her whipped cream [not a euphemism, how many times do I have to tell you?] and licks it clean [all right, so it does sound kinda filthy, you're right]. "Okay, talk me through this fear of yours. Why are you so goddamn terrified?"

I explain to her the thing about my personality, and also my lack of political knowledge, my inability to resist sarcasm. She nods sagely as I do, then lays down her mug. I am impressed but not surprised to see she's already finished her entire whisky hot cocoa. The woman is a machine. A very faulty machine with no instruction manual, but a machine nonetheless.

"I wish your mom could see you now," Betty says, voice slow and soft, eyes wistful. "Well, both of your parents really. But especially your mom. She was a feminist to her core, you know, always calling your dad on his crap." She chuckles, her massive chest rising and falling. "Whenever he got caught up in that macho alpha bullshit that came with working with a bunch of mechanics, she'd make him sit down and watch a romantic movie and talk about his feelings. And if he pretended he didn't have any, she'd withhold sex until he opened up." Another chuckle, followed by a head shake. "My daughter was a real firecracker. What a woman."

I let all this sink in. This is the first time we've talked about my mom since Betty and I sat in that graveyard all those months ago and agreed something had to change. That we had to be open with each other no matter how painful it might be. And this is painful, of course it is. My chest aches and aches whenever I think about how much I've lost. How much Betty has lost too.

But through the ache there's something rich and tender. I love hearing about what my mom was like, how much like her I am. I wish, more than anything in the world, I could have just one day with her. One day to discover the similarities for myself. To laugh and cry and celebrate and commiserate. I want it so badly, so viscerally, that the tears start to flow before I can stop them.

"Do you believe we'll all be reunited someday?" I say, wiping my cheek on the soft cotton sleeve of my hoodie. "In the afterlife, or whatever."

"I don't know, kiddo. I don't know." Betty's eyes are dry, but her voice betrays splinters of sadness and longing. Dumbledore hops onto the sofa and wriggles between us, licking my knee as is now customary. "But in some ways I feel like we're all united already. Maybe not in body, but in spirit. Your mom's soul lives on in you, and in me. Every time I see you fight back against the patriarchy, against the corrupt system we find ourselves living in, I know that for sure. I know she's still with us."

Dammit, Betty. The tears evolve into Niagara-style waterfalls. "And my dad?"

"Are you kidding me? I can't even look at Carson Manning without thinking how much like your father he is."

Her statement cleaves my heart in two, but in a good way. "Forreal?"

Betty chuckles again, stroking Dumbledore's chubby belly. "Oh, forreal. He's sweet and loyal and protective. Hard-working. Always putting others first. Often there with the alpha bullshit. He's your father, all right."

We sit in contemplative silence for a while, and I feel like Betty is right. I can almost sense my parents here with us, not as ghosts or poltergeists or any of that nonsense, but as a thrum of energy, something that flows both around me and through me. They're in my blood and my skin and my thoughts. They are me and I am them. Nothing can ever take that away from us. No drunk truck driver can ever sever that connection.

"I like this," I mumble, swallowing a mouthful of salty tears. "Being able to talk about my parents with you."

"Me too." Betty nods, eyes pink but cheeks dry. "Although it helps that this is my ninth whisky of the day."

9.15 p.m.

Gahhhhhhh. It all comes down to tomorrow. Real talk, I don't think I've ever been this nervous in my life. Because I know deep down the success of the rally will depend on whether or not I can nail my speech.

I want to do it. I really do. I want to open up to a crowd of strangers and talk about how much this matters, how much it nearly destroyed me. I know we need that emotional resonance to push the campaign to the next level. But can I do it? My track record suggests not.

And yet something Meg said when we were discussing the *SLUT* screenplay is still reverberating in my brain. "*Like, maybe this is the thing that'll make you more comfortable talking about it — if you explore it through fiction.*"

Maybe I just need to get in character. Maybe I should write a speech and learn it like I learn lines. Maybe I should write this part of the movie script now.

So I take out my laptop, and I start to write.

11.36 p.m.

The speech is written. The lines are learned. And I think I'm ready.

I'm excited and nervous and scared. I want so badly for it to go well. I want this to succeed more than everything I've ever wanted in my life, with the sole exception of wanting my parents to be here to see it.

Sunday 19 February

10.00 a.m.

So I'm gonna skip over the morning of extensive protest preparation, because I don't know about you, but complex stage assembly and spot visits from risk assessment officers aren't really my jam, and honestly I could try my very best to make it interesting – stage assembly in particular is rife with phallic innuendos – but I must protect my wrists at this point.

Instead let's do a fade-in at around one thirty, about a half-hour before the rally is due to kick off.

Picture the scene: it's snowing, because of course it is, and there's a state-wide shortage of salt to grit the roads, so essentially we're operating on an ice rink. Minus the skates. One member of the BBB team has already slipped and broken her ankle, to the point where she has to be whizzed away to the emergency room in an Uber, because really, who can afford ambulances in this day and age? They are accessible to Mark Zuckerberg and nobody else.

All the food and drink stalls are set up in the town square, which serves as both the start and finish line of the march. We planned the route as a half-mile loop – this does not sound very far, but you forget we are in snowy Narnia at this point, and we can only walk by taking very small steps and looking remarkably like we've shit our pants. Perhaps some of the richer attendees will have fancy snow boots, but your average povotarian cannot afford such luxuries.

The square already smells of roasting coffee and onions being fried for hot dogs and cheese melting on pizza and fresh waffles and sweet, tangy lemonade. This is a highly confusing sensory assault, because if you closed your eyes and disabled your heat receptors, you would a hundred percent think it was a summer barbecue or festival-type scenario. Then you'd open your eyes and see that the middle-school pupils have made an ice fort surrounding the lemonade stand, and nobody can access it without scaling a snow wall and immediately falling to their death. Which, okay, but I would quite like the site of my first ever rally not to descend into a mass grave. Maybe that's unreasonable, I don't know.

In the center of the square, where there's usually a small grassy park but is currently just an extension of the ice-rink situation, we've set up a raised stage where I'll be standing with Ajita and Meg come 2 p.m., giving an impassioned speech before the march begins. This is, of course, providing I manage to avoid shitting my pants for real.

As Ajita and I sit on giant speakers and watch the crowds begin to form the nerves become almost unbearable. Okay, so I say crowds, but what I really mean is small clusters of bored-looking humans. And most of them appear to just be here for the free food, judging by the beeline they make for the pizza stall.

"Fuck," I mutter to Ajita, taking a swig of scalding-hot cappuccino from my paper cup. "What if the turnout sucks?" In all the disastrous possibilities we'd considered during the planning, low turnout was not one of them. With all the media coverage and support/outrage we'd kind of assumed it would be pretty busy in the square. Again, my intense narcissism scuppers a perfectly good plan.

Ajita rolls her eyes. "The turnout will not suck. Give it time. Would you arrive a half-hour early when it's below freezing out? No, you'd stay in your house until the last possible minute like a sane person. So relax. You're being ridiculous."

She seems remarkably calm, but that's probably because I'm the one who has to do all the talking when the moment comes. Also, my face is the face of this entire campaign, so it feels like if the rally fails, I fail too. It's a lot of pressure. Mostly self-induced, but still. Pressure nonetheless.

"Oh, look, here come some people now!" I say, cheering up at the sight. My vision isn't amazing, and coupled with the falling snow it's hard to tell what their banners say, but my spirits are buoyed by the sight of real-life people.

"Uh, Iz . . ." Ajita, who has much better vision than me, trails off.

"What? What is it? Who are they?" Suddenly I'm terrified it's the police in their riot gear. I mean, it would be grossly unnecessary on account of the fact almost everyone in the square is a volunteer wearing a pink BBB hoodie, but still. What if they felt like escalating a perfectly pleasant afternoon for no good reason? That does seem within the realm of possibility.

Ajita doesn't need to answer. As the group of people come into view it's clear they aren't police.

They're counter protesters. Vaughan's counter protesters.

There are around a hundred of them, bundled up in ski jackets and wooly hats and thick scarves, fancy snow boots firmly in place. They're mostly white men in their fifties and sixties, but I'm pained to see at least two dozen middle-aged women in the crowd, pasty faces scowling and full of hate. I recognize too many of them – some people from Betty's community center group, a few Martha's regulars, a member of the school board.

Around ten signs and banners stick stubbornly into the air. The largest says: "YOUNG WOMEN SHOULD MAKE LIKE HILLARY AND #COVERITUP" I mean, this is just confusing. Do they mean she's covering up crimes? Or her boobs? Or both? Are they passively endorsing and advocating for the covering up of crimes? Get it together, angry fascist morons!

The other slogans all center around young women being

respectable, around bringing back old values, around the idea that no decent man will ever marry a slut.

And the worst part? Their numbers dwarf ours. The counter protest is bigger than the protest itself.

"Okay, don't panic," Ajita mumbles in my ear, obviously sensing the fact that I'm on the brink of hyperventilation. "There is nothing to be gained by panicking."

"Ajita, what do we do if nobody else turns up for us? Am I hell getting on that stage!"

The group of counter protesters stand in silence, holding up their hateful signs stoically, death-staring us until they're blue in the face. Of course, due to the extreme cold, they're probably blue in the face anyway.

"Do you have a passport?" Ajita asks earnestly, sipping her vanilla latte. "I'm thinking we run away to Canada and start a new coven with the grizzly bears. They may be more receptive to our progressive feminist notions."

"Ajita. Now is not the time for jokes."

She stares at me in disbelief. "You are fucking unreal. Literally. Why am I even friends with such an unbelievable hypocrite? It's astounding. Really, it is."

Like it always does, though, cracking jokes relieves some of the tension in my chest. I smile and resist the urge to throw my arms round my wonderful best friend who never fails to lighten the mood. Instead I sniff away the cold and say, "Hey, if things go south, we can definitely write a stand-up set about the experience. I had a pretty entertaining thought about mass graves earlier."

"Wait, can you hear that?" Ajita asks suddenly, sitting up straighter, straining to hear. If she was as much of a St Bernard as her tongue length would suggest, her ears would be pricked up right about now.

"No, what —"

But then I hear it. The sound of a crowd. A loud, fierce, passionate crowd.

The source of the noise is somewhere to the southwest of where we're sitting, which makes no sense. [I literally made this up; I have no clue when it comes to navigational stuff. You could not pay me one million American dollars to point north.] That's weird. I can't figure out why there would be so many people on that random side street.

Then, at the exact same time as Ajita, I remember what's down that random side street.

We both look at each other and gasp. "The bus station!"

The 1,440 people coming from the city. In all the panic and stress I'd forgotten about them.

The huge mass of bodies rounds the final corner into the square, and a cheer goes up when they see the setup: the giant stage and speakers, the mini village of food and drink vendors, the ice wall constructed by young kids still old enough to know the difference between wrong and right. And then they flood in, and the counter protesters are immediately lost in the swarm, and our rally is alive and breathing.

Over the next five minutes Ajita and I watch in enraptured silence as hundreds and hundreds more people spill into the square. Teachers from Edgewood; and journalists who interviewed me; and kids from our school and other schools; the girls from Martha's; and Mrs Crannon and her amazing wife; Rosa Garcia, the Democratic opposition to Vaughan, and her teenage daughters; Danny, who I exchange nods with; Betty. Oh, my heart. Betty. The pride on her face fills me with joy, warming my insides more than whisky hot cocoa ever could.

There are people I've never seen before in my life, people who are young and old and somewhere in between. Mainly girls and women, but a few guys stand by their friends or girlfriends or mothers or daughters. This is the best kind of people-watching in the entire world. With the exception of the police in riot gear. There aren't many of them, but still enough to intimidate. The sight of them leaves me uneasy and nauseated.

By the time 2 p.m. rolls around I have to take the stage. Meg's mom pushes her through the rapidly deepening snow to the stage, then the three of us give each other a steadying head nod, like holy crap we're really doing this, and head up the ramp to the platform.

Oh god, oh god, oh god. I'm going to fail again.

Another chorus of cheers, screams and kazoos erupts as I step to the front and take the mic, fighting the urge to break down into tears.

I go to talk, but no words come out. Fear grips me in a vise. Thousands of sets of eyes stare back at me. Waiting. Judging.

Suddenly I'm excruciatingly aware of my own physicality, of the space I take up. Of the spread of my hips and the weight of my breasts, of the tightness of my jeans and the size of my chunky sweater. Of the thudding in my ribcage and the pounding of blood in my ears. I feel the power of gravity with every tiny movement. It's not an out-of-body experience – more like an intense, suffocating bodily awareness. With it comes the sharp realization that every single one of the girls before me have seen this body naked. They've discussed the spread of my hips with their friends and judged the weight of my breasts from the comfort of their own bed. They know exactly what lies beneath my tight jeans and chunky sweater; they know every tiny, painstaking detail. Every single one of these people has seen me naked.

But they're still here, O'Neill. They're still here. In fact, they're here because *they saw you naked, and they know that isn't right.*

The realization uplifts me, gives me the strength to speak, to use the power and the voice this shitty situation has gifted me with. I bring the mic closer to my lips. All I have to do is recite the speech I wrote. I'm a character in a movie. A movie about my own life, and the power that life can have.

Then slowly, clearly, powerfully:

"My name is Izzy O'Neill, and I slept with a senator's son on a garden bench."

Booming and echoing around the square, my words have the desired effect. The quiet chatter falls silent. Everyone is enraptured, hanging on my next lines. Even the counter protesters seem reluctantly interested in what I'm about to say. The snow continues to fall, soft and bewitching.

"And the truth is? I enjoyed it." A small ripple of laughter. "And that in itself is a shameful statement, or so society would have us believe." I glare at the cluster of nervously defiant counter protesters. "Hell, there are people here demanding I cover myself up, I censor myself, I deny myself – because the simple idea of a young woman owning her sexuality makes them so uncomfortable they can barely stand to look me."

A gray-haired woman without a banner shakes her head in disgust, averting her gaze. I address her directly. "You . . . you would rather girls like me didn't exist." I pause, because what I'm about to say is more than I've ever admitted out loud. To anyone. Even Betty and Ajita. "And you nearly got your wish. Because when my nude picture leaked I was destroyed."

A lump of emotion bobs in my throat, and I lean into it. Allow the cracks and wobbles into my voice, to show them that this is real, this was a real person they tried to annihilate.

"When something like that happens it really does feel like your life is ruined. Everything you wanted for yourself is taken away. You're no longer a human being. You're an object." The square is deadly silent, but instead of feeling lifeless it crackles with intensity and underlying energy. "And because you once chose to share your body with someone you trusted, because you once gave yourself willingly, the world believes you're public property. They assume you gave yourself willingly to millions of people just because you gave yourself to one. They believe you belong to them. And that can never be undone. You can never take yourself back. The world can look at your naked body whenever they want, and you can do nothing to stop them. Just stop for a minute and imagine how that feels."

I scan the crowd. "Seriously. I want you all to imagine how that would feel. All of you, even those carrying counter-protest banners. Just imagine how it would feel if everyone in the entire world could look at your naked body whenever they wanted to, and you could do nothing to stop them."

As people in the crowd picture themselves in the same scenario, shoulders stoop, heads tilt shamefully down, faces contort in second-hand pain. They experience a vicarious glimpse of the weight I've been carrying for months and months.

The snowfall intensifies. I let the pause stretch out until it's uncomfortable, because, fuck it, I want every single person here to experience a mere fraction of the discomfort I've been dealing with for so long.

I know what most of the counter protesters must be thinking: *So what? She deserved everything she got. She put herself in that position by sending the nude in the first place. I don't have to imagine what that would be like, because I would never be so stupid.*

But if I can get through to even one of them? To make them see or imagine or *feel* how brutal what I went through was? It'll be worth.

Eventually, when the air around us is taut and tense, I raise my voice and say: "What happened to me is legal in this state. Make some noise if you believe that should change."

Immediately, intensely, the uproar is thunderous, fists pumping the air, banners thrust to the sky, kazoos . . . kazooing?

"I slept with a senator's son," I practically yell, all self-consciousness gone now. "And it was to that very same senator that we appealed for change. But our requests were met with silence. Apathy. Because the pain of teenage girls is irrelevant to people like him. Bitches, the Ted Vaughans of this world will never listen until they have something to lose. And so we take matters into our own hands. We take change into our own hands. And we show those in power that if they don't start to take us seriously, we'll vote them out of office faster than you can say 'slut'."

The roars are deafening. And that's when we shoot 5,000

boob balloons out of a giant cannon and into the crowd. Pink and brown and beige and yellow, big Sharpie nipples, small Sharpie nipples, saggy Betty nipples. The counter protesters look suitably disgusted, so, mission accomplished on the inflatable tits.

As the balloons fall softly with the snow, the crowd starts a huge game of boob balloon volleyball, jumping and cheering and whooping under the vast white sky. They roar with such ferocity and intensity that it sets my heart alight. My skin crackles with energy and fury. As the righteous roars wash over me it feels like rebirth. It's beautiful, wild, passionate chaos, like being in the most spellbinding snow globe in the world.

The moment I exchange with Ajita then is pure magic. Our eyes meet across the stage, sparkling, fizzing with the energy and joy we created. And, wordlessly, we say to each other: Look. Look at this thing we did. Look at everything we survived in the process.

A thousand other moments flash between us: my gulping tears when I told her about my parents for the first time; sitting in the graveyard and sharing with her how scared I was for Betty's time to come too; her grandmother dying back in Nepal, and her pain over having never really known her. Newer moments too: the agony of accidentally outing her; standing on the street outside her house begging for her forgiveness; her anger when she learned Danny was behind the World Class Whore website; my intense vulnerability a few weeks ago, sitting on the street in the freezing cold, not believing I could really do this.

And I know other countless people made this day happen, not just Ajita and I. Meg with her enthusiasm and digital savvy, Bella with her relentless championing, Hazel with her business liaison and refusal to stay a victim. The hundreds of bitches volunteering, the food and drink vendors, the generous journalists who supported us from the start. Rosa Garcia. Carson and Zachary and Betty and Mrs Crannon. So, so many people to thank.

But this moment? This moment between me and my best friend in the entire world, eyes glittering with unspilled tears? This moment means more than anything.

I turn back to the crowd, and yell into the mic: "And now, we march!"

Led by Ajita and I – the deep snow plays havoc with Meg's wheelchair, so she and Betty stay in the square to chat to other non-marching protesters – the march takes over an hour. Yes, to travel half a mile. Hey, you try and lead thousands of people through a blizzard!

Every single step is a step of triumph, of progress, of victory even though victory is not yet ours. It's the show of feminist support I've wanted from the very beginning. That's one thing I've learned: if at first nobody stands with you in your fight, it's okay to demand better from them. And sometimes, better is exactly what you'll get. And it will feel extraordinary.

As we continue through the streets we're joined by random residents spilling out of coffee shops and grocery stores, journalists snapping their cameras and thrusting mics into the crowd for live-action voxpops.

Then, a hundred yards into the march, we're joined by a person I'd lost all hope of seeing today: Carson Manning. Carrying a beautifully illustrated sign saying GUYS CAN BE BITCHES TOO. Oh, and wearing the beanie that makes me want to jump his bones.

I emit a pathetically excited whoop at the sight of him, waiting for us outside a smoothie bar, a giant grin on his face, beaming with pride. The temptation to run over to him and hurl myself into his arms is quickly overridden by the self-preservation portion of my brain, which tells me I would either immediately a) plummet to my death on the ice rink or b) crush him to death beneath my curvaceous frame. Instead I settle for a sped-up penguin shuffle, because there is nothing sexier than the constipated Pingu aesthetic.

"You came!" I exclaim as I finally reach him, throwing my arms round his neck. [Not in a violent way, you understand.]

He laughs into my wild, snow-filled hair. "Wouldn't miss it. You amaze the hell outta me, you know that?" Carson says, looking over his shoulder at the vibrant throng of protesters cheering and chanting at the top of their lungs.

"Why's that?" I laugh, letting his words warm my freezing bones.

"Pullin' all this off. Like, no big deal. Just gonna launch a game-changing political movement while also workin' your ass off in the diner and studyin' for midterms."

"You wildly overestimate how much I studied for midterms," I snort.

As he leads up the march with Ajita and me, our gloved hands intertwined and our faces wearing matching beams of pride, I can't help but think about that moment in the school hallway back in the fall, right after my nude was leaked, when his teammates ripped into me with brutal jokes and he said nothing to stop them. What a contrast to today – cheering proudly alongside me at a political rally, supporting instead of hiding, despite the fact the stakes are so much higher now. We've come a long way, Carson and me. And I can't wait to see where we're going next.

He turns to me, a weird look in his eyes. Says: "You're . . . a force, man. An absolute force. You definitely don't need me. You out there kickin' ass all on your own." His tone is strangely . . . wistful? No, not wistful. But I can't quite place it.

Then it hits me. He *wants* me to need him. I think of how put out he seemed every time he offered help and I told him we didn't need it.

And it makes sense, you know? That's his role, and always has been. His mom needs him, his brothers and sisters need him,

304

his teammates need him, hell, his friends need him if they want any hope of surviving geography class without slipping into a humorless coma.

But that's not our relationship. And it's new territory for him.

"Okay, first of all, I wasn't on my own. This took a village. And second . . ." I'm not sure how to phrase this next part so that it doesn't sound douchey, so I just come right out and say it. "I don't *need* you." His face falls. "But that's a good thing, Carson. It's how relationships should be. We're independent people. We function both separately and together. We're both perfectly capable of living without each other, if we have to. And that's healthy." I lean over and plant a peck on his cheek. "Doesn't mean I don't *want* you, though. Because I do. Very much."

Carson smiles, staring at his feet. Whether because this conversation is a little too deep, or whether just to find his footing on the treacherous ice, I don't know. "Guess I'm just used to being the guy people count on. And . . . I dunno, man. Everyone likes feeling needed once in a while. 'Specially guys."

I remember what both Danny and Zachary have said in the last few weeks, about how guys don't really support each other the way girls do. They have a whole different set of pressures on them. We're allowed to show emotion and allow ourselves to be taken care of, whereas guys have to be the alpha, the hunter-gatherer, the provider, the support system — but never the person who needs support in return. It's a crushing amount of pressure, and I guess because I never grew up with a father figure or any other male relatives I've never really thought about the flipside of feminism before.

And, like, not to give Danny a scapegoat for his shitty behavior or anything, but all this toxic masculinity shit is probably what led him to doing what he did to me. Having to be a certain way, and falling short. The frustration, the anger, feeling constantly at war with who he is – or who he's not. And then he saw me fall in love with a guy like Carson, who *does* fit that arbitrary social concept of what a man "should be", and it pushed him over the edge.

Rounding the final corner back into the town square, the non-marching protesters let out an almighty roar. The marchers roar back, so loud it's deafening. My roar rises to meet the crowd.

You know what that roar feels like?

It feels like taking ownership of the throbbing orb of anger in my chest. It feels like making my fury work for me, instead of against me. It feels like rousing the same anger in all of these amazing young women and allies, and giving them an outlet, a cause, a target for the rage. It feels like hope.

And as soon as this change happens in me, the orb takes on a different weight; it's lighter, and brighter, and it glows with energy and passion. A purpose, not a poison.

12.37 p.m.

Sorry, after that dramatic final line I had to take a break from typing, and you know, dunk my wrists in an ice bath for a while. [Not really. I ate cold pizza and let Dumbledore suck my ankle for a bit.]

Anyway, proceedings yesterday wound down at around 5 p.m., after everyone had their fill of the free food and drink and the frostbite had claimed the fingers of several innocent victims. [Again, not really. You are aware by now that I'm prone to exaggerate for comedic effect. Apologies if this is offensive to Everest climbers. But I mean, really, what are you doing?]

The hundred-strong band of volunteers sticks around for a while to clean up as best we can – easier said than done when half the litter has already been covered in a fresh layer of snow – and help the tech crew pack up the stage and sound equipment. Then Meg, Carson, Ajita and I get picked up by Ajita's parents in their fancy four-by-four and chauffeured back to Ajita's house for celebratory drinks.

After we've all taken turns in the luxurious rain shower with underfloor heating and have finally regained feeling in our limbs, we hang out in the basement with wet hair and tired bones and huge smiles. Ajita and Meg take one sofa while Carson and I take the other, and I can't even tell you how good it feels to be warm and cozy with my favorite people in the world.

I'm not naive enough to believe the hard part is over – I'm

307

still too scared to check the online response to the rally – but the sense of relief and pride in the room is palpable.

Ajita's dad brings down a small crate of beer, and gives us the usual speech about not posting about our alcohol consumption anywhere on social media. We toast to the rally and to Bitches Bite Back and to amazing allies, and that first sip of lime-infused lager is probably the most delicious sip of anything I've ever tasted.

Too emotionally drained to discuss anything real, we're chatting inanely about what movie to see next weekend when Prajesh, Ajita's younger brother, dashes down the stairs and grabs the TV remote.

"Whoa, where's the fire, my dude?" I ask.

"Izzy, I've asked you very politely not to say 'my dude'," Ajita retorts. "You just can't pull it off. I'm sorry. As your best friend, I feel it's my duty not to let you embarrass yourself any further. But seriously, Praj, what's occurring?"

"Hang on," he answers impatiently, which is precisely two more words than I've heard him speak this entire year. He stabs a few buttons on the remote, finds a news channel, then flumps down into the beanbag.

The channel he switched to is a local news station. In the bottom bar are the words:

BREAKING: VAUGHAN ANNOUNCES REVENGE PORN PROPOSAL

Meg gasps and claps her hands to her face, eyes wide. Carson laughs triumphantly and squeezes my thigh as I stare at the TV in disbelief.

"Following today's protest, it's become clear that this is an issue my constituents feel passionately about." Surrounded by his senior advisors – all white men, because obviously – Ted Vaughan looks incredibly sour and displeased, with the facial expression of a man in the process of chewing a wasp. "Your voices have been heard. Your demands have been heard. My office will be drafting a new legislation proposal in the coming weeks. Thank you."

And then he exits the stage in a flurry of camera shutters, refusing to answer any follow-up questions.

"We won," I murmur, still staring at the TV in a trance. "We actually won."

Ajita and Meg are laughing and high-fiving and hugging, and Carson is saying something in my ear, squeezing me tightly in a proud cuddle, but it's all a blur around me.

We did this. I did this.

Overwhelmed with emotion and pride, I start to cry.

Sure, there are no guarantees. The bill might never pass. But we forced that first step.

We, a group of teenage girls, a combination of people so often dismissed by society, made a change. A real change. We have more power and agency than I ever could have imagined, and it feels fucking *amazing*.

My phone buzzes with a text from Hazel: **WE DID IT!!!!! Thank you, thank you, thank you. You're an amazing person, Izzy O'Neill, and it's an honor to know you.**

There are hundreds of other messages, but that one? That one means the most.

Over the next few hours we watch in slightly buzzed amazement as the rally and its outcome makes state news, then national news. This round of media attention feels entirely new. It's on *my* terms, and that makes all the difference in the world. And yeah, as a result, my naked body is on show once more. This time, though, I don't care. Because my body is mine again. My anger is mine. My life is mine.

And nobody but nobody can ever take that away.

Wednesday 22 February

6.14 p.m.

After the high of the rally and our miraculous political victory wears off, I'm left feeling a little flat, arriving back into reality with a crash. Life once again becomes school, diner, school, diner, obsessing over the future and my distinct lack of prospects, repeat ad infinitum. But the existential inertia does not last for long.

[Prepare to literally shit yourself with second-hand excitement. If you don't I will take it as a personal sleight, because if you have made it this far into my story without becoming completely invested in my life, you must be dead inside and/or the High Bishop of Rudeness.]

I get a call from Eliza just after final bell rings, when Ajita and I are making our way back to our lockers. It goes something like this:

Me, equal parts hopeful excitement and sheer unadulterated panic: Hello?
Eliza: Hey, Izzy! Is now a good time to talk?

Me, thinking it is literally always a good time to talk where Eliza is concerned because she holds my future in her perfectly groomed LA hands: Sure!

Eliza: Great. So, I have some news.

Me, internally screaming: Okay . . .

Eliza: Okay, first off, it's not a screenplay option. I just want to manage your expectations a little.

Me, all hopes being shot down like a clay pigeon: Oh.

Eliza: No, but it's still cool news. Are you ready?

Me: Yeah.

Eliza: So there's this new production company being set up in LA by a famous actress and comedian. Her focus is going to be feminist narratives with a ton of humor, reinventing the romcom genre, super-zeitgeisty stuff. Right up your alley. Naturally I thought they'd be a great fit for Love for Hire, so I sent them the script and your idea for SLUT. I didn't hear anything for a while, because these people are busy and take forever to respond, but after your amazing success with the revenge porn rally I decided to nudge on Monday morning by sending them a link to the CNN coverage. I was all, look, this girl is making waves, she's exactly the kind of fresh talent you need to sign, like, yesterday. And they got back to me this morning!

Me, gripping Ajita's wrist so tightly she's dialing 911 to report me for assault: Okay . . .

Eliza: So with all that in mind, they want to offer you a summer internship!

Me, heart both rising and sinking at the same time: Oh. That's great. I mean, I can't afford to move to LA and work for free, but that's such an awesome vote of confidence.

Eliza: Okay, maybe I should've led with this, but it's a paid internship. The founder is so invested in diversity and accessibility, and wants to ensure her interns and staff are from as many different backgrounds as possible. She also believes in fairly reimbursing people for their labor. They're offering minimum wage, plus a weekly travel stipend to help cover commuting costs.

Me, reeling: I . . . wow. I don't know what to say. I'm still not sure I can cover the flights and accommodation — cash flow is pretty tight right now, and, well, always — but I'll try to figure it out.

Eliza: Awesome! Okay, can you get an answer to me by later in the week?

Me: Sure.

After I hang up, Ajita, still at the mercy of my vice grip, is rooting around in her pencil-case for an instrument with which to amputate her own hand. I save her the trouble of pulling a *127 Hours* and release her, then fill her in on what just happened while she massages the feeling back into her thumb.

"Well shit, dude." Ajita fiddles with the combination on her locker and swings it open, then proceeds to stuff all manner of miscellaneous snacks into her backpack for the walk home. "That's . . . legit. Do you know which actress it is?"

"I mean, do you think maybe we can focus on the HUGE IMPACT THIS HAS ON MY FUTURE rather than celebrity gossip? You know, just if that's cool with you."

Ajita rolls her eyes, taking a ginormous bite of a half-eaten Snickers. "Okay, okay, huge impact on your future." She sprays peanut everywhere as she talks. "Let's do this. Are you going to take it?"

I lean back against the lockers and sigh, staring at the needlessly aggressive strip lighting. "I want to. I want to so badly. This could be it, you know? It could be my way in. Paid internships are like buried treasure in Hollywood, and somehow I just unearthed one. Turning it down would just be . . . sacrilege. I'd regret it for the rest of my life. A life I'll probably spend serving waffles in the diner unless I grab this opportunity with both hands."

Ajita ditches her textbooks to make more room for snacks. There's now a chocolate splodge on her navy cashmere sweater. "That seems pretty cut and dry to me, but I know how much you love to complicate things, so let's hear it. Why aren't you going to take it?"

"Money, dude. Money. That thing you can exchange for goods and services."

She frowns. "I don't understand – isn't it a paid internship? All you have to cover is the flights. And, you know, find somewhere to live. But your wages will cover the accommodation. Can't you just borrow some money from Betty to get yourself set up?"

I love my best friend, but she definitely has a blind spot where money is concerned. I guess if you've always had it, you can't ever fully fathom *not* having it. I've often tried to describe it as having one percent charge on your phone and never being sure when you'll be able to find the next socket. Just constant, underlying stress that impacts everything you do and say and feel. I wish it wasn't such a defining thing, but it really is.

"It's cute that you think Betty has that kind of cash just lying around waiting for me to borrow and/or steal. The problem with being this broke is that there's just no cashflow. So even if you know you'll be getting paid in the near future, it's almost impossible to take that first step. Or book that first flight. Or buy dragonhide shoes."

"Credit card? Then pay it off as soon as you get your first paycheck?" Ajita finishes packing up and we head to the exit, through the throng of cross-country freaks panting by the water fountain. It's finally stopped snowing, so they're back to being unbelievable masochists and participating in voluntary trail running. I mean, really. Why. [No offense if you're a cross-country freak. It's just that I don't understand your life choices at all.]

"Nah. We got ourselves in a pretty bad debt hole a few years back. Nearly turned into a loan-shark-smashing-our-kneecaps type situation. Had to sell basically everything we owned. After that, we cut up all our credit cards and vowed never to take out another loan unless it was a life and death situation."

We spill out onto the quad, the punishing cold hitting us square in the face.

"Martha's wages?" Ajita asks, wrapping her scarf tighter round her neck and stuffing her hands into her pockets.

I pull my knitted hat down over my ears. "They might be enough to cover half a flight, but I am not sure half a flight is a thing you can purchase. Think they'll just open the door and let me parachute out over Arizona?"

7.19 p.m.

Over a dinner of last night's watered-down soup leftovers, I explain the latest heart-pounding developments to Betty, and brief her on my half-baked plan to skydive into the Grand Canyon and hitchhike from there. I tell her that while I am aware of a few flaws in this scheme, I would appreciate her unfaltering support nonetheless, because as my grandmother that is her sole duty in life. To validate my ridiculous behavior and pat me on the head when it all goes frighteningly wrong.

"So, in summary, the opportunity is too good to pass up, and therefore I plan to hurtle to the ground at terminal velocity and roll the dice on whether or not I'm intelligent enough to operate a parachute while under severe duress. Sound good?"

"Well, this is a lot to take in, kid," Betty says, pouring yet more salt into her soup in a desperate bid to add some flavor. "But first, I have some things to tell you." She shuffles awkwardly in her chair. "I perhaps should've shared this a few weeks ago when it first happened, but I really wanted to be able to surprise you with some college money."

I frown, vaguely remembering the time she recently tried to sit me down and get me to commit to the idea of college. "What the hell are you talking about? Did you win the lottery and decide not to tell me? Did the secret millionaire pay us a visit?"

"Yes, and I seduced him into the boudoir, took all his money, chopped him up into several bite-sized pieces and stored him in the freezer. You think we've been eating beef casserole this last week? I got news for you, kid."

I laugh, choking on a chunk of overcooked carrot. "Really? Cannibal jokes?"

"You wouldn't have me any other way," the crazy old bat says proudly, shooting me a cheeky wink. "No, what I want to tell you is this. Over the last month or so I've been working a second job from home. Freelance social media manager for a bingo company. It fits around the diner. Keeps me out of trouble, for the most part."

I almost spit my soup/piss water everywhere in astonishment. "You? Social media manager? *What??*"

"Yes, me, social media manager. Is that so hard to believe?

Apparently they like my sass when dealing with complaints. One of my tweets even went . . . what is it you kids say? Bacterial?"

"Viral," I correct her, but judging by the self-satisfied smirk she already knows. She's just winding me up, top-notch wind-up merchant that she is.

Slowly the pieces line up. This is why she's been hogging my laptop so much lately. She needed it for work, and doesn't have one of her own.

Wait, didn't Carson's mom apply for the same job a few weeks back? She must've lost out to Betty. The thought makes me feel guilty, remembering how disappointed Annaliese was. It would've been a game changer for them. Then again, it's a game changer for us. Still, I hate the idea of our situation improving at the Mannings' expense.

"Like I say, I was planning to start a small college fund for you with the extra income." She slurps the last dregs of soup, lifting the bowl up to her face. Lays it down again. I'm still staring at her in cautious disbelief. "It wouldn't have been much, a few thousand maybe, but enough to get the ball rolling. Anyway, my first month's pay check will be enough to cover a one-way flight to LAX, and I'll save the next few months' wages up so we can find somewhere affordable for you to move into with some roommates. Between now and summer, with you working at Martha's too, it's more than achievable. If that's what you want, of course."

Tears sting behind my eyes, and I have to lay down my spoon. Dumbledore is apoplectic with excitement over the prospect of leftovers, squirming at my feet.

And I think it *is* what I want — I'm almost positive it is — but the idea of leaving Betty behind is agonizing. She's been the center of my universe my whole life, and I can't imagine not coming home to her every night, or making waffles and coffee with her every morning while she sings her fucked-up renditions of popular nursery rhymes.

Plus, if anything happens to her while I'm gone . . .

I chase the thought away. It's too excruciating.

But now that she's computer literate I guess we could Skype and email and whatnot. She can still serenade me every morning, although I'm not sure my potential roommates would especially enjoy hearing "Incy Wincy Spider Is a Creepy Little Trash Bastard" over loudspeaker.

I mean, what's the alternative? If I decide I never want to leave Betty, it means staying in this dead-end town for the rest of her days. Sure, I could write in my free time, but would I really be happy with that? One of the things I love most about writing is watching my work come to life — acting out my sketches with my friends, filming them for our YouTube channel. All that would go away as my friends move on to bigger and better things, and it would just be me in my bedroom with my laptop, night after night after night, struggling to find anything funny at all.

And . . . LA would only be for a few months, right? I don't have to decide my whole future this very second – just the upcoming summer. I might hate LA, hate working for a production company, hate the traffic and the weather and the desperate Instagram models, and all the other things people claim to hate about it.

Or I might love it. I might love the palm trees and the beach and the delicious iced coffee and the creative, passionate people and the sense that your dreams are right round the corner. I might never want to leave.

I don't know which is more terrifying.

Finally, I whisper, "It's what I want."

"Then that's what we'll do." Betty grins warmly across the table, completely oblivious to the shred of cabbage wedged between her front teeth.

Friday 24 February

5.58 a.m.

TED VAUGHAN RESIGNS FROM OFFICE.

That's the headline I'm greeted with when I peel my eyes open this morning.

Heart racing, I speed-read the article: "Senator Ted Vaughan has resigned from office after it emerged that he used taxpayer money to fund a counter protest in the revenge porn case. After an anonymous source provided evidence to the State Attorney's office – in the form of an invoice bearing the former senator's signature – ASA Julianna Blake will be investigating the case. It remains to be seen whether or not the SA will press charges."

My initial reaction is this: YAAAAAASSSSSSSSSSSSSS.

But then something twinges in my chest. Will Ted find out his own son is behind the leak? What will happen to Zachary then? I find myself genuinely caring about the answer.

6.49 p.m.

Nothing restores your faith in the world quite like watching two of your best friends fall in love. And, you know, having all your wildest dreams come true. That helps too.

When I stroll down the stairs into Ajita's basement – having been gifted one of Prajesh's horrifying spinach smoothies at the door, RIP me – Meg and Ajita are curled up together on the love seat, mid-smooch, Meg's wheelchair abandoned in the corner.

Neither of them even notice me come in until I stop halfway down the steps and slurp my smoothie so aggressively they cannot fail to hear it. They both look up at me, sheepish and yet clearly proud of themselves, and I can't help but turbo-grin right back at them.

"So . . ." Ajita says, an adorable smile spreading across her face. "This is A Thing."

"It is indeed A Thing," Meg confirms, blushing slightly. Three, two, one . . . yep, she brushes her bangs out of her face.

"As far as Things go, this is one of the best," I say. "I promise you, I only look like I've recently contracted the bubonic plague on account of the taste of Prajesh's smoothie, which in itself reminds me of the Black Death. I assure you it's nothing to do with your PDA."

Although outwardly sarcastic as ever, inside I'm fizzing with joy. This is all I wanted. For them to be able to tell me about their relationship of their own accord. Not because I stumbled upon a picture on a laptop, or because I found myself wedged under a tinsel tree at the worst possible moment. Their love for each other feels like their thing, not mine. And that's exactly how it should be.

As I flump down into the vacant beanbag I grin again and take another swig of smoothie, despite my screaming taste buds. "So. What's new? Other than the obvious."

Ajita and Meg shift in the love seat and rearrange the cushions. They're both flushed and beaming, with an honest-to-God glow around them. On anyone else it would be sickening, but on them it's . . . no, still sickening.

Monday 27 February

8.32 a.m.

The hallways at school are the busiest I've ever seen them as I'm walking from geography to math, having miraculously passed both midterms. The only midterm I flunked was chemistry, which, obviously. I don't even fully understand what the periodic table is at this point.

There's a rumor going around that Danny failed his midterms and lost his academic scholarship. A few weeks back, this would've made Angry Me absolutely delighted and triumphant, and I probably would've thrown some kind of celebratory fête on the football field to mark the occasion, but now I just feel vaguely sad for the guy.

Hey, maybe Carson's pep talk about having an outlet for your anger actually got through to me! Come to think of it, I haven't felt the sharp barbs of anger thorn in my chest for a while. Not even toward Danny. In fact, all I hope for Danny is not that he succumbs to a slow and painful death, but instead that he gets the help he needs and can move on with his life too.

What. The. Actual. Fuck.

Did I just have a mature thought? What is happening? Am I being possessed by a particularly sensible and reasonable demon spirit? Should I arrange an exorcism?

As I'm grabbing my textbooks for English Carson appears from nowhere. Bounding over to me like he's ingested vast quantities of energy juice in the last few minutes, he presses me up against the lockers with a thud, and kisses me. Hard. But before my inner nymphomaniac can awaken . . .

"Come with me," he says breathlessly, tugging me down the hallway.

Confused, I follow him, trying to fight the urge to tell him to slow down on account of my total lack of cardiovascular fitness. As we reach the art studio, he bursts through the door and lets go of my hand, dumping his backpack on the nearest surface. Then he immediately starts fumbling with the zips in an overly enthusiastic attempt to wrestle the thing open.

"What's going on, goofball?" I laugh, more confused than a confused person on National Confusement Day. [I have been made aware that "confusement" isn't a word, but new words have to start somewhere, so I'm calling it.]

Carson grins, pulling a familiar-looking book out of his bag. "Here."

Where do you hide a poo in a zoo?

by Izzy O'Neill and Carson Manning

Only now, the front cover is adorned with an adorable bunch of cartoon animals, each holding a very distinctive-looking poo in their hands/paws/hooves. There's a pink hippo, a green snake, a purple gorilla, a blue rhino . . . I recognize the exact hues from the paint stains on his hands over the last few months.

His face is so adorably excited I can barely stand it. Eyes wide, he looks at me expectantly, gauging how happy I am on a scale of one to nacho mountain.

"So *this* is what you've been working on all this time!" I grin, amazed at the detail and the imagination that's gone into it. Flipping through the pages I wrote months ago, I'm stunned by his talent. Each illustration is both intricate and bold, both vivid and precise. Every animal has a distinct personality, whether goofy or forlorn or cheeky.

"I love it," I murmur. *I love you*, I think.

"So I got some news," he says, rubbing the back of his neck bashfully.

"Me too," I reply, suddenly terrified of telling him about the internship. I don't want this to be the end for us, but I don't know if he's willing to do distance. "You first."

"A'ight. So there's this new art gallery opening up in town, next to that pretentious-ass smoothie bar where they charge,

326

like, nine bucks for some blended banana." Vaguely I remember him standing outside that smoothie bar when I met him at the rally. "And the gallery's curator wants my work to be one of two launch exhibitions!"

"Carson, that's *incredible*," I gush, throwing my arms round him. "You're incredible. Is this your Black Lives Matter stuff?" His ridiculously amazing Statue of Liberty piece is my all-time favorite. His talent blows me away.

"Yup! There ain't no money upfront, but they're gonna be selling my work, and we share the money they get, and, ahhhhhhhhh!" The grin on his face is ginormous and adorable, dimples in full flow. "I can't believe it, man!"

"I can," I say, kissing him on the cheek, hugging him so tight. "You're amazing. Your work is amazing. You deserve this, Carson. You really do."

"Thanks, my dude. It's pretty cool, huh? Now what was your news?"

Stepping back and leaning against the bench, I shakily tell him about the internship, about the production company and what it stands for, about Betty's job and the fact they're going to be paying me, about how excited I am but also how scared I am. I rush out all of this without drawing breath, without even looking at him once.

I don't want to see his face. If he's sad or abandoned or any of that, I'll hate myself for crushing him right after he shared his amazing news.

I need not have worried.

"SHUT THE FUCK UP!" he yells in my face, grabbing my shoulders, eyes wide and euphoric.

"NO, YOU SHUT THE FUCK UP!" I yell back for lack of anything better to say.

"I FUCKING LOVE YOU!" he yells in return, and my heart bursts out of my chest.

"I FUCKING LOVE YOU TOO!" I yell louder, having never felt so happy in my life as I do right at this moment.

Friday 14 April

7.04 p.m.

Carson's exhibition opens at the gallery tonight, and I got the
night off work so I could come to the event with his mom and
older siblings. And now that we've decided to try long distance
and see if we can hack it I can't wait to kiss his beautiful face later
for the millionth time today. Like, the millionth. I currently
have a red mustache, thanks to kissing-induced stubble rash. It's
an incredibly strong look.

I'm waiting outside the school entrance for them to arrive,
freezing my ass off despite the fact I'm wearing every single
jacket I could find in the apartment. In a twist surprising to no
one Betty still hasn't made it yet. I swear the woman would be
late to her own funeral.

Then I hear them coming round the corner; Carson, his mom
and his four eldest siblings. They look even happier than usual,
all wrapped up in winter clothes, skipping along and laughing at
a joke Carson probably told. When he sees me standing at the
front entrance he kisses his mom on the cheek, ruffles his kid

sister's hair, and dashes off ahead, speeding through the gates at a pace he usually reserves from the basketball courts.

"Hey, Speedy Gonzalez." I laugh as he sprints up to me and grabs me by the waist, picking me up and swirling me around despite the fact I weigh more than your average Olympic wrestler. "Nervous?"

"Hell yeah. But excited too, y'know? How do I look?"

I take in his appearance – black pants, blue button-down shirt, brand-new sneakers – and grin. "You look perfect."

He grins back twice as hard. "See you in there."

"Good luck," I say, pecking him on the lips. "I love you."

Tagging along behind his mom, his brothers and sisters giggle playfully, sending a burst of warmth through my heart. Everything is so good. So, so good.

7.43 p.m.

The event is about to start, and Betty is still not here. Checking my phone anxiously, I start to fear the worst. What if she slipped in the snow? What if it's even worse than that? [This sounds dramatic, but it's what happens when your only family in the world is very old and working herself to the bone. Your worst-case scenario is legitimately a real possibility at any given moment. And it's terrifying knowing your whole world could die in an instant. And also I watch too much TV, so.]

That would be just like the O'Neills. Things finally start

going right, and within two nanoseconds tragedy strikes.

Carson's family are already inside, and I'm going to have to join them any second, with or without my grandma. But just before the doors close two figures appear round the corner. One is Betty. The other looks . . . vaguely familiar?

I squint down the street, trying to work out who the hell is accompanying my lunatic grandmother to a gallery opening. Did she get a nurse and just not tell me? Or meet a new pal at the community center? A work colleague, perhaps?

As they get closer I see that the person beside her is a man. A man in a long trench coat, with a newspaper tucked under his arm.

The penny drops, and I collapse into a fit of laughter.

"It's Frank!" I splutter aloud, barely able to breathe I'm laughing so hard. "Betty and Frank! Betty and Frank!"

They make it to the door after seven years of shuffle-walking, Betty in her nicest floral dress and Frank immaculately shaven as always. My grandmother, the absolutely bonkers old bat that she is, calmly says to me, "I believe you know my friend Frank?"

"What the fuck?" I mutter in response.

"Well what the fuck to you too, sweetheart!" Frank replies with his genial smile. He turns to Betty. "Vegetarians are very strange people, aren't they?"

"Betty, dearest," I manage to say. "Do you mind telling me what on God's green earth is happening right now?"

Betty loops an arm through Frank's and squeezes his non-existent bicep. "Frank and I met on Tinder. Have you heard of it? It's really very good." And then Frank winks at her. Actually *winks*.

Honestly. I can't speak.

Betty and Frank ease into the gallery, tripping over each other several times as they do so. We're just in time and pick a spot next to Ajita and Meg, who are holding hands and whispering sweet nothings to each other.

Carson takes to the makeshift stage beneath a warm spotlight, smiles his easy smile, and begins to talk about his work. And as I listen to his powerful, passionate, hilarious words I'm so unbelievably proud to be his girlfriend.

For the first time in months there's not a single trace of anger anywhere in my chest. My heart feels light and free, and full of hope for the future. Tears silently start to flow down my cheeks. They're happy tears, though. The very happiest.

I look around the gallery, at Carson and his family, at Ajita and Meg, at Betty, at Frank. And I feel like the luckiest girl in the universe. My world is a small one, but right now it is perfect. It won't necessarily stay perfect forever; change is the only constant, after all. Still, maybe change isn't universally awful.

It can be bad, yes. Can take the form of a car crash or a leaked nude picture or a best friend's betrayal. But it can also be politics and internships and pink hair dye, screenwriting competitions and art exhibitions and LA. Hope and laughter and forgiveness.

My future is still a giant question mark. Yes, going to college one day would be amazing, but it's not the *only* amazing. I might become a famous stand-up comedian, or a struggling screenwriter, or I might kick ass at this internship and decide that producing is the right move for me. Bitches Bite Back might take off, or I might open my own diner, or I might become a drama teacher like Mrs Crannon. I might marry young, have kids young, or have no kids at all. It doesn't matter. Because I know, without a shadow of a doubt, that if I have these people around me, I'll be happy no matter what.

Maybe . . . maybe this is growing up. Maybe you realize that you don't have to have the "best" life in order to have a great life. Maybe you embrace the mess, embrace the unknown, embrace the good and the bad and everything in between. Maybe you learn how to channel anger, how to survive grief, and how to walk away.

Maybe you realize that coming of age means you're allowed to go on pretentious rants about the meaning of life, as if you have all the answers.

Fuck it. All I know is that right now? There's nowhere in the world I would rather be.

Epilogue

Hey Izzy,

Hope your internship is going well? I spoke to your boss last week about a mutual project, and she mentioned how impressive and tenacious you are. I knew you'd take Hollywood by storm!

So I'm not just getting in touch for a catch-up. I actually have an interesting proposal for you.

An editor from one of the biggest book publishing houses in the world just reached out to me. She saw your story on the news, and she thinks you have so much to say – with the perfect voice to make people sit up and pay attention.

She especially loved this line: "Because the way the world treats teenage girls – as sluts, as objects, as bitches – is not okay. It's the exact opposite of okay."

Izzy . . . they're wondering if you might like to write a book about your experiences?

Eliza

Acknowledgements

Acknowledgements are weird. It kind of feels like an Oscar acceptance speech, except I'm alone in my pyjamas at three in the afternoon, eating popcorn and trying to resist the lure of video games. Ah, author life.

First up, the hugest shout out to my literary agent Suzie Townsend. We've worked together for five years, sold eight books during that time, and it's not hyperbolic to say I wouldn't have a career without her. And the rest of the New Leaf family – in particular Cassandra, Pouya, Maíra and Veronica.

Next up, Team Egmont: the biggest champions of Izzy O'Neill since day one. Ali, Liz, Sarah – your editorial insights are sheer magic. Siobhan, you're the best publicist to drink rosé, do bookish tours and terrifying school visits with. Thank you for repeatedly talking me down from the ledge. And to all the members of marketing, sales, design, PR . . . you're all bloody brilliant.

Over the last few years, I've met some incredible writing friends, both online and in real life. My agent sisters Victoria Aveyard, Emma Theriault, Claribel Ortega. Rebecca McLaughlin, PitchWars mentee turned lifelong friend. My ambitious badasses, Sasha Alsberg and Francina Simone. Our group chats and Skype hangouts give me life. The world is not ready for us. *yacht emoji*

There are so many others, and to have enough paper to thank them I'd have to murder an entire rainforest, so let's just say: the entire YA community, on both sides of the Atlantic – authors, bloggers, readers, reviewers, agents, editors, event coordinators and all-round champions. Thank you for welcoming me with open arms.

Then there's the unfortunate bunch who have to put up with me in real life, which I assure you is no mean feat. Firstly to my dog, Obi. Truly the best colleague on earth. Mum, Dad, Jack, Gran, Harry (who is also a dog) and the rest of my huge, mad family. The best pals a girl could ask for: Toria, Nic, Hannah, Lauren, Lucy, Steve and Spike. And Hilary, even though you technically come under the Mad Family header. To Millie – I hope the world is a better place for young women by the time you become one.

And to Louis, who will be my husband by the time this is printed. Wtf. Thank you for the nacho-fuelled life talks, terrible puns, hilarious cases of the zoomies, karaoke-filled road trips, endless back tickers, always doing the dishes, and for making me smile no matter what. There's nobody else I'd rather have by my side.

LAURA STEVEN

Laura Steven is an author, journalist and screenwriter from the northernmost town in England. *The Exact Opposite of Okay*, her YA debut about slut-shaming and the Friend Zone, was published by Egmont in 2018. Before taking the plunge into full-time writerhood, Laura worked for a glossy lifestyle magazine, then spent three years at *Mslexia*, a non-profit organisation supporting women in the arts. She has an MA in Creative Writing, and her TV pilot *Clickbait* reached the final eight in British Comedy's 2016 Sitcom Mission. Laura's journalism has been featured in *The i Paper*, *Buzzfeed*, *The Guardian* and *Living North*. She won a Northern Writers Award in 2018.

The scandal that started it all . . .

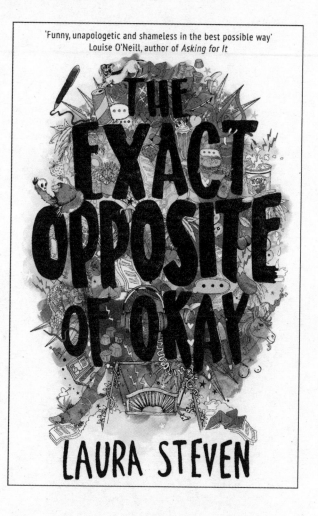

'Funny, unapologetic and shameless in the best possible way'
Louise O'Neill, author of *Asking for It*

THE
EXACT
OPPOSITE
OF OKAY

LAURA STEVEN

AVAILABLE NOW